UPPERCUT PRINCESS

THE HEIGHTS CREW
BOOK ONE

By
E. M. MOORE

This book is a work of fiction. Names, characters, places, and incidents are the product of the author's imagination or are used fictitiously. Any resemblance to actual events, or persons, living or dead, is coincidental.

Copyright © 2020 by E. M. Moore. All rights reserved, including the right to reproduce, distribute, or transmit in any form or by any means. For information regarding subsidiary rights, please contact E. M. Moore at emmoorewrites@hotmail.com.

Manufactured in the United States of America
First Edition February 2020

Edited by Heather Long

Cover by 2nd Life Designs

Also By E. M. Moore

The Heights Crew Series

Uppercut Princess

Arm Candy Warrior

The Ballers of Rockport High Series

Game On

Foul Line

At the Buzzer

Rockstars of Hollywood Hill

Rock On

Spring Hill Blue Series

Free Fall

Catch Me

Ravana Clan Vampires Series

Chosen By Darkness

Into the Darkness

Falling For Darkness

Surrender To Darkness

Ravana Clan Legacy Series

A New Genesis

Tracking Fate

Cursed Gift

Veiled History

Fractured Vision

Chosen Destiny

Order of the Akasha Series

Stripped (Prequel)

Summoned By Magic

Tempted By Magic

Ravished By Magic

Indulged By Magic

Enraged By Magic

Her Alien Scouts Series

Kain Encounters

Kain Seduction

Rise of the Morphlings Series

Of Blood and Twisted Roots

Safe Haven Academy Series

A Sky So Dark

A Dawn So Quiet

Chronicles of Cas Series

Reawakened

Hidden

Power

Severed

Rogue

The Adams' Witch Series

Bound In Blood

Cursed In Love

Witchy Librarian Cozy Mystery Series

Wicked Witchcraft

One Wicked Sister

Wicked Cool

Wicked Wiccans

PROLOGUE

The atmosphere in the old, abandoned warehouse pricks my skin. The giant, industrial room is alive with electricity. Like it has its own heartbeat for the damaged, raucous crowd. I stand at the edge, aware every single person in this room thinks I'll get my ass kicked tonight.

A smile flickers across my face, but I hold it back. Cockiness isn't part of the plan...yet. Instead, for those who even glance my way, I feign an air of scared-out-of-my-ever-loving mind, even though I'm comfortable in places like this. Places with an undercurrent of weed and BO. The sweet scent of sweat a haze over it all. The people here thrive off of fights, and so do I.

They just don't know it yet.

Brawler approaches me, and I pretend I don't have

a lady hard-on for him. I also pretend I'm nervous as shit. "Is it...is it soon?" I ask.

He tips his head toward the fight currently going on in the makeshift ring. The bigger dude has a huge gash over his brow. Blood leaks into his eyes, but his opponent doesn't go easy on him. Instead, he tries to open the cut up further with two quick blows, but the bigger dude blocks each one and retaliates, the sight of his own blood making his attacks almost feral. Once he's seen it, he can't contain his madness. He delivers blow after punishing blow to the bridge of his opponent's nose until blood splatters everywhere.

Brawler smiles at the carnage, an evil glint in his eyes. "As soon as Rascal takes care of that guy, you're up."

I move my head from side-to-side, cracking my neck before staring down at the stained floor. Dried, crimson circles mar the floor at my feet. Like most other underground fighting venues, they're not ones for cleanliness. It doesn't bother me. It only adds to the animalistic nature of it all.

Brawler claps me on the back with a devilish grin. That same look is common in places like this. If you're not the predator, you're the prey—and everyone fancies themself a predator. "Chin up, Kyla. I have a feeling it won't last too long."

He walks away, his demeaning laughter coating me in his wake. I don't know why his amusement at my upcoming demise thrills me, but it does. I can't wait to prove him wrong. I can't wait to prove everyone wrong. I stare after his retreating, muscled form, my mouth watering for him.

That's not a part of the plan though. Definitely not part of the plan. I can't get mixed up with any of the Heights Crew.

Not when I plan on ruining them all.

I slip into the shadows where no one can see and start warming up. Through the gaps in the crowd, I spot my opponent Cherry, so named because Rocket was her first. Or at least that's what I hear. Anyone and everyone in the Heights has a nickname with a story. Why hers is attached to Rocket taking her virginity, I don't know.

Cozied up in the corner, a hand turns her chin. Her lips part, staring at someone in the shadows. I can't see his face. I squint, trying to place him without even really seeing him, but I only make out the color of his shirt, partial chest, and a leg of his jeans.

I know who I want it to be though.

I shake my head, focusing on the present. I have a fight to prepare for. Lunges, squats, and tuck jumps are my friend as I limber up. I windmill my arms around, loosening my shoulders, and then crack the knuckles on every one of my fingers and shake them out. The background is just that: background. I tune out the sounds of the current fight and the crowd to mentally prepare myself for what's about to go down.

I'll have to take a few punches. I already know this. It's the only way to make it convincing at first, but then I'm going to switch the tables on Cherry. I'm going to be the worst nightmare she won't ever see coming. Because in that ring, it won't be me and Cherry, it'll be twelve-year old Kyla wanting vengeance on everyone and everything that has to deal with Big Daddy K.

Fuck that murderer.

I let the rage seep deep into my marrow. I let it fill me, my hands already clenched to fists. My body turning to steel like iron-clad armor.

"Kyla," Brawler roars.

I turn, purposefully loosening my fists and looking at him like a deer in the headlights. He shakes his head like he might even feel bad for me, but in the next second, all that vanishes when his predatory smile comes out to play again. He crooks a finger at me, and I step toward him in my oversized shirt and joggers. "You're up."

I make a show of letting my gaze wander, stopping to stare at the unruly crowd perched on wooden crates.

The square slats of wood stacked on top of one another like poor men's bleachers.

Brawler sighs as he takes me in. He lowers his lips to my ear, whispering, "Just turtle up when she comes at you." He gives me a wary once-over, like he's afraid I might get seriously hurt.

"But—"

He cuts me off. His momentary lapse in better judgment now gone. "It's your funeral, New Girl."

I bite my lip, but in my head, all the taunts, all the petty bitches and dicks from Rawley Heights flit through my head, and I know I'm about to get my revenge on them. After tonight, I won't be the object of their utter humiliation and bullying, I'll be their goddamned *Princess* for real.

The sick satisfaction fills me, and when Brawler pushes me toward the empty circle in the middle of the room, I stumble forward. I must look like a blithering mess and that part wasn't even faked. I really did trip over my own feet. That fucker has big hands and more power than he knows.

Unless he does know, and he's just being a dick.

Come to think of it, I'm sure he knows, and he definitely means to be a dick.

Cherry enters through a gap in the crowd like the queen bee. She has on a cherry red robe as if she's an actual boxer showing up for her title match. A guy in her corner even slips it off her shoulders for her. A skimpy sports bra and shorts round out the ensemble, but I can't stop staring at the cleavage she's showing off. Is this a fight or a wet t-shirt contest?

She throws her arms in the air, and the crowd roars. Mostly man sluts hoping she'll slip a tit. I bet they're looking over at me thinking that's the only excitement they're getting out of tonight.

They'd be wrong.

I stop myself from jumping up and down, the way I get rid of pre-fight jitters. Instead, I toe the ground and do some basic stretching. I'm talking hands over my head, twisting this way and that. Basically, the kind they taught us in Kindergarten, so everyone thinks I look like a dumbass newbie.

Cherry sneers at me. "This is what you get for coming to the Heights, Bitch."

I've had to tone down my snarky ass for days. My tongue is practically salivating to talk back. I can't wait until this fucking fight is over, so I can verbally eliminate all these fucking wannabe thugs.

"Aww, do you need to run back to Mommy?" Cherry snickers, an exaggerated frown playing over her pouty lips.

My blood boils. This bitch's mom is probably

doped up on crack right now. Or spreading her legs downtown. She probably never had a mommy to console her...

But I did. She's just fucking dead.

Bitterness makes my body flash hot and cold. My gaze zeroes in on Cherry's perfect, upturned nose. I stare straight at it, imagining what I'm going to do until Brawler breaks my concentration. He steps into the middle of the ring, looking back and forth between us. His lips move, but a rush of nothing but rage overwhelms me.

This bitch mentioned my mom.

A raging storm kicks up in my brain. A swirling mess of devastating wind and waves roar between my thick skull and ears until he steps back and yells, "Fight!"

My plans have left the building.

I rush her. Her eyes flare with anticipation, but she isn't that good of a fighter. I'm fast and skilled. I slip under her lame ass attempt at punching me, pop back up, and give a good right hook to her fucking ribs.

The crowd gasps. The moment lingers in the air, suspended. Sure, Cherry's not their number one fighter. Everyone knows that. I was a gimme to her. Someone she could steamroll through to climb ahead in the rankings. Well, good fucking luck after this, you dirty fucking hoe bag bitch.

I grit my teeth, punching the same spot two more times until she cries out. Her sharp squeal brings me back to reality. I step back. Trying to dampen my initial reaction, my mouth falls open in abject horror. I really do have to stick to the plan. I drop my hands to my waist, making my eyes round.

"You cunt," she seethes.

She lunges for me, and I let her. She gets in two good punches to the side of my face before I veer around her, bringing my forearms up to block. To my right, Brawler eyes me. Maybe he saw my initial attack for what it was. A deliberate, skilled offense.

Cherry's fingertips dig into my shoulders before pulling me down, landing a solid knee to my gut. Mouth next to my ear, she says, "You piece of fucking trash. Bitches like you don't make it in the Heights."

I look over her arm, scanning the crowd again until I see *him*. There. Exactly who I needed to make sure was watching as I do this.

Now that I have his attention, I push past her hold, slip under her arm, and lock my arm around her outside forearm. I hold her in place, battering the side of her head with hard-hitting blows. Every time she tries to squirm out of it, I move with her, keeping out of her reach while she's well within mine.

She's not so talkative anymore. Now that she's getting her head beat in.

I trip her and throw her to the ground. She lands on her back and stares up at me, round eyes meeting mine. Her skimpy bra has inched lower, showing the top half of her areola, but she's not giving a shit about that right now. She runs her hands over her face, wincing when it meets the cut I've given her over her eye.

My stare moves up, catching on the most important person in the room. He glares at me with dark eyes, and I shed my oversized shirt, wiping my face with it before throwing it on the ground while he eyes me.

The crowd nearly trips over itself before the comments start flying and the decibels double from the roaring and clapping. They didn't expect this from me. Not the fight, and not my body. My sports bra and low-slung joggers show off my toned physique, which I've kept under wraps from the thugs at school. I needed to play this my way.

I like being the underdog as long as I come out on top, and I *will* come out on top.

Cherry tries to scramble to her feet. Real fear dancing in her eyes.

I kick her, and she sprawls out again. When I move in, she tries to kick me in the face, but I throw her feet to the side and pounce on her, elbowing her in the forehead. In this moment, I don't even care that Brawler's in the room or Cherry or any of the other fuckers I have to go to school with every day. This is about me. This is about my plan. About my vengeance.

Next thing I know, I'm being pulled off her. The tangy, copper taste of blood coats my mouth. I reach up with my fingers to touch my lips and realize it's not mine. It's Cherry's. I spit the shit out and look up to lock gazes with *him*.

"Fucking shit," Brawler mumbles behind me, his fingers tightening around my upper arm.

I blink, staring down at an unmoving Cherry. She's not dead. I don't think, anyway. If she was, it wouldn't matter to me. I have one job here at Rawley Heights, and she was in my way.

He doesn't even spare her a glance before stepping over her feet to make his way toward me.

Well, happy fucking day to me. The game is on.

1

Two days earlier...

THINKING ABOUT VENGEANCE IS ONE THING. Training for vengeance is another. Actually being here at Rawley Heights? Holy. Fucking. Shit. These kids aren't imposters. They aren't fake or pretending to be badass. They're seriously tough. The rough and tumble type of delinquents moms from the suburbs warn their privileged womb warriors to stay away from.

Me? I'm walking straight into the hornet's nest.

I approach the metal detectors. A kid in front of me slips a knife into his shoe to hide it. Just about everyone around us notices, but the guards don't. Or, they look the other way. I haven't identified him as a member of the Heights Crew yet, but that doesn't mean he isn't. Their reach is far, open-ended, and scary as fuck.

The guard waves me forward, and my stomach clenches. Maybe I should've thought harder about bringing a blade with me and hiding it somewhere. The dude in front of me is already walking around the detectors with a nod at the guard. Instead of freaking out, I toss my bag on the table, so they can go through the contents while I walk *through* the detectors. I swear to God the guard who checks my bag licks his lips and fondles the tampon I have in there. Fucking creep. He gives me a toothy grin, and I practically yank my bag out of his hands and walk away.

My tiny outburst is nothing like the shit the other students are giving the uniformed showpieces. You only have to watch the nightly news to know the guards aren't stopping a lot of the shit happening here. In fact, a few lines over from me, a girl is bitching a guard out because he found a baggie of weed in the front pocket of her book bag. It's not that he found it, it's that he's threatened to flush it. He's about to stand from his stool when she tears the baggie from his grip and runs through the parking lot until she's out of view.

No one gives the scene a second glance.

It's a huge difference for me. Though, I'd die

before I show it. My aunt and uncle brought me up in the life of private schools and dinner parties, but I never fit in with their world. I knew what I was getting myself into when I decided to enroll here. I'd do all this and more just as long as I get to do what I came here to do. And trust me, I'll be doing shit a hell of a lot worse than pulling my bag away from a potential child molester before the year's out.

While I walk down the graffitied hallway, angry looks follow me everywhere. Trust me, I've changed schools before, I know what the normal looks should be. They should be curious. Sizing up, even. Not these. These are straight up nasty from the beginning. Like, how dare I set foot on their turf kind of bullshit.

In Rawley Heights, you're an enemy before you're proven worthy. I have a plan to get on their good side, but I have to let this charade play out for what it is.

"Eat a bag of shit and die," one of the mouthier bitches says, knocking her shoulder into mine as she passes.

I look away, bringing my bag closer. On the outside, it looks like I'm scared to death. Tactically, I'm just making sure no one uses my own bag as a weapon against me. I don't have time for that shit. It's barely eight in the morning, and I'm fucking tired. And cranky.

Fuuuuuck. I forgot to eat breakfast. No fucking wonder I'm jittery. Note to self for tomorrow: Breakfast really is the meal of champions.

Another girl walks past me and clips my shoulder with hers. I stumble forward to keep my feet underneath me, but I don't make eye contact. That would just be asking for trouble.

Behind me, a male voice cuts through the air like he's the emcee at a party. "New pussy!"

Students around me chitter like it's the funniest thing they've heard all day. I mean, it may be. Did I mention it's only fucking eight o'clock in the morning?

The crowd parts, and a guy at the very end of the hall leans back against his locker, one leg quirked with his foot planted on the metal behind him. He's staring down the hallway like he owns the place before zeroing in on me: New Pussy, apparently.

Holy hot shit. Hopefully I'm as good of an actress as I think I am, otherwise, he'll see the spark of acknowledgment in my eyes. Private school assholes never did it for me. Guys like this though? Damn. Yes. Just fucking yes.

I reach up to pull my hair around my ears. A gesture I hope looks hesitant. I know who the guy is. I've done my research. I just didn't expect to have this much of a visceral reaction to him.

He quirks an eyebrow, and I wet my lips. He's tan with dark hair shaved at the sides. The top is longer and slicked back. He has bottomless pits for eyes that should make me think he's definitely an enemy, but it doesn't. It makes me wonder how deep his pit actually is. I'd be willing to bet it's not as deep as mine, but we all have secrets, don't we? We all have things we'd rather not remember. Memories we hold tight to but wish they would blow away like smoke on the wind.

Just how bad are you, Oscar Drego?

A hand shoves me from behind, and I sprawl toward him. I end up within a couple of feet of his casual stance and look up. I suck in a breath. The energy coming off him sets fire to my nerve endings. He's wearing a cheap ass Rawley Heights letterman jacket he got for playing football. Quarterback to be exact. Last year, he left to go to Spring Hill, chasing rich girl pussy. When he got back, he paid for that shit. At least, that's what I hear. He had to make ties with the Heights Crew to stop his ass from being fucked up every day.

Not that you'd know it from the look on his face right now. He looks smug as all shit.

The same person who pushed me forward grabs a hold of my neck, forcing me closer to Oscar. "Say hello to your master, little cunt."

I grit my teeth, but Oscar just beams at me like he's won the fucking lottery.

The fingers tighten around my neck. "I said...say hello. Or are you too much of a princess for us?"

I swallow down the bile rising up my throat. I want to tell both of these assholes to get fucked, but that won't bode well for me here. I can't make enemies. I need to sneak in the backdoor, not come in guns blazing. Not yet anyway. "H-hello," I say.

My voice makes Oscar tilt his head. "Hello what?" His eyes almost twinkle. I swear he's getting off on this.

The richness in his voice makes me squeeze my legs together. For fuck's sake. I need to get a hold of myself. *I'm* getting off on this shit. "Um, excuse me?"

Oscar snickers and kicks off the locker before stepping forward. Whoever has my neck in a vise loosens his hold and backs away until it's just Oscar and I face-to-face.

I smile tentatively. "I'm Kyla."

His lips turn up. "You think I give a fuck?" He moves around me, staring me up and down while walking around me in a wide circle. We've attracted a crowd now. As much as I'd love to demolish these guys, I keep my mouth shut and my arms pinned to my sides. When he moves around to face me again, he shakes his head. "You're not giving us anything, are you?" His stare drags down my oversized t-shirt, which is cleverly hiding my body away from everyone. I'm pretty much dressed the exact opposite of every other female in this school. On purpose.

I pretend I don't know what he's talking about. The truth is, if I came in here dressed like everyone else, I'd be on their radar for the wrong reasons. I'm going to be on their radar, sure, but by my doing.

I try to walk away, but the same guy from before grips my neck again, forcing me to stay in place. My face reddens, and I let the heat crawl all over me until my skin is hot and itchy.

A throaty laugh rips from Oscar. "I give her two days."

The guy behind me, most likely someone trying to get into the Heights Crew since he's acting like Oscar's little bitch instead of standing next to him, roars. Somehow, the sound is more infuriating than Oscar's guess at how long I'll last here in the Heights.

"We'll let the girls deal with her," Oscar says, nodding at me. "She's not worth our time."

The grip on my neck loosens for a fraction of a second before I'm pushed to the side. I stumble, catching myself on the intersecting hallway wall. I look over my shoulder at the douche who keeps manhandling me, solidifying his face in my memory, so I can kick his ass when I get the chance. Hmm. He has a lip ring. That could be fun.

And no, not to kiss. To tear it the fuck out. Men don't need to be handling women that way, especially to pretend like they're fucking cool.

Afterward, I focus on Oscar. He's eyeing me still, but nothing in his face gives away what he's thinking. I guess we're both good like that. From what I've already gathered about Oscar, he'll pretty much do whatever it takes to make his life better. Including succumbing to the whims of the Heights Crew for protection.

Throughout the day, the insults get worse. It hasn't taken long for word to spread that it's open season on me. Guys sit back, watching the girls try to tear me to shreds on my very first day. Some get physical. Some just use their words. The only respite I get is while I'm in class, but even then, it depends on the teacher. Some teachers don't have control of their classrooms at all. It's anarchy in English. People come and go as they want, and not one time in any of my classes do any of the teachers ask who I am.

I'm getting the impression no one gives a shit about these guys, not even themselves.

At the end of the day, I try my locker again. I haven't been able to get the fucking thing open all day, which isn't going to work for me. I need some place to store my shit, maybe hide something contraband in case I need it. After the fifth time trying to open it, I groan. *Fuck me.* I look around, only to find Oscar walking down the intersecting hallway. He's got one of the other Crew members next to him: Brawler.

I blink at him. He's bigger up close. With a name like Brawler, he had to be chiseled and muscled in all the right places, but within twenty yards, he's a sight to behold. I won't ever deny what fighter's physiques do to me. I've spent my fair time in gyms across this state, and I've seen some banging bodies. This guy? He's right up there at the top.

A split second of warning is all I get before my head slams into my broken locker. I grunt, bringing my hands up to prevent another go. When I realize it isn't coming, I turn to find one of the crew cunts smiling at me. Girls aren't usually let into gangs like the Heights Crew, but I know this type of chick. She hangs on the guys, mostly for protection. She throws her weight around like she means something to them, but she doesn't, only a lukewarm hole to stick their dick into when they want it. The only chicks who make it into the Crew are either as badass as the guys, legacy, or girls who are going to end up tied to a member for life. Traditionally, we'd call that husband and wife, but for the Crew? It's more than that. You can't just divorce the Crew if you want out.

This girl wants in. Bad. She smirks down the hallway at Oscar and Brawler when they stop to look back at us. The flow of the other students moves around them. Now that she has their attention, she returns her stare to me. "I guess you are a princess, huh?"

My jaw locks. I now have a raging fucking headache. I knew I wasn't going to get out of today unscathed, but fuck. I have to remind myself that it's all part of my plan. I reach up, feeling the bruised skin that's already forming a welt above my eyebrow. "What was that for?"

The girl laughs, cocking her head back. She has huge hoop earrings in, which is the dumbest fucking thing I've ever seen. She has to know the second she gets into a fight, someone's going to rip those out of her fucking ear. She must be under more protection than I thought. "Bat says you won't last two days." She steps in closer. "I'm making sure that happens."

I sneak a peek behind her to find Oscar, a.k.a. Bat, and Brawler openly watching us still. They don't move to the side of the hallway or try to hide what they're doing, they just stare. Because they're looking our way, everyone else does too.

Moving to look back at the desperate girl, I raise my eyebrows at her. I take a quick look, scanning down her body, trying to figure out how much of a problem she's going to be. With the way she keeps checking over her shoulder, it's apparent she's all bark and no bite. She just wants to put on a show.

Well, so do I. I step back against my locker, holding my book bag to myself again. I keep my hand on the lump forming on my forehead. I've had far worse injuries, but they don't need to know that. "This has been the shittiest day," I groan.

The girl in front of me looks over, eyes gleaming. "It's only going to get worse from here."

"Why?" I ask, pretending like I can barely even meet her eyes.

"Because you're in Rawley Heights now, Princess." She gives me a dismissive look. "We don't fuck around."

2

The first thing I need to do when I sneak my way into the Heights Crew is get rid of the fucking name Princess.

The asshole who thought that up deserves a fucking nut kick.

After the girl who slammed my head into the locker decided it was much more fun to cozy up to Oscar and Brawler than to fuck with me, I walked toward the main office. It's not my first choice to find myself heading this way on the first day, but I need a lock. Surely, just because this school is filled with gang bangers and miscreants doesn't mean they don't have a maintenance department, right? They must have extra locks somewhere.

I shake my head as I walk close to the walls. I can

imagine what any of the stuck-up rich assholes I went to school with once upon a time would look like here in Rawley Heights. Comical. Downright hysterical. *Yes, please, sir. I don't seem to be able to utilize my locker. May I get reassigned?* The thought is almost enough to make me smile. Almost.

The Rawley Heights High School Office is just a singular, solid door. To the right, a ripped computer paper sign that looks as if it's been taped a handful of times says, you guessed it: office. It's not even capitalized. Paint chipping on the side of the door makes me think there used to be a legit sign here once, but who knows how long that's been gone. I double-check the area to make sure I'm in the right place. It's unlike any Main Office I've ever seen. Usually, they're encased with windows that look out into the hallway or flanked with school spirit signs. There is none of that here. They've basically made it as unwelcoming as possible.

I turn the knob and push the heavy door open. Once inside, I take note of the dirt brown, threadbare carpet and the overall seventies coloring of oranges and green that cover the walls and aesthetics. My gaze traces over a hallway that branches out. It's dim, as is the entire office itself. Most of the lights are off. The doors are shut. "Hello?"

A musty smell barrages me, like this place doesn't

get used often. I wait for a response, but there isn't one. I walk farther in. An empty sunburnt-colored desk sits front and center. Piles of paperwork are strewn over it along with several wire baskets filled with more papers.

I sigh. There's literally no one around. The bell only rang five minutes ago. Shouldn't administration be staying later than the students? That only seems logical.

A creaking noise interrupts the stillness. I tilt my head, trying to figure out where the sound came from. It's then I notice there's an open door just to the right of the empty desk. I walk forward right before a hissing sound pours out of the room followed by a masculine "Oh, fuck yes."

I stop. Curiosity burns through me. It can't be what I think it is. I glance up just as the blinds on the window that look out into this room fly upward.

My heart falters in my chest as I stare into the eyes of Johnny Rocket. My skin turns cold then heats when I read the pleasure in his eyes. My gaze drifts lower, and my stomach clenches. I press my lips together to keep from spewing the empty contents of my stomach everywhere.

Johnny's sitting on the edge of another sunburnt orange desk. His feet propped up on the open bottom drawers on either side of the desk, he's tilted back slightly, and a head is going to town on his dick. His eyes gleam. "We're going to need a minute."

The woman startles when she realizes he's talking to someone. She tries to pull away, enough so that the crow's feet at the corners of her eyes are clearly visible, which tells me she's a lot older than Johnny. She's also wearing a collared blouse with her hair in an updo that Johnny demolishes when he pulls her mouth back to his cock. I swear he pulls her so hard she had to have gagged, but instead, she moans like she loves being manhandled by this spawn of Satan.

My surroundings burn hazy at the edges. All I can see is him. I don't register that he's getting head from a secretary or some other administrator. The darkness in his eyes has captured me in place. The rueful play of his lips have stolen my breath. In my head, I imagine an older version of him, and my blood boils.

"You can watch if you want," he suggests, his hand still on the back of the woman's neck while he gives me a slight shrug.

His words are like a douse of reality. In a snap, my vision expands, and I remember where I am and what I'm doing. I turn away from the audacious scene and exit out the nondescript wood door. Leaning against it,

I bring my hand to my stomach as if to hold its contents in.

Not exactly the way I wanted to handle meeting the son of my parents' murderer.

I close my eyes, and the rest of the school disappears. In my head, I singsong, "One Kyle-and-An-na. Two Kyle-and-An-na. Three Kyle-and-An-na." When I get to five, I open my eyes again. The picture is clearer. My focus restored. I shift on my heel to walk out of this ridiculous building they call a school. I'll head to Walmart tonight to grab a fucking lock and maybe even some bolt cutters to get the old lock off my broken locker myself.

I push the image of Johnny Rocket away and store it for another day. Another time to come back to for analysis. I can't get ahead of myself. Not yet. Not ever.

The empty halls greet me like a barren cave. I have a suspicion the only ones left are students and teachers who actually give a shit about being here day in and day out. Not counting the fucking bitch who's in there with Rocket for extracurricular activities.

"Crazy first day?"

I jump. Spinning, I glance up to find a girl walking past me in the hall. She has a pair of holey jeans on, a chain looping from her front belt loop to her back belt loop. A tight black shirt rounds out the outfit. I narrow my gaze, but first impressions tell me she won't be one of the ones trying to mess with me so she can get on the Heights Crew's good side. "You could say that."

She walks past me, only giving a cursory glance, but then she stops suddenly. Sighing, she turns toward me like it's really the last thing she wants to do yet feels compelled to anyway. "Watch out for Nevaeh. She'll do anything to get into HC."

I rack my brain. There were so many wannabe gang bitches today who tried to make my life a living hell. I don't have the foggiest which one Nevaeh is. I lift my shoulders.

The girl sighs again, mumbling something to herself. When she finally responds to me, she's more clear. "Neveah's the one who slammed your head into the locker."

Ohhhh. I file that name away. My head's still thumping from that bitch move. "You saw that, huh?" Real embarrassment crawls over my skin. I do have some pride after all. I'm just willing to overlook it for the greater good.

"Stay out of her way. And if you tell her I said something, I'll..." She trails off, then looks up like she's trying to figure out the best threat to make. Clearly, she doesn't have a lot of experience with this.

I like her immediately, which means I need to stay

the hell away from her. "Thanks," I tell her, before stepping toward the main doors again. I need to get home, put some ice on my fucking forehead, and regroup before I do this all again tomorrow.

The big reveal can't come soon enough.

I walk around her toward the doors. Her stare is like a hot poker burning a hole into my side, but I don't slow up or try to be nice or try to make a friend. In any other world, I would have. I'd want a friend to get through Rawley Heights with, but I've never been all that good at having friends, first of all, and second, it's just not the time.

I have only one goal here, and it's not to find something real.

My life in Rawley Heights is fake. It'll be raw and dirty and bloody. Filled with betrayal, revenge, and fucking satisfaction. I don't need to add another casualty when I leave this fucking place with murder on my hands.

Behind me, the girl groans. Her footsteps slap the worn flooring as she catches up to me. "Don't ever go out the main doors by yourself when security is around. They're fucking child rapists, you understand?"

I turn toward her, eyebrows in my hairline, which

really fucking hurts by the way. I can look up and see the goose egg on my forehead. "Good to know."

"If you're alone, go out the side door. I'll walk out with you tonight though. Don't make eye contact with them. Or bait them either. You look like trouble follows you everywhere. At least it will in the Heights."

"So I've noticed," I deadpan.

We walk through the glass doors. I don't look around, but the hair on the back of my neck stands, so I know what this chick has just told me is correct. The security team are predators living right with the prey. And the school doesn't give a fuck.

We part ways in the parking lot without a word. She doesn't try to talk to me again, and as I said, I don't need real friends. My life can start after I've finished what I've come here to do.

My aunt and uncle have no clue why the hell I'm here. They think I'm throwing my life away at a shitty school that won't impress any colleges. They're wrong. Well, they're right. Rawley Heights doesn't impress anyone, but I'm not throwing my life away. I'm making sure I actually have one. One where I can live without regret. Without terror. Without what ifs.

Once I kill Big Daddy K, head of the Heights Crew, I'll finally be able to start my life. It'll be like a rebirth. A christening. Sure, not any christening I've ever been to unless it's blood they're using to bless people with instead of holy water. But to me, this is everything. I've bided my time. I've made my plan.

Now, I just have to execute it.

3

As soon as I get home, I place a bag of frozen vegetables on my face.

I spend a half hour just sitting on a hand-me-down armchair I got at the Salvation Army, the footrest kicked out, eyes closed, and face tipped toward the ceiling in the middle of my living room. Eventually, condensation builds up and trickles of water drip down the side of my face. That's my cue to stop replaying the day in my head. My replay isn't a scene-for-scene reenactment of what actually happened though, it's better than that. I imagine what I would've done if I wasn't playing a part. It turns out much more fun for me. One, there are no frozen vegetables needed at the end of the day, and two, I kick that Nevaeh girl's ass. The preening bitch.

The second-hand chair groans as I push the footrest down and stand. I open the freezer and toss the buttered corn back inside. Turning, I take in my new apartment. It's not half bad. The inside looks better than the outside of the building, that much I know. I can tell they put down new carpet and painted in here right before I moved in. I mean, it's not the Taj Mahal. It vaguely smells like mildew and a crazy amount of bleach, which makes me wonder what it was like before I got it. But listen, I'd rather it smell like straight up caustic cleaner than something else.

The faucet in the kitchen leaks. The caulk in the bathroom is an off-white, not chosen by color aesthetic, but lack of cleanliness, and the walls are super thin. Next door, a couple argues about money, and the distant sound of a baby crying carries from down the hall.

If the life I grew up in was Neverland, I'm definitely in Hell. None of that matters though. I'll wade through the flames and pitchforks all day every day to come out the other end safer and stronger.

I go to the small, separate bedroom and pull down the secret compartment on the ornate shelf I have hanging on the wall. I ordered it brand new off the internet from a nut who has a conspiracy theory website. When it came in, I had to rough it up so it would go with the rest of the decor. Chips in the wood mar the surface, and I did a really shitty job of painting so it blends in. But what still works perfectly is the hinge that drops down a secret compartment where I keep my sacred things.

I check the phone I have stashed inside. That and the picture of my parents I have sitting on the shelf are the only things I own in here that connect me to my old life. A text awaits me from my aunt, telling me she hopes I'm okay. I send her a quick one back telling her I'm fine and that I started school today with no issue.

She hates that I'm here, but I also know she and my uncle never wanted kids. They took me in after my parents died because that's what you do, but I never fit in with their upscale life, and I don't need any ties to that life here. As soon as I'm done here, I'll go back to being Kyle and Anna's daughter again. I'll go back to the life I should've been living all this time. Which means this one needs to stay completely separate from the other. They cannot mix. No one can find out who I really am.

Keeping the phone out, I make sure my aunt's not going to text me right back. When a response doesn't come within ten minutes, I shut the phone off and put it back, sliding it next to the sweet silver pistol I have there, which was surprisingly too easy to buy on the street. Sure, it's not legal. The scratches over the serial number tell me that, as did the shady-as-fuck guy who sold it to me, but I'm okay with that. This gun represents Kyla Samson's life—her goal—and as soon as I'm done with it, I'll toss it into a sewage drain.

I push the compartment closed, making sure it looks like a regular old shelf before heading into the bathroom. My head still throbs, so I open the medicine cabinet and take out a couple of Advil. When I move the mirror back into place, I stare at my reflection. Well, honestly, the glaring blue and purple bruising over my eye catches my attention more than anything else.

I sigh. The girl didn't even shove me that hard. It must've been the angle. Looks like I'll have to use a shitton of makeup tomorrow to try to cover whatever the frozen vegetables don't help with. Though I'm pissed I have a shiner, it probably works in my favor. What makes a girl look more defenseless than bruising from a fight? A fight I didn't even react to?

The thing is, I get how the Heights Crew works. I've been studying them from afar, standing in the background like a shadow. I'll need to get to the top to take my revenge. But in order to get to the top, I have to start at the bottom. If I came into Rawley Heights with a chip on my shoulder, no one would've let me in on the underground fighting biz they have going on. At least not for a while. They don't like newcomers. They don't trust them. To them, things are black and white. You're either a friend or a foe, and if they don't know you, you're automatically placed in the foe category.

But, by playing the victim, they'll let me in quicker. All I have to do is play soft, act like I don't know what I'm doing. I've already caught the eye of Oscar and Brawler. The latter arranges the fights in the underground fighting ring. He'll throw me in as a gimme to one of the girls who wants to climb to the top. Or, I'll seek that girl out myself, get under her skin, and make it so she wants to take me on. When she calls me out, that's when I'll step up. I'll make them see me. From that point on, it'll just be about ascending the ranks, capturing their trust, and then using it against them in the end.

My mind flicks back to Johnny, a.k.a. "Rocket", getting head in the fucking Rawley Heights' Main Office. He isn't even a student there anymore. My skin pricks at the way he looked at me. At the desire in his eyes. I clench my fingers, and they bite into the skin of my palm. Johnny Rocket is vile. He's disgusting. He's—

Three heavy knocks sound on the apartment door. The crying baby's lungs expand at the intrusion, making the cry worse and testing the limits of my hearing. I stomp out into the main living area and head toward the door. Another three knocks sound before I even have a chance to get to it. "Hold on," I snap. I take a quick peek through the peephole and freeze. "Shit," I mutter under my breath.

The view outside the door is distorted in a way only peepholes give, but Brawler is most definitely standing outside my door right now. *The* Brawler. *Fuck.* Before I can start freaking the hell out, convincing myself that he knows who I really am, I pull the door open, my heart lodging itself in my throat.

He looks lazily over at me, but then his eyes widen a fraction before he schools his features.

"Hey," I say. I tug at my clothes and run my hands through my hair like I'm worried about my appearance. Then, I cock my head. "You go to Rawley Heights, right?" Like I wouldn't have recognized him. He's exactly my type.

He peers behind me. "Everyone in this shithole our age goes to the Heights."

I shift ever so subtly to impede his view. I've tried to nail the shitty home life, but I also don't want to get found out on a technicality.

"Oh right," I mumble.

"Here." He thrusts a package at me.

I take a step back, my hands immediately moving

up to take the paper plate wrapped with foil. I look up from it, blinking at him.

"My mom likes to welcome the neighbors. She heard someone moved in down the hall."

Well, shit. I was not expecting that. Everyone else I've walked past in this building has either looked the other way or stared me down to prove their dominance while I avert my gaze. "That's really nice," I say.

His voice remains curt. "Don't get too sentimental. She can't cook worth a shit."

Okay, then. I see he's all about the warm and fuzzies. I shrug. "It's the thought."

When I look back up at him, I catch him staring at the goose egg above my eye. When he sees me looking, he casually slides his gaze away and looks into the apartment over my shoulders. It would be too obvious if I tried to block his view now.

His eyes burn with questions, but he doesn't say anything as he easily peruses what he can see behind me. I lift the foil on the plate and find a heap of chocolate chip cookies stuffed inside along with a very distinct burnt smell coming from them. I package it back up and set it on the small table just inside the door.

I peer down the hallway looking for any sign of where Brawler lives. I knew he lived in this building, along with a bunch of other Rawley Heights students and members of the Heights Crew, but I didn't know he was on the same floor as me. "Should I come thank her?"

"No," Brawler says definitively.

I widen my eyes at him like I'm a little too innocent.

His face darkens as shadows descend over his gaze. "Look, are your parents around?" he asks. He takes a quick look behind me again. Then, his gaze moves to the door.

"I don't have parents," I tell him. It feels good not to lie about this one thing. I even let some of my natural anger about that seep out.

He looks me up and down again. "You look like you have parents."

"I don't," I snap. "I have guardians, and no, they're not here. Why? Are you planning on coming in here to finish what your classmates started earlier?"

Okay, I was wrong about the shadows before. Now his eyes are truly black. "I don't hit women." Anger wafts off him. So much so that it pricks my nerve endings again.

Brawler's drop dead gorgeous. It has to be the eyes. Blue. But not light or dark, they're more like turquoise that turn into sapphires when he's pissed. He's wearing a wife beater, and a chain of tribal tattoos adorn his upper arms. If I didn't already know he was a fighter, I'd be able to tell now. His fists clench and unclench, causing his biceps to pull tight, his tattoos rippling with the movement. "The girls take care of their own," he says finally, flippantly.

"They don't seem to like me very much."

He laughs, the sound ricocheting through the barren hallway and temporarily overpowering the screaming baby a few doors down.

He doesn't follow that up with anything insightful, so I give him a look. "You seem to think that was a given."

He shakes his head. "You stick out like a virgin in a whorehouse."

"Um, I think that's a compliment."

He twists his head to the side. "To them it's not, Princess. To them, it's a threat."

He shows off a set of white teeth, but his smile isn't jovial. It's predatory. Him standing here in his wife beater, his tattoos showing, and that smile make my stomach tumble over itself. The fact that I know he's a fighter makes it all the better. Yes, I have a type. A definite type, and Brawler ticks all my sweaty, spasming, sheet-twisting boxes.

His jaw ticks the more he stares at me. The smile

melts until he's glaring. "You give other guys that same look, and they won't walk away like me. Buy an extra lock for your door. Don't open it when your *guardians* aren't home. Stay out of trouble."

With that, he walks away, his giant stride taking him quickly to the stairway door at the end of the hall.

Now that it feels like an entire bucket of ice water has been thrown on me, I step back and slam the door shut. I lock the five locks I have on the door already. Two I installed myself, thank you very much. And then I sit back down in the recliner.

He read me like a damn book.

I spend the next half an hour schooling myself on how to keep my thoughts in check in front of Brawler before I fall asleep for an hour and wake up in time to take the bus to the parking garage where my car is parked. I can't have anyone knowing I have a car a forty-year-old would drive. Plain, but nice. A tad fancy, but more economical than anything else. It was a gift from my aunt and uncle, but it screams another life. One I can't show here. I take it to Walmart to grab the lock and bolt cutters, and then I return to the tiny apartment to spend the rest of the evening watching murder mysteries with a bag of frozen vegetables over my forehead.

Before I head to bed, I throw away the cookies

Brawler's mom made. I smile when they thunk one-by-one into the trash. He wasn't kidding. His mom can't cook. He probably saved me from chipping a tooth.

Him walking away also saved me from getting involved in something I shouldn't. I have one focus and one focus only while I'm here.

4

The swelling in my face has gone down the next morning. Heavy makeup hides some of it but it's still noticeable that I got my ass beat yesterday. It's a fine line I'm trying to walk, actually. I want to seem demure, but at the same time, I can't become a target. If I become a target, they'll stop at nothing to take me down. People prey on the weak. It's just the hierarchy of things. It's like the food chain. The lions eat the smaller animals and the smaller animals eat the even smaller animals, plus plants and shit.

I can't be a plant. Or shit.

I hike my bookbag up my shoulder as I fall in line with the other kids who live in my building who are now making their way toward school. The back of my neck heats. I have no doubt several people stare, wondering why the hell I'm even bothering with school today. Though rough, Rawley Heights isn't that big. Everyone knows I'm the new girl, and everyone knows Oscar made that declaration about me only lasting two days. Maybe they're trying to find a way to make that happen. Everyone wants to get on the good side of one of the Heights Crew.

I run my hands through my hair and casually look over my shoulder. Instead of seeing some sharp-eyed bitch making plans for me, I find Brawler. He's not looking at me. In fact, it's like he's making a point not to look at me, which makes me think he was definitely the one giving off the vibe that I was being watched.

His attention unnerves me. It's what I want—what I need—to accomplish what I've come here to do, but I think I've gained his attention in a way I didn't mean to. I should've known better than to show my attraction to him, but it was literally impossible to deny. He basically personifies my entire wish list—and he's in the flesh, not just in my head.

I move to the edge of the sidewalk and slow down, pretending I have to tie my shoes so he'll pass me. He turns his head to glare at me, and I give him a disinterested look as I kneel. He walks past, and I get a glimpse of his threadbare shirt that's doing a terrible job of covering up his sinewy muscle. His jeans hug his ass with perfection, and he strides like he's a runway model though he'd kill anyone who made that reference. It's the confidence in the way he walks that gives me that vibe, not a flare for the dramatics. He owns himself. People part for him because of who he is, but also the way he carries himself. When he gets to the next street, he stops to lean against the pole littered with rusty, leftover staples, a representation of party fliers from the local bar and clubs.

I know that because that's where I did my research. That's where I learned about the Heights Crew. It's amazing what you can pick up by standing in the shadows of a disgusting bar, watching and listening. Drunk girls have no filter, so it was easy to listen to the names I needed. From there, it was just putting the faces with the names.

A few weeks ago, I witnessed Brawler fight. Well, I witnessed him *almost* get into a fight which was scary as fuck—and a turn-on. The anger that washed over him crept out of nowhere. Even now, I don't understand his trigger only that it had something to do with a girl. A girl I don't even think Brawler is seeing. From what I've heard, he's one of the unattainables. He's like the guy every girl wants to fuck but can't get because he always has a girlfriend. With Brawler, there's no girlfriend, but there's that same air of *don't even bother*.

No one gets close enough to him despite rampant attempts by desperate girls.

Before I know it, we're walking side-by-side on the way to school. Actually, he's even dropped back a few steps to the same position he was in before I stopped to tie my shoes. I clench my jaw. He must be playing at something. He must be paying just as much attention to me as I am to him, or how would we have ended up there *again*?

Worry seeps into me. Kids from the Heights are cutthroat. This could be about anything. Brawler could be setting me up. Sure, he didn't seem all that bad yesterday when he delivered his mother's terrible fucking cookies to my apartment, but that was outside of school, outside the crew. Family shit doesn't have anything to do with gangs. They're two separate entities. A gang banger could do a drive-by and then go home to his kids, reading to them before bed. Does that make him less of a killer?

No.

"Your neck's all red," a gruff voice remarks.

The tenor makes my joints lock up. "I'm hot," I lie. It spews from my mouth on its own accord. I sigh, wanting to take it back. Right now, I'm supposed to be scared Kyla. I should've told Brawler the second day at

Rawley Heights doesn't sound appealing to me, but instead, my real personality came out.

He casts me a sideways glance but looks straight ahead again. With the look on his face, I would think he'd be going back to ignoring me, but that's not the case at all. Brawler's like a silent killer. Unless he's in full-on fight mode, of course. When he's out of the ring, he's more like me. He's aware of his situation. He doesn't boast or talk just to hear the shit that comes out of his mouth. People know he's a threat because of his past actions, not because of the threats that pour out of his mouth over every little thing. It's people like Brawler you need to watch out for.

Brawler walks just behind me until we get to the metal detectors in front of the school. There's a back up this morning, and I realize I've gotten here a little later than I wanted. I might not have enough time to switch my lock out before first period.

When it's my turn, I drop my bag on the table. It thunks, and the security guard raises his eyebrows at me. "What the fuck are you packing?"

I don't answer, preferring to let him look through my bag himself.

He smirks as he pulls out the head of the bolt cutters. He shakes his head while turning his gaze to me. "No weapons in school."

"It's not a weapon. It's to cut off the broken lock on my locker."

He makes a humorless noise in the back of his throat, clearly telling me he doesn't believe a word I'm saying. Without uttering another word, he pulls the bolt cutters out and starts to chuck them in the trashcan next to him.

I stare him down. There's no way I thought they'd give me trouble for these. It's not like I'm packing a knife or a crude shiv. "Look," I say. "It's not a weapon."

"Sorry, Princess." The guard winks at me.

My hands turn to fists. I glare at him as he moves the bolt cutters over the trash. He looks to Brawler with a smirk, like he should get extra points for this, but instead, his lips thin. My body tenses as the large expanse of Brawler's chest crowds me. "Those are fine," he says.

The guard looks from the bolt cutters to Brawler again. "You trust this chick with these? I heard she gave Nevaeh a hard time."

"Nevaeh shouldn't start fights if she's worried about someone stopping them."

The guard shrugs like he could give a fuck and places the cutters back in my bag slowly, deliberately, like he's doing what Brawler told him to do, but he's not very happy about it. When he's done, I snatch my bag out of his hands and walk away. My skin's flushed. My mind is whirring. Why would Brawler follow me to school and then vouch for me over the bolt cutters? He has no idea what I'm going to do with these, and now that I think about it, hitting Nevaeh upside the head with these is a really good fucking idea. It would teach her not to attack from behind.

Footsteps thud behind me. They stay there until I get to my locker and stop when I stop. I spin on my heel, facing Brawler. I'm about to open my mouth to tell him to back off, but he's already ripped and roaring to go, effectively shutting me up. "The Heights isn't like wherever you came from."

"Shit, really?" I feign surprise. "My bad."

When I cross my arms, his jaw ticks. He reaches out, snatching my bag off my shoulder and unzips the main pocket. He pulls out the cutters, makes quick work of the broken lock on my locker, and turns to leave before the broken lock can even hit the floor.

"Hey, those are mine," I shout after him.

I don't expect a response, and I don't get one either. A girl walking by kicks my book bag down the hall. She crows in laughter when I hurry to retrieve it, grabbing it just as the bell rings.

"Shit," I grumble, hurrying back to my locker and fishing through my bag to put the new lock on it.

I just slide it through the hole when a voice behind me says, "Second day, Princess." I look over my shoulder to find the asshole who coined the nickname for me. I still owe him a nut shot for that and for manhandling me. Oscar's next to him though, his dark eyes boring holes into me. His friend asks him, "You still stand by your assessment, Drego?"

I watch Oscar carefully as he answers. He's the loud one. He's the one who talks fear into people. I'm not saying he can't back it up because I'm sure he can, but it's harder to understand who he is because talking is a front. It's our show to the world.

It's even harder to make him out because he was forced to join the Heights Crew so he wouldn't keep getting his ass kicked. Despite that, he seems to have taken the role seriously.

Before he can answer, a girl wraps her arms around him, draping herself over him like she's his blanket. "Hey, Baby," she coos.

I turn. There's no reason for me to watch this show. Plus, I'm finding it difficult to hide how interested I am in them. They can't know how badly I need them to accept me because they'll turn on me in an instant. What I've experienced so far will be nothing. It'll be a cake walk compared to what they'll have in store for me.

"What are you—? Oh," the girl says. Her displeasure makes me think she's spotted me.

"Hey, Nevaeh," douchebag says. His voice is low, flirty. It's like he can't even see she has a lady boner for Oscar. Or maybe she just has a lady boner for anyone who has power in this school. "I was just asking Drego if he still gives new girl two days."

"Well?" Nevaeh asks like I'm not standing right there. I hurry, throwing shit in my locker, locking it up, and then starting to walk away, but douchebag gets in my way.

"We're talking about you," he says, eyes glistening. "Don't move."

I tentatively look toward Oscar. He's assessing me. Not in a humiliating way. He's not undressing me with his eyes he's just watching, waiting. It's like he's content to sit back and see how this plays out.

"Actually, she needs to get the hell out of our way," Nevaeh says. "She looks like shit warmed over." Her sneer at my oversized shirt tells me exactly what she thinks about my choice of clothes. She's wearing a short, black skirt, a body conforming white tank and a gold necklace dipping into her cleavage, so it's easy to see why she thinks my clothing choices leave everything to be desired. "Oscar doesn't need to look at this fugly chick."

Oscar licks his lips. He leans away from Nevaeh like she suddenly smells bad. "Jealousy looks like shit on you," he says, his voice even and sure.

Nevaeh's jaw drops. She pulls out of his grip, wobbling a little in her tall heels. "What's that supposed to mean? She may as well be wearing a paper bag."

"This isn't about her," Oscar says, turning his full attention toward Nevaeh. "This is about you trying to claim me when I know who you've been spending time with."

There's something in Oscar's eyes. It's not just anger. He looks pained. A pain he seems to hate himself for feeling.

Nevaeh has the sense to look demure. She's definitely not dumb. She's smart. She knows who she needs to suck up to in order to survive this place. But I don't just want to survive. "It was a mistake."

Oscar laughs, loudly. "Once is a mistake. Twice could be an accident. But ten times? That's with intent."

I want to roll my eyes at his assessment of cheating, if that's what this even is. He probably just wants her to hang off him and only him. To be there when he deems it necessary to show her affection. I can't help but feel bad for her. In places like the Heights, the girls have to be as bad as the guys or they have to be someone's *someone*. The one person they'll crawl through fire for. The girl they'll take a bullet for.

Nevaeh's definitely not it for Oscar. She's better off trying with douchebag here and then hope he actually makes it into the Crew.

A hand smacks me in the chest. "What are you looking at, Skank?"

I fly back into my locker. I take a moment to breathe before glancing at Nevaeh. Her red-rimmed eyes are glassy. It's obvious she's taken what Oscar said hard, and now she's taking it out on me.

I shrug, then try to move around them, catching Oscar's eye as I do. He's looking on with interest—and possibly a smirk—as Nevaeh uses me as a play to get him back.

"Don't you dare look at him. You should be kissing his fucking feet."

Her hand slams down on my shoulder and pushes. She succeeds in making me stumble, but it doesn't take me to my knees like she wants. I try to shrug her off. "I'm just trying to get to class," I say, even though I'm twitching to retaliate.

"You can go to class as soon as you kiss Oscar's shoes," Nevaeh says loudly enough for everyone to hear.

The douchebag laughs like he's never had this much fun before first period. I'd wish for the bell to ring, but I don't think any of these guys give a shit whether they show up to class at all, let alone care if they make it on time.

Nevaeh tries to force me down again, this time buckling my knees for a second. I pop right back up, turning toward her. I draw the line at kissing fucking feet. I won't be humiliated like that. Oscar reaches out for me, and everyone pauses. The laughter slows and then dies. Nevaeh stares open-mouthed at his gesture. He takes my arm, sliding his around mine.

Nevaeh gasps behind us. "Oscar..."

"Who knows," Oscar says. "Maybe Princess knows how to treat a man."

We walk around the corner, leaving the scene behind us. As soon as we're out of sight, Oscar immediately lets me go. He walks off like he didn't just make me enemy number one in Nevaeh's eyes, but that wasn't what his goal was. He was doing this for him. He was showing her he doesn't give a fuck. That he can move on to the next girl because she means nothing to him. But I suspect the opposite is true. I suspect he actually really, really cares that he was runner up to someone else.

Who doesn't? We all want to be number one. A long time ago, I was.

I grip the side of the locker and stare after Oscar. Cement hardens my veins, strengthening my purpose. I want revenge on the person who took the people who thought I was number one away from me. He deserves it.

5

You know that feeling when people keep looking at you and you're afraid they know something you don't? I get that for the entire day. In class, the other students blatantly watch me, most of them snickering, some just with looks of disinterest.

In the halls when I change classes, I get the same treatment. I don't ever think of myself as someone who fears a lot of things. I've already been through the worst parts of my life, but today? Today, I'm worried about what the hell kind of shit is about to go down.

Right before lunch, I stop at my locker to drop off my book bag. It crashes to the bottom with a metallic clank. School seems like such a waste at the moment. Not only do the classes suck, but it's basically impossible to learn anything. Plus, school isn't the most important thing going on in my life right now. I'm only paying attention in class to wonder why everyone keeps watching me. I'm basically just waiting for the other shoe to drop.

A tickle of awareness cascades down my shoulders. I turn, slowly, so it doesn't look like I'm afraid, but when I finally do see who's behind me, my stomach bottoms out.

"The fuck are you doing?" Brawler seethes.

He grips my wrist, shuts and locks my locker with his other hand, and pulls me behind him to the stairwell at the end of the hall. It smells like a mixture of must and lingering smoke in this corner. Dust bunnies scatter along the walls. There are so many of them it looks as if they haven't swept back here in a year. I yank my wrist out of his grip, certain I'm only able to because he let me. "What the fuck?" I growl back.

Brawler leans over me, his blue eyes blazing. He's effectively cut me off from escaping. My back's to the wall as he fills the gap between the wall and stairs. Voices linger in the hallway, but not enough that I would feel safe if I called out. Not to mention that would be a stupid idea, anyway. No one's helping me here. I'm on my own. It's Heights Crew territory, and I'm no one.

"Are you insane? Or just plain stupid?"

I rub my wrist for something to do. He didn't really hurt me all that much, which makes me wonder what he's playing at. I sit back on my heels and stare into the inky depths of his eyes. I want them to tell me all of Brawler's secrets, but I keep coming up with nothing. "What are you talking about?"

He lets out a breath. "Nevaeh is what I'm talking about. She wants to challenge you to a fight."

My heart starts to pound. This is what I wanted. This is my in. Go to the Heights. Act like a doormat. Find a back door into the underground ring. "A-a fight?" I stammer out, and the tension is real, not faked. I'm not worried Nevaeh will beat me. She's straight up amateur, but the fact that on my second day at school, what I needed to have happen is already happening is fantastic. It just needs to play out the way I want—no, need—it to.

"Yes," he all but growls. He runs a hand through his hair. "I know you're fucking new here but listen up. If you get challenged to a fight, you *have* to fight. You don't show your face after passing on a fight. You won't fucking last. They'll make sure of it."

I bite the inside of my cheek. Brawler's concern warms my insides. A fleck of fear for me passes in our heated gaze. I wouldn't have pegged Brawler as a weak link. Not that concern should make you weak, but he's the one who puts on the fights for crying out loud. You would think he'd want to see this. "Why would she want to fight me?"

Brawler's wide shoulders relax in defeat. He checks over his shoulder. "Oscar. Did he pick you over her or something? What went down?"

I pretend to think, drawing it out, which only makes Brawler more and more agitated. "He accused Nevaeh of cheating on him, then he did walk me down the hall a little way. I didn't think that meant we were..."

I trail off, but Brawler doesn't waste any time. "Nevaeh's been going after Oscar since he got back. Her older brother's in the Crew, and she wants in too. She'll only be able to get in if she wifes up."

"Wifes up?"

Brawler sighs. "Just forget it. Can you just please stay the fuck out of her way? When you see her coming down the hallway, move. If she's in one of your classes, skip. If she comes at you, fucking run."

I run a hand through my hair. Brawler watches the movement as I wonder what he's playing at. I must've missed something important. I didn't think any of these important players would be trying to help me. I can't let Brawler get close. I have to make sure I fight. "Why do you care?"

Brawler snaps his mouth shut. His eyes shutter. There's some definite emotion there for a split second before he shields himself, cutting me off from his real emotions.

"I'm a big girl. Brawler, right? That's what they call you?" I don't wait for an answer, and he's not forthcoming with one, anyway. "This is just ridiculous," I laugh. "She doesn't want to fight me. I didn't do anything to her. Oscar did this. I'm sure he'll fix it."

Brawler's head snaps toward me. "If you think Oscar gives a fuck about anyone but himself, you're mistaken."

"Again," I say, losing patience. I can't have Brawler interfering in this. "Don't worry about me."

"Don't be dumb, New Girl."

"My name's Kyla, and I'll be sticking around, so you might as well learn it."

I try to push past him, but he's like an immovable wall of muscle. His muscles flex as soon as I graze them. "Don't do anything stupid. Take my advice."

He gives me space to move out of the way, and I push through only to stop short when I see who's standing only a few feet away. Oscar's leaning back against a locker, looking much like I saw him on the first day of school. He kicks off the row of metal as soon as we spot one another. "What's this?" he asks, looking between Brawler and me.

The heat from Brawler's torso warms my back as soon as he steps behind me. When he speaks, his voice sounds gruffer. "I was warning her to stay away from Nevaeh."

A cocky grin stretches Oscar's lips. "Yeah, I guess she really didn't like what happened earlier, huh?"

Brawler nods. "That's the word being passed around."

Oscar reaches out to play with the short hair around my temple that's escaped from my ponytail. "I guess I should've seen that coming. Nevaeh doesn't like being taken down a peg or two. Even when she's in the wrong."

"She wants to fight Princess here."

My jaw locks. That fucking name needs to die. Instead of blowing up, I smile sweetly at Oscar. "I told Brawler it was a misunderstanding."

Oscar's arm drops down to his side. He peeks over my shoulder at Brawler then back at me. "Whether it was or wasn't, doesn't change anything."

The look in his eyes is cold. A familiarity seeps through me. I recognize some of myself in him.

"You can fix this, man," Brawler says. "Look at

her," he says, motioning toward me, "She's going to get seriously hurt. She doesn't belong here."

I guess no one has ever told these guys that appearances aren't everything. Wasn't that something we should've learned a long time ago? Don't judge a book by its cover and all that jazz? These guys are going to have a rude awakening when I step into that ring.

Oscar laughs. The sound chills me. He's perfected the art of not giving a fuck. I suspect a lot of the people here have—except Brawler. I still can't figure out why he's even giving me the time of day. "Why would I do that? I said she was going to last two days, today's the second day. She'll probably run home tonight after the threat of violence and beg her parents to take her the hell away from here."

"I don't have parents," I say

Brawler talks over me. "This one's on you then, man. Remember that."

"Isn't everything on me?"

Brawler and Oscar stare at one another. Unspoken words pass between them. Their eyes flare, their muscles bunch. They're having a battle of wills I'm not privy to, but I can taste the testosterone they exert on my tongue. It smells like bad decisions and musk.

My heart flutters.

I don't dare speak or move while they eye one

another. It's Oscar who moves first. He holds his arm out to me. "Lunch?"

I stare at his offered hand and then up to him. "Um, what?"

"Sit with me at lunch."

"Isn't that just going to piss Nevaeh off more?"

"Yes, but I suspect it's also going to piss someone else off." His eyes flick behind me. "Which makes it that much more exciting."

I look over my shoulder to find Brawler shaking his head. He walks away, his long strides taking him away far quicker than if I were to hurry off the same way.

A grin teases Oscar's lips. "I swear I'm a nicer guy than Brawler makes me out to be."

"Didn't you just say that I was only going to last two days and you were okay with that?"

"That's just years of experience talking." He drops his voice, murmuring into the now empty hall. "There's no shame in running away." Even though he offers it with a grin, I'm not meant to take him up on it.

Despite myself, I'm more curious than ever about these two. Oscar seems lost, and I never would've guessed that the guy who puts on the Crew fights has a conscience. He's worried for me, and if I had to take a stab at what he was doing this morning on our way to school, I'd bet he was watching me to make sure I made it okay.

Oscar leans over as we start walking down the hallway. "Do me a favor. If Nevaeh calls you out, make sure you kick her ass for me."

He keeps his head facing forward, but I turn to look at his profile. His eyes are dark, clouded over with a mixture of anger, self-loathing, and something much fiercer.

There's definitely something more to these guys than I originally thought.

Like this morning, Oscar drops my arm like he never even wanted it in the first place. I stop just outside the lunchroom as he walks in, greeted by a myriad of other students. In there, there's no trace of the guy who wants revenge on the girl who wronged him. In there, people fall all over him because of who he is.

Back in my old school, the only ones who were treated like that were the ultra-rich. Here, Oscar's three rungs from the top on the gang life pyramid, which makes him a damn hero. Those who don't like him still tolerate him because they know what he has at his disposal.

An arm moves around my shoulders, dropping there like it belongs. I immediately jump and stiffen when I see who it is. The guy's eyes widen with recognition. "Ahh, you get around, don't you?" His snicker makes me want to vomit. "I see you've met Oscar, probably in more ways than one already. No wonder why I hear Nevaeh's gunning for you."

My lips move without saying anything. The skin he just touched crawls with confusion. It's repulsion, yet warmth at the same time. Stomach rolling, I attempt to get myself together. "I'm new." I swallow, hoping I sound authentic. "I just met Oscar yesterday, if you can call it meeting at all. He thinks I'm only going to last two days in this school."

Rocket looks me up and down, his perusal slow, steady, and unnerving. "He was generous." I can't help the annoyance that flits across my face. It makes Rocket laugh. "I can see why he's all up in your business though. Oscar's always liked shiny things. He likes to chase better tail, and we can tell you're not from around here from a mile away."

No kidding. Having an admin go down on someone in the main office who isn't even a student never would've happened in my old school. Hell, it shouldn't be happening in this school either.

"I wonder how jealous I can make Oscar..."

Rocket reaches out, but I move out of the way. "I don't know Oscar. I don't even know you."

"You remember we met yesterday though, right?"

"Was that a meeting? From what I could see, you were busy."

Rocket's eyes dance. On the surface, they're a similar color to Brawler's, but Rocket's are lighter like swimming in the Caribbean Sea. "I'm Rocket," he says, inclining his head.

"Kyla," I tell him. My fingers clench and unclench. I know he didn't kill my parents. He didn't pull the trigger, but he comes from the deranged man who did, and it's hard to separate the two. I've seen blurry pictures of both. Their bone structure is similar, but Big Daddy K, leader of the Heights Crew, has thirty pounds on his son and thirty years. Neither is in the positive column.

I'm trying to accept the fact that Johnny Rocket is good looking. My brain tells me that. My eyes tell me that. But I can't help but wonder if his soul is as dark as his father's.

"Good to know," Johnny says. He rakes his gaze down me, making me want to take these clothes off and burn them. He's having entirely too much fun trying to see under them.

"What year are you in?" I ask because that sounds like a reasonable question for someone you've just met who's standing in a school, even though I know he shouldn't be. "I don't think we have any classes together."

The corners of his lips tip up. "Oh, we won't be having any classes together. I graduated two years ago. I just like to stop by to check on my guys."

"Your guys?"

"Friends," he tells me, shrugging off the question. It looks like even he isn't arrogant enough to spill that he's a part of the Crew even though everyone knows it. Hell, he's second tier. He's runner-up to his father. In the years to come, he'll be groomed to take his father's place. He'll reign supreme over all this. The school, the city, the people. There's not a single person around that won't be out of his reach.

Johnny Rocket is everything. And he knows it.

6

Seeing Johnny Rocket unnerves me for the rest of the day. Brawler follows me home, the whispers of Nevaeh and I fighting still thick in the air around us. I should be happy about this because this is what I wanted. I needed an in to fight. I have one. I'm not worried about fighting Nevaeh at all, I just didn't think I'd see Johnny the first day I got to the Heights—or the second.

What if his father is around, too? Like a fly on the wall? Or the boogie man in the shadows? What if he's around, and I just don't know it?

The thought follows me all the way home, and even though Brawler stomps up the steps behind me since we live in the same hall, I go right to my apartment, lock all my locks, and walk right into the small bedroom to lie down, dropping my book bag on the carpet in the process. I feather a breath out, staring up at the ceiling, but not seeing it. Instead, I'm imagining everything that's gone down in the years since my parents were taken from me. That's how I get through times like this. Times when I wonder what I'm doing this for. I mean, I want the outcome. I want to have Big Daddy K's life in my hands at the end but getting there is the problem. Every little step makes everything I've worked for and trained for all that much more real. The path is opening ahead of me like I thought it would, and I can't help but second-guess things.

One Kyle and An-na. Two Kyle and An-na. These words are my calming motto. My reminder I have more to live for.

I fall asleep thinking about all of this, but I'm awakened later by hard knocks on the door. My eyes flit toward the hidden compartment below the shelf, wondering if I should grab the gun there.

It could be Nevaeh.

It could be Johnny.

It could be Big Daddy K, and somehow, they've put it all together and know what I'm here to do.

The banging persists, so I get up, tiptoeing my way to the door while straightening my clothes.

I'm about to peek through the peephole when a gruff voice says, "I know you're in there, New Girl!"

I close my eyes briefly. Brawler's on the other side of the door. I recognize the annoyance in his voice. Out of everyone it could be, he's the safest to open the door for. In his way, he's tried to protect me. Just to be sure it's him, I check the peephole and then go through the process of unlocking all the locks when I recognize the tribal tattoos flowing up his arms. I pull the door open. "I hope you aren't dropping off more cookies. I threw the last ones away."

His gaze narrows at me, but then moves behind me, once again looking into my empty apartment. "No guardians again?"

"They work a lot."

"They must have shit jobs."

"Doesn't everyone around here have shit jobs?"

His lips purse. Instead of responding, he pushes past me like he owns the place.

"What the fuck?" I growl.

He turns toward me, pushing the door closed to enclose us in this space. He checks the locks before turning a calculating gaze on me. "We have a problem."

I try to keep still. I hope this is it. My chance to get into the depths with them, but in the Heights, who knows what this could be about? He could be pissed I said his mom's cookies were shit. I don't know. "You and I have a problem?"

"No, *you* have the problem."

I fold my arms over my chest. "Is this about Nevaeh because I really don't think that's going to be an issue," I lie. My skin tingles at the prospect. *Please. For the love of God, let me fight her.*

"It was about Nevaeh, but it's not anymore." Brawler does a once-over as he shakes his head.

Well, fuck. I try not to look put out.

"There's some shit you don't understand about your new school. Even if you heard people whisper about it, you still don't know shit. Trust me."

I just stare, waiting for him to keep going, trying not to look at the ink on his forearms.

"In Rawley Heights, we have the Heights Crew. For lack of a better term, it's a gang."

"Okay…"

His jaw clamps shut. I can't help that I find Brawler intriguing. I totally had him pegged wrong. Here I thought he was going to be a badass fighter, which I'm sure he is, but he's more than that, too. Or maybe I've just done my part well, looking like a pathetic scared kitten, and he feels like he needs to warn me about the dangerous side of the Heights.

Still, it doesn't add up. I've seen him around the

other people in school. I've even watched him interact when I was gathering information about the Crew. He barely talks. He's talked more to me than I've seen him talk to anyone.

Passing his thumb over his lip, he says, "Nevaeh took her beef with you to Johnny Rocket. Remember when I told you that if you got called out, you have to fight?" He waits for my nod, then continues. "After she took it to him, he agreed you're fighting, but not with Nevaeh."

This time, the look of concern that passes across my face is real. If not Nevaeh, then who? "And...?"

"Cherry."

I rack my brain, trying to remember if I've come across the name Cherry, but I come up with nothing. "Does she go to our school?" I ask.

Brawler shakes his head. "Used to. Not anymore." He runs his hands over his blond hair. "Fuck. I was hoping I'd have more time to introduce you to all of this, but for some fucking reason, you stick out to everybody."

"Introduce me to what?"

"The fight ring," he says, gaze meeting mine. The struggle in his blue depths is real.

"You already told me if people get called out, they

have to fight," I tell him, spilling out everything I'm supposed to know.

A low chuckle spills from his mouth, and for the first time since I've laid eyes on Brawler, his eyes are practically dancing. "It's a lot more than that, Princess."

"Stop calling me that," I snap. I hate that we're talking about fighting and I'm being called Princess in the same damn sentence.

"I like it," he says, shrugging. "I like it even more because you don't." I bite my lip at the look of fiery excitement in his eyes. He immediately drops his gaze to my mouth before continuing. "The fights are how the Heights Crew makes money. People can call people out, but you have to pay to fight. Sometimes with money. Sometimes with other things. It's the betting that they make the big bucks on though. It's made the Crew one of the wealthiest and most dangerous around." He swallows. "If you'd stuck around, you would've figured this all out on your own. I'm giving you a crash course because you're on the card tonight."

"I'm what?" My eyes round. Excitement and uncertainty clash inside me.

"Unless you're out," he says. He looks around my empty apartment. My stomach tightens. It might be me, but I think he sees more than he should. He's perceptive. He's never just looking at the surface. If Brawler's looking at you, he's going deep.

"I can't be out," I tell him. "I live here now, and I don't want to fucking move again." The irony that I'm arguing to stay in this shithole is not lost on me. I'm probably the only one in this world who would pick this life over the other one waiting for me if I choose to go back to it.

I won't until I get this shit done.

"Then you don't have a choice. And when I say you don't, I mean it. If you don't at least show up and put up a fight, consider yourself enemy number one, Princess. We don't play games here. You might have heard of bullying at your other schools. Maybe even witnessed it." A dark smile stretches his face momentarily. "Ours is more like a hazing. If you survive, you can stay, and I do mean *survive*. There's no PTA or administration who's going to save you. The teachers don't care. They're scared, and if they're not scared, it's because they're in the Crew too. There's only two ways out of this shit you find yourself in. Fight in the fight. Or fight for your life. Both are going to suck, but at least if you show up to the fight, you have a chance of survival."

Goosebumps spread over my body. I pass my palms

over my skin, trying to calm the chills, wondering how many students at the school have been run off because of what the Heights Crew has going on here. If you think about it, it's the perfect setup. They own the people here. The fights keep everyone in line and makes sure only the strongest survive. It gives guys like Rocket the perfect opportunity to pick the best people to join the Heights Crew ranks. Not to mention the money they make out of it all.

"So, who's this Cherry?" I ask.

Brawler drops into my recliner and ignores the evil eye I give him. "Now that would be cheating."

"You don't think she's going to know everything about me?"

"No one knows anything about you. You just showed up." He eyes me like he's trying to look deep under my skin again. It's unnerving.

I move to the bar separating the small kitchen from the living room and lean against it. "That happens, doesn't it? People just move places. That's not unheard of."

"It doesn't happen in the Heights. You think people want to just move here? The people who live here are stuck, and there's more than one way to be stuck."

He looks away. I'm burning with curiosity about all

his secrets. I can't help myself. I thought I would hate everyone here. I thought everyone who had anything to do with the Heights Crew would be outright terrible. Like I could look at them and just know their dirtiest secrets. If Brawler has dirty secrets, they're hidden underneath his fine exterior and conflicted gaze. "Fine. I don't get information on Cherry. How does Nevaeh feel about this? She wanted the fight, right?"

"You're still on her shit list. You better be careful with that one. Oscar's been at the top of her list for a while. That asshole hasn't done you any favors."

That's an understatement. He basically sicced every female at the school on me on day one. Then, he used me as bait to get back at someone else. I'm beginning to think that Brawler's assessment of Oscar only being out for himself is all too true.

"So, you said I have to pay to fight, right? I—"

Brawler waves me away. "Only the person who wants the fight has to pay up." He stands from the armchair. "Have you ever fought before?"

He steps closer, his looming presence hovering over me.

I shrug, a smile plays over my lips. "You think I'm going to tell you?"

"Why wouldn't you?"

"If I don't get to know anything about Cherry, why

would I tell you something about me? Something you could take back to her?"

He purses his lips. "Why would you think I'd do that?"

It's hard to concentrate when he's around. I've almost forgotten we're even having a conversation. He just has this aura about him that makes me want to take him in. Inspect him without using words. "Just being cautious," I say finally.

He gives me a short nod. His intrusive blue eyes make me want to fidget under his inspection. But if I do that, he'll know I have something to hide.

"You know, you never really answered the question about why you're helping me. This isn't the only time. You practically walked me to school this morning. You warned me about Nevaeh. Now this. What's the deal, Brawler?"

He steps back on his heels like I've shoved him with my words. "I don't know," he says. Pure honesty flickers in his gaze before he covers it up, placing on a controlled mask I can tell he's perfected. "You remind me of someone, I guess. Someone who never belonged here. Who put on a facade, but..." He trails off. "That's all."

Jealousy burns in the bottom of my stomach. Whoever Brawler is talking about, he loved this person very much. The wound he's carrying is raw, open, and seeping. I haven't loved someone like that in a long time. "Sorry," I say automatically because it's clear he lost this person and that he has to deal with the loss every day.

Just like me.

"Be ready in an hour," Brawler orders. "I'll take you to the place."

I peek at the neon clock lights above the stove. It's six already. I guess I definitely did take a nap when I got back from school. "I'll be here," I tell him, gesturing like I have nowhere else to go.

He gives me one last look before walking around me, leaving a trail of controlled sadness and resolution in his wake.

When the door closes behind him, I drop down into the recliner he sat in and breathe in deep. It smells like him. Like sweet sweat and musk.

I didn't expect to find someone who gave a shit about anything here. Even less so someone who might look out for me. I have no idea why Brawler would be doing this, so I have to believe what he told me. I remind him of someone...

The lies I've worn and spewed make my stomach churn with guilt. Isn't that one of the first things we learn when we're little? Not to lie? I have to though. I have to bury the truth inside me, so it doesn't come up when I least want it to. My truth will kill me. It doesn't matter if Brawler acts like he gives a shit what happens to me. I have one goal and one goal only. Take Big Daddy K down. And if someone else in the Heights Crew gets in my way, I'll take them down, too.

I can't have any regrets.

I turn my music on and start warming up. I have a lot riding on this fight, and I can't leave anything to chance.

7

The Heights Crew's underground fighting warehouse reeks of desperation and excitement. It sits smack dab in the middle of the city, which happens to be the most rundown, forgotten, dilapidated area. Broken windows and graffiti would ward me off the place if it weren't for Brawler accompanying me, but inside, all that washes away. The buzz sets my skin afire with recognition. Sure, I've never fought *here* before, but places like this are the same. The energy, the mystery, the darker side of life thrive here. It's thrilling and scary. The feelings pounding in the walls have their own alluring heartbeats that bring me back time and time again.

Since Brawler and I showed up, I've stayed in the background, avoiding everyone. A lot of familiar faces from school stride in, hanging out in groups. To the side, there's a makeshift bar, mostly serving up bottles of beer, but there are shots, too. Brawler sits on the very last stool, staring out at everyone clamoring inside for a place to sit. Every once in a while, our gazes meet. He's the only one who knows I'm back here. He probably thinks I'm hiding. I kind of am, but I also want to warm up in peace.

People approach him while he sits, leaning over to whisper in his ear and greet him with knuckles or bro hugs. As soon as we got here, it became apparent Brawler ran the fights. Not that I hadn't already known that, but he'd left that conveniently out of the conversation earlier when we spoke. Like me, he thrives in arenas like this. He becomes his nickname, dominating the space in his makeshift black tank top with ripped out arm holes. He's the person everyone wants to see. The guy everyone flocks around.

Not that I'm noticing when I should definitely be concentrating on my fight. Right? Right.

I glance that way again, but find his seat occupied by a girl in a black bikini top, a blinging necklace hanging in her cleavage. Scanning the area, I search for him, telling myself it has nothing to do with the fact that I think he's hot as fuck and everything to do with the fact that I need to know where Brawler—the guy who runs the fights—is at all times.

He appears to my left, and I almost jump. He casually strides toward me, giving me ample time to watch him approach. The shirt he chose displays his tattoos just as appropriately as a significant artifact in a museum display. I want to ask him about the black, twisting ink. I want to know what they're about because guys like Brawler don't just wake up one day and get a tattoo. They have meaning, like a story to his soul.

He stops a foot away, and I pretend I don't have a lady hard-on for him. I also pretend I'm nervous as shit. "Is it...is it soon?" I ask, twisting my hands. He must think I'm pathetic, which pains the pride in me. In another life, Brawler would well know by now how much I want to jump his bones.

He tips his head toward the fight currently going on in the ring. The bigger dude has a huge gash over his eyebrow. Blood leaks into his eyes, but his opponent isn't going easy on him. Instead, the sight of blood makes him almost feral in his attacks. He keeps delivering blow after punishing blow. "As soon as Rascal takes care of that guy, you're up."

I move my head from side-to-side, cracking my neck before staring down at the stained floor. The dried crimson circles at my feet tell me exactly what kind of place this is, and it thrills me more than it should. I'm having a hard time keeping my excitement to myself. Adrenaline shoots through me, making me want to bounce on my toes.

I hate having to be this other person. This person who acts like she's scared of everything. I'm hardly scared of anything. The worst possible thing has already happened to me, so what's there to be scared about? The Heights Crew? Please. The worst thing they could do to me is kill me, and who would care?

Nobody. Least of all me. I haven't had a life since they took it away from me.

Brawler claps me on the back with a devilish grin, but a hint of concern stretches underneath it all. "Chin up, Kyla. I have a feeling it won't last too long."

The spot where he touches me burns. His hand lingers there, our gazes connecting once again like two magnets that keep getting pulled together without thought. He walks away, leaving demeaning laughter in his wake. That should be my signal that he's dangerous. He should be automatically moved to my "don't fuck with" list, but I can't sweep the warnings he gave me away. In his way, he's tried to help. Though, admittedly, that was earlier. Something else entirely has come over him since stepping foot in here. He's Dr.

Jekyll and Mr. Hyde. Outside of this place, he wanted to help. Now that we're here, he's ready to throw me to the wolves to see how I fare.

I slip even farther into the shadows and start warming up like I should have been all along. Through the gaps in the crowd, I spot Cherry. We haven't been introduced, but Brawler goes to her next, leaning over to whisper in her ear. My hackles raise, jealousy burning through me, but when Brawler straightens, he greets a guy standing in the shadows much like me. The guy's hand moves around her possessively, and she easily melts into his side.

Thanks to the drunken girl who walked past with her friend only a few minutes ago, I found out Cherry's the nickname Rocket gave her the night he popped her cherry. If some guy is going to nickname her that after sex, I imagine he'd be the one with his arm around her right now.

My temple throbs with my own pulse. I had not planned on meeting Rocket the way I did. He'd caught me off guard, and dammit if ever since then I can't stop thinking about that rather than him being the spawn of the evil that's been lurking in the background of my life since I was twelve. Since then, it's hard not to wonder if we're caught in this tangled web together, both of us victims of our own circumstance.

I shake my head, focusing on the present. I have a fight to prepare for—a fight to win. Lunges, squats, and tuck jumps are my friend as I stretch my limbs. I windmill my arms, loosening my shoulders, and then crack the knuckles on every one of my fingers and shake them out. The background is just that: background. I tune out the sounds of the other fight and the crowd and mentally prepare for what's about to go down.

I'll have to take a few punches. I already know this. It's the only way to make it convincing at first, but then I'm going to switch the tables on Cherry. I'm going to be her worst nightmare she won't ever see coming. Because in that ring, it won't be me and Cherry, it'll be twelve-year-old me wanting vengeance on everyone and everything that has to deal with Big Daddy K.

Fuck that murderer.

I let the rage seep deep into my marrow. I let it fill me, my hands already clenched to fists.

"Kyla," Brawler calls out.

I turn, purposefully loosening my fists and looking at him like a deer in the headlights. He shakes his head like the Brawler who was inside my apartment earlier might show up, but in the next second, that vanishes when his predatory smile comes out to play again. He crooks a finger at me, and I step toward him in my oversized shirt and joggers, sweat already rimming the collar. "You're up."

I make a show of staring at the crowd perched on wooden crates. They're stacked on top of one another like poor men's bleachers. They're oblivious about the fight that's about to happen. They're still talking about the last one while downing their drinks or sharing a joint.

Brawler sighs as he takes me in. "Just turtle up when she comes at you." He gives me a wary once-over, like he's afraid I might get seriously hurt. The old Brawler's back, making me even more curious about what goes through his head. He told me I remind him of someone. That someone had to have been so important to him. Ridiculously, I'm attracted to both his sides, whether they're complete opposites of one another or not.

That doesn't matter right now, though. And not ever. I have one fucking thing to do while I'm in the Heights, and it's not to bang Brawler. "But—" I start to protest.

He cuts me off. His momentary lapse in better judgment now gone. "It's your funeral, New Girl. Remember what I said. You only have two options, and you won't survive the other."

I bite my lip to keep from smiling. All the taunts,

all the petty bitches and dicks from Rawley Heights, like Nevaeh and the douche who coined me Princess, are about to see a side of me they never saw coming. I wish I could record what's about to go down, cameras focused on their reactions. I haven't seen Nevaeh, but I have no doubt she's here. Oscar, too. I doubt he'd miss this, whether I'm fighting the girl he wants me to beat up or not.

Brawler pushes me toward the empty circle in the middle of the room, and I stumble. I must look like a blithering mess, but before I get pissed, I remember that's exactly what I want to look like.

The crowd crows. Blistering heat warms my cheeks. the embarrassment eating me up from the inside out. They start to chant, "Prin-cess. Prin-cess."

Seriously, did Brawler tell them how much I fucking hated that?

Anywhere else, Princess might be a compliment, but to them, it's far from it. It denotes a life of privilege they never had. They hate me. All of them.

Cherry enters through the crowd like the queen bee of Rawley Heights. The crowd roars. She's a favorite of theirs. It's not difficult to figure that out. A cherry red robe drapes over her shoulders like she's an actual boxer. A guy from her corner slips the silk material from her shoulders revealing a skimpy sports bra. It traps the majority of her breasts away, but ample cleavage still pours out. The crowd's cheering intensifies. My guess is it's mostly man sluts hoping she'll slip a tit in the fight. They're probably looking over at me and thinking that's the only excitement they'll get out of tonight.

Now that we're facing each other, it's getting more real. Who would've thought two days in and I'd get my chance to show the Heights Crew's leaders what I'm about? Fighting is my only chance in. If I had to wait to endear myself to them in some other way, it could take years and years for them to trust me. Call me self-serving, but Big Daddy K has already taken six years of my life. He doesn't need more than that.

I stop myself from jumping up and down, the way I usually get rid of pre-fight jitters. Instead, I toe the ground and do some basic stretching. The kind they taught us in Kindergarten, so I look like a dumbass newbie.

Cherry sneers at me. "This is what you get for coming to the Heights, Bitch."

I've had to tone down my snarky ass for days. I can't wait until this fucking fight is over, so I can verbally eliminate all these fucking wannabe fighters. Instead of tearing her down, I flinch.

"Aww, do you need to go hide back to Mommy?"

My blood boils. This bitch's mom is probably doped up on crack right now. Or spreading her legs downtown. She probably never had a Mommy to console her, but I did. She's just fucking dead because of people like her.

I search the crowd behind Cherry, looking for Rocket and hoping he was the guy cozying up to her before the fight. At the same time, I'm begging for him to appear so I can be sure he's watching, I'm also wondering how many girls he's fucking. The secretary at the school, for sure. Cherry, obviously.

Get a fucking grip, I scold myself. Rocket's sex life is none of my concern. Nor is Brawler's, or anyone else's for that matter. I'm only interested in him being here because he needs to see me kick his girl's ass. He and Brawler need to give me more fights, so I can move up and make my way as a serious player for the Heights Crew.

Brawler steps into the middle of the ring. His lips move, but I look past him toward Cherry. She winks, still smirking over her Mom comment. A rush of nothing but rage fills me. How dare anyone here mention her. A storm rages inside my head until Brawler steps back and yells, "Fight!" Then, the storm unleashes.

My plans have left the building.

I rush her. Her eyes flare with anticipation, but she isn't good. I'm fast and skilled. She's just an amateur, a wannabe competitor dangling from the coattails of Rocket. I slip under her lame ass attempt at a punch, pop back up, and give a good right hook to her fucking ribs.

The crowd gasps. Sure, Cherry's not their number one fighter. I get that. I was just a gimme to her, a steppingstone. Someone she could use to climb the trellis of the Heights Crew hierarchy. *Well, good fucking luck after this, you dirty fucking hoe bag bitch.*

I step back after my body reacts on autopilot. My fist connecting with her midsection a third time brings me back to reality. I can't just come out here and kick her ass. Not until I'm sure Rocket's here. Trying to stifle my reaction, I leave my hands down at my waist and look petrified at what I just did.

"You cunt," she seethes, blinking

She lunges for me, and I let her. She gets in two good punches before I veer around her, bringing my forearms up to block my face. Brawler eyes me from the outskirts of the crowd. I definitely didn't do a good job of hiding my prowess. He saw my initial attack for what it was. A deliberate, skilled offense.

Cherry pulls on my shoulders and lands a knee to my gut. With her mouth near my ear, she says, "You piece of fucking trash. Bitches like you don't make it in the Heights. Consider me your gatekeeper, and you're not in."

Her confidence is growing. Good. I look past her arm, scanning the crowd again until I finally see him. There. Exactly who I need to see this. Now that I have Rocket's attention, I push past her hold, slip under her and then lock my arm around her outside forearm, holding her in place as I batter the side of her head with hard-hitting blows. Every time she tries to squirm out of it, I move with her, keeping out of her reach while she's well within mine.

She's not so talkative anymore. Now that she's getting her head beat in.

I trip her and throw her to the ground. She lands on her back and stares up at me, wide-eyed. Her skimpy bra has inched lower, showing the top half of her areola, but she's not giving a shit about flashing the crowd right now. She runs her hands over her face, wincing when it meets the cut I've given her over her eye.

I glance up again, staring at the most important person in the room. He glares at me with dark eyes, and I shed my oversized shirt, throwing it to the ground as he eyes me.

Brawler may make the fights happen, but Rocket is

the true leader here. Everyone takes their orders from above, and short of Big Daddy K himself being here, Rocket's number one.

The crowd nearly trips over itself. Comments start flying, and the decibels double from the roaring and clapping. I've kept my toned physique under wraps from the wannabes at school. I needed to play this my way. None of this would've happened if they knew I could fight. Nevaeh wouldn't have challenged me and Rocket certainly wouldn't have pushed his number one contender to be the one to welcome me to the Heights.

I don't mind being the underdog as long as I come out on top, and I'll always come out on top.

Cherry tries to scramble to her feet. Real fear blazes in her eyes. They bulged out of her sockets when she saw me take my shirt off. Now, she's running scared. I kick her as she tries to move away from me, and she sprawls out again. She flips to her back, and when I move in, she tries to kick me in the face, but I throw her feet to the side and pounce on her, elbowing her in the nose, feeling the sharp bone of my own body connect with hers. At this point, I don't even care that Brawler's in the room or Rocket or any of the other fuckers I have to go to school with every day. This is just about me. This is just about my plan. About my vengeance.

Next thing I know, I'm being pulled off her. The tangy, copper taste of blood taints my mouth. I reach up with my fingers to touch my lips and realize it's not mine. It's Cherry's. I spit the shit out and glance up to lock gazes with Johnny Rocket who's finally moved to stand on the outskirts of the circle.

"Fucking shit," Brawler mumbles behind me, his fingers tightening around my upper arm, letting me know he was the one to put a stop to the fight.

I blink, moving to stare down at an unmoving Cherry. She's not dead. I don't think, anyway. If she was, it wouldn't matter to me. I have only one job here at Rawley Heights, and she was in my way.

Rocket doesn't even spare her a glance. He moves toward me, stepping over her feet like she's just an inconvenience to him. Brawler tries to tow me backward, but Rocket holds his hand up to stop him. Mirth dances in Johnny's eyes. He reaches down to take my hand, squeezing my fingers in his. "It's nice to formally meet you, Kyla. I enjoy surprises."

Behind him, Cherry groans. He's forgotten all about her though. I straighten my spine when his gaze doesn't leave mine. "Sorry about your girl."

Though he's not acting like he cares now, that was his girl who's currently trying to get to her feet without anyone's help. Her face is bloodied, and her nose is definitely broken. She's just fallen so far no one dare tries to step in. She let the "Princess" beat her. She didn't stick up for Rawley Heights.

Then again, they're all wondering about me now. If I can fight like that, I must be one of them. How quick the tide changes.

"I only have one girl," Johnny says, his smooth voice like aged bourbon. "And she's standing right in front of me."

Brawler's grip around me tightens for a split second before letting me go. His absence leaves a cold shiver running up my arms. Johnny's *girl*? That's not the plan.

I stutter for a moment, not sure how to react. The plan was to get into the gang through fighting. Work my way into their trust by winning them lots of money. If Johnny does this, that's not fucking happening anymore.

My stomach clenches. The enemy's DNA runs through him. If I have to gain their trust by sleeping with the enemy...

"Brawler," Johnny finally says after he waits for a response I never give. "Get someone to clean Kyla up, will you? Then bring her to me."

Brawler only grunts in response. Not that Johnny waits for any at all. He turns on his heel and steps around Cherry, still avoiding her like she's invisible to him. She gazes up, hopeful, like he's coming to help her, but he doesn't even give her a second glance.

I blink at her, expecting her to turn her rage on me after being cast aside so quickly, but she doesn't. Instead, she looks broken. Her head drops between her shoulder blades, and my heart grows heavy.

Brawler gives me a gentle tug as he wraps his fingers around me once again. He scoops down to pick up my shirt as we go, and before I know it, I'm in a back room that's much nicer than the industrial look of the warehouse proper in the center. It takes me a moment to realize it's a locker room. Fighters stretch and warm up. A row of lockers fill one wall.

"Get out," Brawler orders as soon as we walk in.

The fighters stop to look at him, but they don't move.

"I said, get the fuck out!" he roars.

They all jump. The few guys and women in the room pick up their towels and water bottles as they make their way to the exit.

When the door closes and I'm stuck here with him, he turns toward me. "What the fuck was that?"

"What the fuck was what?"

"You can fight," he accuses, as if he's just confronted me about something terribly illegal.

"Yeah," I tell him.

He shakes his head. "You never said a word." The disappointment lacing his voice unnerves me.

I don't have an excuse. I purposefully didn't tell him, but no way in hell am I admitting to that. "What? Do you want me to say sorry for not getting my ass kicked?"

"You can't *just* fight, Princess," he spits, still using the name I fucking hate. "You beat Cherry. She's not the best, no, but Johnny only puts her up against people he knows she can beat."

"I guess everyone should stop judging people they don't really know," I tell him, motioning toward my baggy shirt. It's evidence of their prejudice. Just because I don't look like them doesn't mean I'm not like them. I'm as angry as they are. I'm as lost as they are. And I'm as stuck as they are. Except, I'm stuck in a mind prison I can't escape from. One that shows me my dead parents every day.

He throws my shirt on the floor, knuckles turning white. When he glances up, he studies my best features. At least, what I think my best features are: my muscles. They show me I'm strong. They show me I can handle myself. When I feel like I can't, like everything's getting too big, I go work out. When I feel like I'm just an imposter, I look in a mirror. The muscles, the bruises that usually highlight my light skin from training, all tell me I can do this.

I glance down. Splattered blood paints my skin as I breathe in deep. Like war paint, it fills me with the thrill of victory and a power I never knew I carried before fighting.

Like Johnny just did, Brawler reaches for my hands. Instead of squeezing them like Rocket, though, he brings them to his face, inspecting them. "I'm fine," I say, trying to pull away.

He tightens his grip. He's looking for evidence of how much I fight. If I was just a novice, I probably would've broken a knuckle or two, but I'm not and I didn't. I spend a lot of time in gyms, and I can't fucking wait to get back into it now that I don't have to hide.

"I see that," he says, finally dropping my hand.

I bend down to pick up my shirt and use it to wipe Cherry's blood off me.

Brawler snickers. "That's not going to be good enough. Johnny wants you back with him, which means you're going to have to take a shower and pretty yourself up."

"Pretty myself up?"

"Didn't you hear him?" he sneers. "You're *his* now."

"I'm no one's."

"Hate to break it to you, but you don't have a choice."

I lick my lips. I loathe to admit it, but he's right. Rocket's made a public declaration. To go against it, is to go against him and the Heights Crew.

I can't afford to do that.

Brawler swallows, taking one last look at me and then spins to walk away, jaw tight. A minute later, a shower kicks on somewhere in the back of the locker room.

This isn't the way I wanted to buddy up to the Heights Crew, but I won't turn it down. I can't. In fact, this could give me easier access to Johnny's dad, and that's all I want.

I can practically feel my fingers on the trigger now.

8

I scrub my skin until it's raw. Not because I want to make sure I look good for Johnny Rocket, but because I'm procrastinating getting out of the shower. Once I get out, I have to play the game. I have to pretend I'm all about the guy who shares DNA with the fucker I hate most in this world. Just because I know I have to do this doesn't mean I want to. I grip the side of the shower while my stomach heaves. There's nothing in it. I can't eat before a fight. I learned that the hard way after puking all over the clothes I was due to wear in my first match a couple of years ago. Now, though, I grit my teeth, waiting for the feeling to pass.

"Princess, I didn't take you for someone who spends hours in the shower."

I close my eyes and swallow. "I didn't take you for

someone who stands outside creeping on a girl while she's in the shower."

Brawler's silent for a few moments. He's not that guy. Not at all. He's just doing as he's told. He stepped out of the room while I undressed, and for the majority of the time I've been in here, he's been outside, but I must be taking too long. Rocket's probably getting antsy.

I reach down to shut the water off. While I squeeze the excess water out of my hair, Brawler says, "There're clothes out here for you. Rocket sent them."

I snap the curtain open so just my head peeks out. "Are you serious?"

Brawler immediately averts his gaze. "He thought you'd look good in them." He takes a deep breath, his muscles taut like he's ready to spring. He motions with his hand to a stool that's been placed by the shower. "There's a towel for you there, too. I'll wait for you outside."

He slips through the door, leaving me by myself. Every time I'm around Brawler, he surprises me. Averting his gaze like I'm a virgin maiden. Helping me ready myself for Rocket, when he certainly could've—and should've—ordered someone else to do it, so he could focus on the fights happening out there. That's not to mention the conflicting emotions in his gaze or the way he held me protectively for a brief second the instant after Rocket claimed me. Like he didn't want to give me up to him.

Then again, I could've been on a fight high and misinterpreted everything.

The towel is surprisingly lush as I dry myself off and pull on the clothes Rocket thinks I would look good in. To my utter surprise and dismay, they fit. Like a glove. There's no bra or underwear, but with how tight the clothes are, I don't think I'd want to be wearing those pieces anyway. The shirt has an open back that ties around the neck. Extra material drapes over my chest, giving it a flouncy look but the rest is skintight. It looks like something Cherry or Nevaeh would wear, so I guess this is exactly what I should be wearing now that Rocket owns me—or thinks he does.

The excitement of the fight still flows through me as I comb my fingers through my wet hair to get rid of the tangles. When I finally pull the door open, Brawler's there, leaning against the wall like he's been waiting for me for a while. "Where do you train?" I ask him. Now that my secret's out, I need to jump back into the gym life. I started boxing and martial arts at the suggestion of a shrink who thought it would be a great way to release my aggression. Soon after, I started taking it seriously, so I could carry out my vengeance plan one day. From the second I stepped into the gym, I loved it like nothing else. Nothing calms me more than hitting pads or feeling the satisfying thwack of my fists against something hard.

"Excuse me?" Brawler asks, his eyebrows inching up his forehead.

"Train? You know, for fighting. You must train somewhere. You don't expect me to think you just someday woke up with those muscles, do you?"

His lips thin, and his gaze narrows as he takes me in. He stops at my shoulders like he wants to graze my entire body but doesn't dare. "When I was a kid, my brother taught me. He took lessons when we were little, but he learned most of it on the street. After him, I trained by myself."

I try not to show the surprise I feel. I didn't know Brawler had a brother. "Do you ever fight here?"

He laughs. "All the time."

"Are you fighting tonight?"

He shakes his head. "No, just running it tonight. Or supposed to be. Now, I'm babysitting you."

My hackles rise. "I don't need to be babysat."

A smirk crosses his lips. "You're going to long for the days when you were just Nevaeh's punching bag, Princess."

"Stop calling me that," I grind out, instead of

focusing on what I should be. What does he mean I'll want to be Nevaeh's bitch again? Just how bad is Rocket?

He grins. "Not a chance. It's even more appropriate now. You've caught the attention of the Goddamn prince. Congratulations."

"Rocket?" I ask.

"You met him before tonight, haven't you?" he accuses.

"Briefly," I shrug, not understanding what the big deal is. "Actually, I saw him getting head from some lady in the administration office when I went to get a new lock the first day of school."

Brawler's eyes cloud over. He runs his hands through his cropped blond hair. "You have no idea what you've gotten yourself into." He shakes his head. "You should leave."

"If you think I'm going to leave, you have no clue the type of person I am."

"Obviously fucking not," he seethes. "You come into town wearing fucking extra-large garbage bags with this meek little attitude. Then, when you step into the ring, you destroy Cherry. He may have chosen you because of it, but he won't let that go. He'll punish you for that." He blows out a breath, his severe look faltering. "What the hell am I even fucking talking about?

He'll be punishing you no matter what. You'll be feared and hated. You'll be put on a pedestal yet treated like shit in the shadows and behind closed doors. You—"

I bite the inside of my cheek. It was never going to be safe for me inside the Crew. I just have to deal with whatever comes. "You seem to know an awful lot about what happens with girls Rocket likes."

"I have eyes," he deadpans. "That's all I need." He breathes out, deep, checking the door behind him. "You should leave. Tell your *guardians* it's not safe for you here. Or if that's a line, which I suspect it is, you'd be smart to get the fuck out yourself. Staying here is stupid."

"Real words for someone who's a part of the Crew. Aren't you afraid it'll get back to Rocket? I bet he wouldn't like it if he heard you warning me off him."

Brawler's blue eyes blaze. It's like someone set a fire to neon blue metal, the sparks simmering in aqua. "I'm *not* part of his Crew."

My mouth drops, but I quickly try to mask my shock at his anger. Of course, I know he's not technically part of the Crew, but why associate with them at all if he reacts like that?

"I run the fights for them, like my brother did before me." Brawler moves forward, crowding me into the wall behind us. "Do you want to know what happened to my brother?" His nostrils flare. Despite myself, him pushing up against me is having the opposite reaction it should. I place my palms against the wall at my back, so I don't do something brash like throw myself at him. This is not the time nor the place. "He's dead." Brawler's tone flattens. "He gave his life up for the Crew, and he died because of it, too."

Okay, this *really* isn't the time.

I search his fiery depths for real answers, but as soon as he's said his piece, he closes himself off. I won't be getting answers from Brawler tonight. Stepping back, he leaves my skin cold and wanting. We're alike, him and I. The connection between us is already burning hot. I've felt it from the beginning but didn't know where it stemmed from. The Crew took loved ones from both of us. That's why he cares. That's why he's warned me off time and again. I recognize pieces of myself in him, and that's why I've wanted to wrap my legs around him from almost the first moment. That, and his fighter physique and tattoos. I mean, I'm not immune to them. I'd have to remove my eyes for that to be true.

I highly doubt Rocket will give me the same feeling. Not that he should, but I'm already missing the ache Brawler's awakened inside me. I haven't felt anything like it yet. A yearning. A safe place to crawl inside that feels like we could understand each other. We're linked in this horrible way.

Rocket's claim won't allow me a chance to explore this eruption of feelings I have for Brawler though. Not that my plan for the Crew would either. I close my eyes, conjuring up the images I've kept with me of my parents. I'm doing this for them. I tell myself there'll be someone I meet after this who will make me feel the same way Brawler does. I don't know much about love, but it's just about chemical reactions and connection, right? Brawler can't be the only guy who's lost someone to a tragedy. Who's also a fighter. And has badass tattoos.

I need to keep my head on straight.

I don't say sorry to Brawler. I don't acknowledge what he's just told me. Something about the way he's turned his back tells me it wouldn't be welcome anyway. He doesn't like to share his secrets, his pain. I know the feeling. And right now, I'm grateful for it. I can't be sucked into him again.

But that also begs the question of why he just told what he did. Despite him not really being in the Crew, he works for them. Talking shit about your employer, especially when your employer is the Heights Crew, is a no-no. He doesn't know me from anyone. I could run right into Rocket's arms and tell him everything Brawler said.

I won't, of course. But *he* doesn't know that.

He's taken a risk. There has to be something he sees in me that makes him want to help. I file that away. I might need help through this. I might need a lot of help. Brawler might just be the one to do it because of his love-hate relationship with the Crew.

"Maybe we could train together sometime?" I offer as he gathers himself.

"That's up to Rocket."

My hands clench to fists. The fuck it is up to Rocket. "I don't want to give up training," I say. I figure he trusted me with a truth, I might as well give him one back. "Sometimes it's the only thing that keeps me sane."

"I guess you better be a good little showpiece then," Brawler snaps. He smacks the locker room door, and it opens for him, banging against the opposite wall. "Follow me."

I run my hands through my hair, tuck my chin, and do just what he's ordered. I don't want to give up training and fighting but depending on how close I get to Big Daddy K, I could end this sooner rather than later. Giving up fights, and the connection I feel with Brawler, seems trivial compared to that. Sure, I'll have to move out of the country and live in hiding for the rest of my life after I've killed him, but I'm willing to do all that for the pleasure of knowing I got my retribution.

Brawler doesn't bother looking behind him to make sure I'm following. He thinks his warnings gave the desired effect of scaring me into submission. At least, that's what I believe until we get to a set of stairs I hadn't noticed in the preparation of the fight. As soon as he steps onto the first step, he turns. When he spots me, he looks pissed all over again. He shakes his head. He wanted me to leave. He was giving me a chance. It's too bad I can't take it. Moving forward, he takes the steps three at a time while I jog behind him to keep up.

Over the railing, another fight is raging below us. Two guys are going at it. Their chests drizzled with bright red blood that leaks from both their noses. The higher we go, the better view I get. Glancing up, a loft looms above it. I hadn't spied this earlier either. I blame it on the butterflies from the fight and the pressure of needing to be noticed. The place is huge, almost like a penthouse or the fancy boxes owners of sports teams use so they don't have to sit with the general public. It denotes exclusivity. Money. Privilege. I'm surprised this goes over in the Heights. They hate everything this loft stands for, except for the Heights Crew.

When we reach the top of the stairs, Brawler hangs a left and knocks on the door. Below, the frenzy of the crowd heightens. Shouting, panting, and a general hum of conversation buzzes through the air like frenzied electrical current. Once we walk into this other room, though, all of that fades away. As does the real world. I've now stepped foot into the nicest place I've seen since coming to the Heights. The place is decked out in leather couches and crystal decanters. Along the side of windows facing the warehouse, barstools sit nestled next to a long bar. The perfect spot to view the fights below. The back of the loft, however, looks more like a party room. Scantily dressed girls bring out glasses of liquor on circular trays.

Before I can move in farther, a figure steps in front of me. He does it so quickly I almost bounce off his chest, but I catch myself at the last minute. My gaze roams over his tight black shirt. It drags upward over a copper-colored beard before hitting a scowl that makes me step back even farther. "Who's this?"

"Mag, this is—"

"There she is," a voice speaks up from beyond this Mag's impressive shoulders.

The tenor is sweet, yet confident. When Mag, who must be some form of security detail, moves out of the way, I stare right into Johnny Rocket's pale blue eyes.

No matter how much I don't want to think so, he's attractive. His dark hair and dark features give him a bad boy persona, which calls to me. I understand there are fucked up parts of me. I give attitude and dwell in the dark side of my mind. Honestly, I would run right over a pretty boy with a heart of gold. Johnny Rocket definitely isn't that.

He comes right up to me to grab my hand like he did before. He brings it to his lips, grazing them over my knuckles. "You fought like a champion."

"Thank you," I tell him. As soon as he lets my hand go, I drop it to my side, heart racing. I can acknowledge how good looking he is, but I would never be able to get over who his father is. With that thought, I refrain from looking for the man who brought me to the Heights.

Big Daddy K. He's like lore. A fantasy. A mystery. Everyone knows of him, but he stays in the background, living in the shadows like a puppet master. I often thought I could pass him on the streets—the man who murdered my parents—and never know. Goosebumps sprout over my arm.

With the way Rocket keeps staring at me, I have to look away. He's a wolf, and I'm what he wants to sink his teeth into. When I glance to the side, Mag is there with his tight black shirt. He narrows his eyes at me. I'm no stranger to the suspicious crowd. Trust me. For someone who's always looked for the guy who ruined her life in everything, I know what it's like to be suspicious of the world, but Mag takes it to a whole other level. His eyes are like stone, his gaze dropping boulders on me that weigh a ton.

I'm not sure there's a comfortable spot for me here. Nowhere to look. Nowhere to feel safe. But I knew that when I made my decision to get my revenge.

Rocket tucks my arm in the crook of his, taking me to the other side of the room. He smells like whatever cologne he spritzed over himself before he came here. It's not an altogether bad smell. In fact, it smells a thousand times better than the BO mixed with skunk fragrance that filters the air below.

From behind us, Brawler excuses himself from the room. I turn to watch him go. At the last second, he looks up to meet my gaze. There's fear there in his sapphire blues, but the unnerving part is that I think it's aimed at me. I watch him as he makes his way down the set of steps and stands at the edge of the makeshift ring while Rocket settles us into a corner on the furthest barstools away from Mag.

Apprehension grips me. I'm in the lion's den with no chance to escape and not a single ally in sight.

When I sit, Rocket moves his stool closer and then settles his hand at the small of my back. "I knew you were something special when I first saw you." His pale blue eyes sink their teeth into me. "Kyla," he muses, like he's trying to imprint my name on his tongue. The thought makes me shudder, but I look up and smile anyway. His face reveals all the interest he has in me, but I don't think it's companionship he's looking for. It's straight up lust.

Well, I can't just sit back and stare into his eyes. They make me want to draw a line in the sand when I shouldn't have a line at all. "So, you like the way I fought?" I ask tentatively.

His hand on my back connects more assuredly. He leans over until his lips brush my earlobe. "More than you know."

I pull away slightly as my body responds to his touch. His lips feathering over my ear felt...nice.

Rocket leans back. I think he's just taken the hint, but it's not that. He stands from the stool, a dark look crossing his face as he stares at the fights below. "What the fuck? I didn't think he was on the card tonight."

I follow his gaze. My eyes round when Brawler drags a guy into the middle of the ring, his fist connecting with his face.

Mag moves closer to the window without a sound. "He's not."

"Christ. Does he think we give out free fights?"

Rocket slams his fist down on the small bar top in front of us. I jump, unable to prepare myself for his outburst. His anger seemingly coming out of nowhere.

When I glance down again, Brawler's looking straight at me. Our gazes collide like warriors throwing down a gauntlet. Then, he turns, a smile playing over his lips as he smashes his fist into his opponent's surprised face.

9

My heart skips a beat as the anger pulsing from Rocket settles over me like a cold chill. I had him pegged as a man that was all show. It's not like he looks like a wuss, but people in positions of perceived power use that power to throw their weight around without backing it up. Instead, he's fuming. A knot tightens my core, a warning that he's not to be fucked with.

"Watch her," Rocket orders Mag as he gets to his feet. "I'm going down to deal with this fucking mess."

I lean over to look back down at the crowd. They're going nuts. Brawler must be a favorite because everyone is yelling and screaming. Even from up here, I can tell the room below is pulsing with violence. The angry shouts permeate this room's sound barrier, muting it to a dull roar. As soon as Rocket makes himself known, though, the cries turn to silence in a ripple effect. Brawler, unable to ignore the reason for the sudden change in the room, lets the guy he dragged into the fight slump to the floor.

Rocket heads out of the main room toward the locker area. Brawler brushes his knuckles against his joggers to wipe the blood away and then follows him. The crowd parts, people giving them ample room to get by.

"Jesus," I mutter, surprised at the show of brutality and respect. To be one, I didn't think you could be the other, but I was wrong.

Mag makes a low sound of agreement. I turn in my seat, forgetting he was still in the room with me. Nothing is going on below now. In fact, the crowd starts to scatter and leave. Looks like Brawler threw in a finale that never should've been.

"He's going to be in big trouble, huh?"

Mag's gaze slices toward me. "He's used to it."

I let that sentence linger in the air. I'm not touching it with a ten-foot pole. I have no idea if I can trust this Mag guy or not. Ha. What am I thinking? I can't trust anyone here. "I'm Kyla, by the way."

"Magnum," he says. He shifts. The hard outline of a gun on his hip I hadn't noticed before protrudes. I'm beginning to think there's a pattern with the nicknames everyone has. Magnum has a gun. Brawler likes to fight. I'm pretty sure I've heard someone call Oscar Bat before. Johnny's called Rocket, which I can only imagine what the hell that means. Several meanings flick through my head, but I don't dwell on any of them.

"You're security?"

He nods but doesn't say another word. He just keeps staring at me, which is as unnerving as it sounds.

"Not much for talking, huh?"

He cocks his head. "Don't mind talking. Just not when I don't trust someone."

I shrug and look away. Instead of staying seated, I get up and look around the room. The ladies who'd been walking around with the trays are now behind the bar, sending me dirty looks. A bunch of questions hang from the tip of my tongue, but I won't be getting answers. Magnum is as tight-lipped as they come, and the girls all look like they would murder me to be in my position.

A phone rings, and I look around to find the source. Magnum pulls a cell phone from his pocket and holds it to his ear. "Boss." He nods. "Of course. Yes. Bye."

Nerves pool in my stomach. Boss could probably

only be one person, and I doubt it's Rocket. He had to have been talking to Big Daddy K.

My heart lurches, and I stare at the phone as Magnum puts it away. I'm a call away from the man who took my parents. Since coming to the Heights, I've moved closer and closer. My plan is working, even if it makes my stomach roil at the same time.

I pretend to not care who he was talking to and walk back to the stool I'd been sitting on. I'm getting antsy. I really don't want to wait around here all night. If Big Daddy K is calling Magnum on the phone, that probably means he's not here.

Relax, I scold myself. It's not like I can just walk right up to him and take him down. I take a deep breath, trying to release all the stress I've been bombarded with. I'm in. I'm close. That's all I need to accomplish right this minute. I don't want to just kill Big Daddy K and get caught. That was never the plan. I have to bide my time. I have to make a concrete plan. I'm not ruining my life just because I want to take his. That wouldn't give me satisfaction at all. I want to live a long and happy life after he's gone, after I've made him atone for what he's done.

The door opens then. Magnum turns stealthily, the first quick movement I've seen him make while he's been here. I look around him, hoping to find Brawler.

I'm admittedly worried about him, but also knowing it'll probably be Rocket who's come back up the stairs.

It's neither.

"Princess?"

I stand from the stool. Oscar's glaring at me with a confused expression. He isn't the only one who's surprised to see me up here.

He looks around. "Where is everyone?"

"Brawler jumped into a fight. Rocket had to take care of it," Magnum answers.

Oscar rolls his eyes. "Always so dramatic, the big lug."

Oscar looks at peace here. Maybe he wasn't at my fight earlier, but he's certainly watched the fights from up here before. The way he joined the Heights Crew would make me believe he would be a low-rung guy, but his attitude at school and familiarity with this place makes me think he has a bigger stake in the Crew than I thought.

He winks at the girls in the back, and they titter. As I'm beginning to notice, Mag doesn't prolong their conversation, so Oscar has to return to looking at me. His dark eyes narrow, taking me in in my outfit that is so different from what I normally wear to school.

"What's she doing here?" he finally asks, inclining his head toward me. His gaze moves down my body, pricking my skin at his attention. In this outfit, I'm exposed. Not that I don't like it. I actually do. But to be this revealed in front of him makes me want to go hide in a corner.

"What? You just get here?" Magnum asks.

"Had to take care of some shit."

Magnum eyes Oscar as he moves closer to me. I stand up straighter. Mag's voice sounds far away as he says, "Let's just say she kicked Cherry's ass. Rocket was impressed."

Oscar's eyes gleam. "Kicked Cherry's ass? Didn't know you had it in you, Princess."

"Don't call me Princess."

Magnum's marble-like face starts to move until I see him almost smile. "If you saw her fighting, you wouldn't use that nickname anymore. She was far from it."

I glance over. The smile of appreciation hinting at his face leaves as soon as he realizes I'm looking at him.

Oscar can't help but to be surprised. His lips part while he studies me again. This time paying particular attention to my arms and shoulders. "That good, huh? It's a shame I missed it."

"You mean it's a shame it wasn't Nevaeh whose ass I kicked."

He winks. "Maybe we could still make that

happen." Moving closer, Oscar's all smiles, slinking in like he's got charm in spades to spare for me.

His heavy gaze drowns me in lust. I felt it the first time I saw him, and I feel it now. This time's worse, though. He's trying to draw me in. The sexy smirk of his plays on his lips like he knows exactly what he's doing, and what girl doesn't want a guy who knows exactly what he's doing?

Before I know it, Oscar's being hauled backward. He's slammed into the opposite wall as I stifle a scream.

"My. Girl," Rocket seethes. "You're already on thin ice, Drego. Don't make me kick your ass for this."

Oscar holds up his hands. He's trying to be his casual, nonchalant self, but his gaze flicks to the imposing body in front of him and then back to me. Magnum's hand hovers over his gun as he eyes Oscar to make sure he won't retaliate, but he doesn't move from his spot either. When Rocket turns to look at me, Oscar drills a hole into the back of his head.

Rocket's pale blue eyes harden to ice chips. "If someone touches you, it's your responsibility to tell me. Got it?"

His curt words drill a warning into me. In theory, possessive guys are sexy. Hell, maybe they can be if I actually had a say in the matter, but it's alarmingly clear Rocket claimed me, and there's nothing I can do or say about it.

I may as well have my muzzle still in place when it comes to Rocket because I'm sure he wouldn't find it endearing if I told him just what I thought of him claiming my body for his and no one else's. Instead, I push my now dry hair off my shoulder. "He didn't touch me."

Behind Rocket, Oscar whispers, "A heads up would've been nice, Asshole."

I peek at Magnum who doesn't respond to Oscar's comment at all. He's too busy glaring at the two of us.

Rocket cups my face, and my stomach bottoms out. He's far too touchy feely for someone I just met, for someone who's staked a claim on me. The thought rattles me. I came here to take back control of my life. Not the other way around.

I peel his hands away from me, hoping I won't get my ass tossed out a mere half an hour after I made it in. Hopefully Rocket likes girls who play hard-to-get because I'm about to be as hard-to-get as they come.

It turns out, I don't have to just yet. Magnum speaks up. "Boss called. There's been an update he needs to fill you in on."

Rocket licks his lips, leaving them glistening as he stares at me. Anger flits through his gaze but it's gone before I can even decipher it fully. "Looks like we'll have to get to know one another better some other time, Kyla. Oscar?"

Oscar clears his throat. "Yeah?"

"Can you see to it that Kyla gets home safely?"

My hands tighten around his. "Don't bother," I say. The last thing I need is for people to be snooping around my apartment. I'm already paranoid about having anything from my other life there. I don't need to have a coronary if someone like Oscar comes into my place. "I can get home by myself."

Rocket cocks his head. "Oh, I'm sure you can," he says, his pale blues practically twinkling. "But I take care of my own."

A warning shiver works its way up my spine.

"I can do it," another voice says. Without even looking, I know it's Brawler's. "She lives in my building."

"Does she?" Rocket asks, smirking. The facial expression is a cover-up though. His gaze hardens again.

I keep my stare trained on him. He's like a feral cat in that moment, letting his eyes do all the stalking.

Leaning in, his cologne coats me again. I close my eyes, and it isn't long before my lips buzz. I squeeze them closed tighter, partly to block out what might happen and partly to keep myself from shying away if it does.

His lips graze mine. A soft caress, a barely there touch I could almost call sweet if I didn't know who it was coming from. "Tomorrow, Kyla," he promises, his lips still brushing over mine.

I can't say he isn't intoxicating. I'm stunned on my feet. Immobile. When he moves away, I sway in place while he leaves the room, calling everyone to follow him briefly.

The door closes, but I can still spy them through the glass. I mentally smack myself to pay attention. Rocket's giving orders, his face fierce while the others nod their agreement or complacency. It's hard to tell which. When he's done, he and Magnum leave. Underneath all that glorious copper stubble Magnum boasts is a ticking in his jaw. They disappear down the stairs, but they must exit through a different door than Brawler and I entered earlier because they don't cross the empty circle in the middle of the floor below.

The door to the loft crashes open. The girls in the back squeal, and it makes me wonder what they see and hear in this room. No one's watching over them as far as I can tell, but that seems unlikely. For the biggest, toughest gang in the area, they have to be a well-oiled machine whether I see all the moving parts now or not.

Oscar saunters in. He bows slightly as if he's an actual gentleman addressing a lady. I might find it more believable if he wasn't wearing a hoodie with a backwards hat. "Looks like we're tasked with keeping you safe, Princess."

"Not that again," I grumble.

"Oh, it's definitely sticking now," Oscar says, a flirty smile teasing his lips. "The Prince just left, and here you are, his new—"

"Oscar," Brawler warns, cutting Oscar off completely.

I study Brawler. He's put together again, very different from the guy who pulled someone else into the ring with him just so he could kick his ass. "Nice fight," I say.

"You weren't on the card tonight," Oscar says flatly.

Brawler swallows. "It was a surprise fight."

"I'll say," I deadpan. "I think that guy shit himself."

Oscar turns his head to gaze at me. His eyes narrow like he's seeing me for the first time. "You have a personality other than scared shitless?"

"She fights, too," Brawler says.

"So I heard. Enough to catch Rocket's eye."

"Who doesn't catch Rocket's eye?" Brawler asks, laying it all out there.

A pin drop could be heard in the small room. Oscar

slowly turns. It's like waiting for the big explosion at the end of an action flick. You know what's coming, but you don't know exactly when it'll hit.

The silence Oscar gives him is even eerier than saying something. To me, I'd rather see the storm coming at me than have to wait for it to suddenly appear. A look passes between them, and I get the feeling that whatever needs to be said between the two is going to wait until I'm out of earshot.

Oscar holds out his arm for me. I glance at it, dismiss it, and walk past him. "Aw, come on," he says, good naturedly, joking, as if Rocket didn't just push him up against a wall not ten minutes ago for touching me. "It's a platonic arm. An arm of friendship. I don't think you can catch sex from forearms touching."

"I don't know," I say. "I think Rocket told me not to touch anybody." I look over my shoulder to find them following me down the steps. It's strange to be in the warehouse with no one else here. Without the thriving pulse of excitement, it just looks like a rundown building in dire need of a sweeping.

"And you're the type of girl to bend to his every whim?" Oscar asks.

He's pushing his luck. There's no way he would be saying any of this if Rocket were still here, but hell, neither would I.

A smile pulls at my lips. "Nope. Not at all."

"Don't fuck around," Brawler warns, his deep voice cutting through the teasing and adding a thick layer of tension.

"Or what?" Oscar asks, turning to drill his dark gaze into Brawler. "Don't forget who I am and where you are."

I glance back at Brawler, spotting the indecision on his face. It's not that he fears Oscar. In actuality, I don't think he does at all. I'm positive Brawler's fears have nothing to do with members of the Heights Crew. They're far deeper than that.

I sigh, loudly, enough to get both of their attention. "I'm not going to have to listen to you two bicker every time we're together, am I? If that's the case, I'm going to ask Rocket for two new guys to follow me around like puppies on a leash."

Both men shift into matching fierce looks.

"Just let's get in the fucking car," Oscar gripes. He doesn't offer me his arm again, which is fine by me. I just want to get home and out of these clothes. I need to dissect everything that went down tonight. I need to go through every scenario and figure out which is the best way to play this.

We leave through a side door, and Brawler locks up behind us. In front of us idles a big, black car. It's by far the fanciest car I've seen in the Heights yet. The kids who have cars at school are lucky, but not in the fashion department or even in a car this decade department. They're all rust buckets. But they're treated as the luxury they are.

Oscar pulls the door open and gets right in, but Brawler stands aside, waiting for me to go in first. When I pass him, he stops breathing. His chest halts, and he tries not to look at me. I don't understand what's going through his head. "Thanks," I whisper.

He doesn't answer as he gets in after me. There must be a driver up front because as soon as the door shuts, the car lurches forward, and we're being taken away from the warehouse. I try to look through the rear window at the three-story building behind us, but the glass must be tinted because I can't see anything in the dark of the night. I just wanted one last glimpse of the place that gave me the only joy I've had since I got to the Heights.

"You must've had fun in there," Brawler guesses.

I sit back in the seat and stare at him. "I want to fight again."

Oscar laughs. The trilling sound catches me off-guard in the narrow confines of the car. "You'll have to get permission from your keeper," he says, sarcasm dripping off him. I get the feeling he's not much of a fan of Rocket's. Actually, I don't think he cares much for Brawler either.

I try not to let my disappointment twist my face. I don't want to show weakness in front of these guys. I want to be taken seriously. Now that Rocket's chosen me as a girl to haul around, I'll be seen as an object. That won't work. I'll have to have everyone's respect. I'll need to gain it, to prove myself worthy.

But how do you gain the respect of those who only respect the one thing you've never had? Power.

10

If I thought I was getting dropped off at the front door, I was wrong. Even Oscar follows us up into the shitty apartment building. I wait by my door, itching to get rid of them, but they both stay with me. "I'm here," I finally say. "I made it safe."

Oscar laughs. "You think you're getting away with that?" He shakes his head. "If we don't come in and make sure no one's here, it's our asses that are going to get reamed out."

"How will he know? I won't say anything." More and more, this being Rocket's girl is grating on my nerves. I really don't need a keeper or two babysitters or someone who thinks they own me just because he likes the way I fight.

Oscar drops his head to the side. "He'll know." His

voice turns smoother. "Just open up and let us do this. If you're worried either one of us is going to touch you, don't bother. You're off limits for everyone in the Heights now. Unless they have a death wish."

He looks away, face tight, and I sigh before opening up my apartment. We all walk in like we own the place when only one of us does. Oscar looks around, nodding, gaze dragging over the very few things I've brought with me. It helps with the backstory that I don't have anything to my name, just like everyone else here.

Brawler pushes past him, going into the bathroom first, pushing the shower curtain aside, and then moving into my bedroom.

"Hey!" I move toward him, but Oscar stops me, his hands on my forearms. "He's just checking to make sure no one's here. Chill."

I grind my teeth together. "Why would anyone be in here? That's the stupidest shit I've ever heard."

Oscar looks at me like I've just lost a few IQ points. "Word travels fast. The Crew has enemies. Those enemies are now your enemies. You're not in Kansas anymore, little one."

I press my lips together. I knew I was getting into a violent situation. There was always a risk, but I've suddenly become a lot more important than I wanted to be. If I'm attached to Rocket, Oscar's right. I could be used in any number of ways. "Lucky me."

Oscar grins, chuckling at my sarcasm. "I knew I liked you, Princess."

"Kyla."

"Princess Kyla."

I sneer at him while Brawler comes out of my room. He holds his hand out, my cell phone in his palm. "Here."

I stare down at it. My heart leaps into my throat, but it's just my decoy cell phone. I try to relax, but Christ, he scared the shit out of me. The cell phone with my aunt and uncle's number programmed into it is the only thing I have in this apartment that leads me to my old life. I snatch my decoy out of his hands. "Why are you touching my shit?"

Oscar tries not to laugh. Brawler tenses. No one gets to say anything, though, because the phone rings in my hand. I stare at the palm-sized piece of technology, reading the screen. Johnny Rocket scrawls across the screen.

"Are you fucking kidding me?" I growl at the privacy violation. I stare at Brawler who looks unapologetically back at me.

"You better answer it," Oscar says, nodding toward the incessantly ringing device.

I swipe the screen, turn away from the two assholes in my apartment, and bring the phone to my ear. "Yeah?"

There's a beat of silence. "Kyla?"

"It's me," I say, not attempting to hide my displeasure.

"Did something happen?" he questions. The fact that he's being nice, almost concerned, is comical to me. Then, it pisses me off.

"Yeah, there are two guys in my apartment. One of them took my phone without asking and put your name and number into it."

"Oh, I told them to," Rocket says nonchalantly.

I try to picture what he's doing on the other side of the line. Me going off about the misuse of my privacy doesn't seem to have bothered him a bit. He's very cut and dry, black and white. It doesn't bother him because he expects his orders to be carried out and for the person on the other side not to give a shit.

"I'm glad we officially met tonight," he says, his voice lowering.

I almost pull the phone away from my ear to make sure it's still Rocket on the other side of the line. This guy is a wooer. A ladies' man. He's suave and cool and used to getting everything he wants, women included.

And he's certainly clueless to the fact that I'm seething on this side of the line.

I bite my lip, reigning my temper in. "It was better than the other way we met."

Rocket chuckles and then he's silent for a few sick moments. I can't tell whether he's thinking about getting head from the administration lady again. Or if he's thinking about getting head from me.

"I have so many plans for you," Rocket says, voice husky. "Meet me after school tomorrow. We need to discuss shit."

My first instinct is to tell him to get fucked, but I can't say that. "Okay... Where?"

"I'll come get you. Goodnight, Kyla."

He ends the call before I can say good night back. I take the phone away from my ear and stare at it. *I have so many plans for you.* His voice rings in my ear. My stomach tightens, wondering what that means. It could have a million different meanings.

"Everything okay?" Brawler asks.

I turn toward them. Oscar's expression is guarded, but Brawler's eyebrows are pulled together in a tight line of concern.

I straighten my shoulders. "Yeah. Good. Fine."

Oscar's phone goes off with a quick shrill. A second later, Brawler's goes off. They both pull their phones out of their pockets and stare at the screen. Brawler's brows arch as he reads. When Oscar's finished, he slips the phone back into his pocket and gives a mock salute. "I'm out. See you at school."

He takes off, and I expect Brawler to follow him, but he doesn't. Instead, he takes a seat in the armchair. It's almost one a.m., so it's not like I want to stick around and have a chat with him. When he notices me staring at him, he says, "I have orders to stay with you tonight."

"Orders? I thought you weren't part of the Heights Crew. How can you take orders?"

Brawler leans back to engage the footrest then puts his arms behind his head like he's settling in for the night. He even has the audacity to close his eyes. "I live closest to you, so it makes sense." He opens one eye. "Plus, he's paying me."

Disappointment fills me. I guess he isn't the nice guy I had him pegged as. Everyone can be bought.

"Can you ask Rocket about training with me?"

"No."

"Why?" I snap back.

"You ask him."

I groan in frustration. "I don't know him."

"I doubt that will last long," Brawler says, both eyes open now, his muscles tenser than I've ever seen. "But if I were you, I'd keep your distance. For as long as you can. Oscar was right when he said you have enemies now. Rocket's enemies, the Crew's enemies, they're now your enemies. And some of them are scary as fuck. If Rocket likes you half as much as he's making it out to be, you're in trouble."

"Likes me? He doesn't know me." I don't hide the fact that I'm laughing about this. It's just outrageous. "It's lust more than anything."

Brawler shakes his head. "Not in this world. Rocket knows three things: gang life, sluts, and possessions. Let's just say he never asked anyone to look after Cherry, and you don't fuck with another man's possessions."

"I'm no one's *possession*." I grit the word out like it's venomous. It is. It means being trapped in a cage again, and I don't want to go from one cage to another.

Brawler snickers. "Don't get me wrong, he won't think of you as a possession. He'll think he's doing right by you. He'll think he's giving you a world you never would have had. He'll even think he loves you, but he doesn't know how to love, Kyla. None of them do."

I press my lips together at his words. He's throwing everything in my court. He knows what he's saying can get him into so much trouble, yet he's saying it anyway. He's trying to warn me off. He's trying to help, but he has no idea I need to do the exact opposite of running away. "And what if I said I wanted to leave right now?"

Brawler pushes the footrest down and leans forward. His sapphire eyes shining brilliantly. "Do it. Do it now." There's so much feeling behind his words that goosebumps course down my body. I should be doing what he says. If I had any self-preservation at all, I'd grab my shit and leave. He'd let me. I know he would. He'd suffer for it, but he'd do that because he doesn't want anyone getting mixed up with the Heights Crew who shouldn't. I'm not going to flatter myself and think it's all me. It's not. It's just that Brawler probably has the best sense of right and wrong than anyone in a three-mile radius. "This is the only chance I'm giving you, Kyla. If you wait any longer..." He sighs. "There's more at stake. But the deeper you're in, the harder it'll be for you to get out. The harder it'll be for me to help you get out. I have others I need to care for," he almost whispers.

His openness guts me. It also makes me afraid for him. Someone like Brawler shouldn't be caught up in all of this. "Are you going to join the Heights Crew one day?"

He shrugs. His eyes tell me he knows he already lost me. I won't be leaving tonight, and the disappointment makes him lean back in the chair. "Maybe."

His answer is guarded and closed off. Not that I can blame him. I just gave him the equivalent of a 'fuck you.'

"You don't have to stay with me," I tell him. "I won't say anything. You should go home to your mom."

"I'm staying," he says, voice firm. "We should get some sleep before tomorrow. I'm assuming Rocket said he wants to meet you after school?"

"He did."

He looks me straight in the eye. "If you're staying, you should do everything in your power to stay on Rocket's good side."

"So, meet him when he wants?"

"Among other things."

It's the "other things" that bother me. Just what am I going to be expected to do?

In my mind, I know it doesn't matter. I came here with one goal, and I'll do anything to make sure I get it done.

Even if that means crossing a line.

11

In the morning, I'm awakened by a quiet knock on my door. I immediately sit up, sheets twisting around my waist. As far as having a roommate, Brawler isn't bad. I didn't hear a peep out of him all night, which makes me wonder what's going on now. I pull the sheet up over my chest. "Yeah?"

"Can I come in?"

His question makes me smile. I doubt Rocket would be asking permission to walk into my bedroom. "Yes, I'm decent."

He walks in, his massive body filling the doorframe and making me drool already, even this early in the morning. He has on a tight wife beater, perfectly displaying his tattoos and muscles, and in the early morning light, I notice some swelling and bruising around his eyes. Remnants of the fight he started last night.

I glance at my alarm clock. My eyes round. He's woken me up an hour earlier than I usually get up for school.

He must read the look on my face because he says, "I'm going to train some. I thought you might want to join in."

I suck in a breath, but I don't want to give away how much of a big deal I think this really is. "Yeah. Yes, please," I say. I pull the covers off me and stand.

Brawler's gaze moves down me, his blue eyes blaze, and then he turns away. The draft on my legs tells me I'm not wearing any pants, just the underwear and a tank top I threw on before bed.

Oops.

"Please," I joke. "Like there's anything left to the imagination after those tight ass pants Rocket made me wear yesterday."

Brawler bristles. I can already tell I said the wrong thing, but I've no idea what part did it. The memory of what I was wearing, the sarcasm, or the fact that Rocket told me what to wear. Instead of dwelling on it, I pull out a pair of joggers and throw them on.

Once I'm dressed, I follow Brawler into the living room. He's already pushed the armchair back, and since there's really nothing else in the room besides a small TV stand, it's a decent sized area to train. Without saying what he's doing, he starts in with jumping jacks, so I start too.

Okay, I'm in pretty good shape. Really decent shape, actually. But Brawler's a beast. I lost count at the number of jumping jacks we were doing after I started sucking in air at five hundred. I'm pretty sure he felt pity for me and stopped soon after.

Next, we run through some more calisthenics. Tuck jumps. Lunges. Surprisingly, there's not much give in the floors of this building. At the time it was built, it was built to last, and it's held up. I doubt even the neighbors under me know what we're doing up here. I'd be more apt to think the neighbors I share a wall with can hear all the heavy breathing going on.

Again, without a word, Brawler starts punching the air, running through different punching combinations. In the soft light, a glow emanates around him from the window at his back. My apartment never looked so sexy. I run to my room, open the closet, and bring out some focus mitts.

When I walk back out with them, his eyes round, and he immediately grabs for them. "Where did you get these?"

His surprise and excitement makes me backtrack. "Gift from my guardians."

His gaze shuts down. The marvel at my training equipment retreats, replaced by annoyance. "You're still going with that?"

Technically, it's not a lie. All the money I have is from my aunt and uncle, so despite the fact that I bought these myself, they're still a gift from my aunt and uncle. I'm just lying about the aunt and uncle part. "I do have guardians," I tell him. "Used to, anyway."

Brawler sighs and shoves his hands into the pads. "You know no one here is going to tell on you for shit like that. For living alone?" He looks up to meet my gaze. "No one gives a shit about us. No one will be paying you any attention to notice you don't have guardians living with you."

"You did," I counter.

"I'm different."

He can say that again.

He holds up the pads, claps them together, then widens his stance, telling me he's ready for me to start hitting them. We fall into an easy rhythm. This is one thing among many that we both have in common. We know how training works.

Brawler and I spend the next hour working out without communicating. We pass the focus mitts back and forth, and even though I tell him he can hit me harder, he's giving me fifty percent strength when he hits while I'm wearing them.

I wish I could take Brawler to an actual gym. He would love it there. He would fall in easy with the type of guys that go there.

In another life... I almost sigh.

By the time we're done, sweat is dripping off us. My tank top clings to my skin. "You can hit the shower first," I say while taking the pads from him. I try to move around him to place the pads on the counter, but my foot catches on his sneaker, and I sprawl forward.

Strong arms move around me. He pulls me back into his embrace, arm moving around my middle to steady me. His fingers scorch my bare skin from where my tank top has pulled up, and I still. His breathing halts at the same time, but then a long exhale hits my shoulder and collarbone, hot breath teasing me. His palm presses into my stomach, moving me back. I'm hit with the hard surface of his abs, and a growing surface as his hips press into my thigh.

I bite my lip to keep from sighing or moaning.

"Fuck!" Brawler suddenly bursts. He steps away, then strides angrily to the bathroom.

The door slams behind him as my body flushes with heat and then cold. I shiver, standing in the middle of the living room while my arms fall lifelessly to my sides.

Shit. That was bad. I mean, fuck. It could've been so good, but I can't trust anyone. Not Brawler. Definitely not his libido. This is a dangerous line we're treading. Whether Brawler wants to admit it or not, he must be closer to the Heights Crew than he realizes. Otherwise, why would he run their fights? Why would he spend the night with me at Rocket's orders if he didn't have to?

I throw the pads up onto the counter and get a large glass of water before guzzling it down. Then, I get another. By the time I drink the second one, my heartbeat has returned to normal, and I don't feel like I'm going to come out of my skin at any moment.

In the bathroom, the shower shuts off. My mind races to think about what Brawler's going to be dressed in when he gets out of there. Does he have any clothes? Do I want him to? I mean, I'm pretty sure I don't want him to, but there's a difference between fantasy and reality. Reality is: nothing can happen between Brawler and me. Period.

After a few more minutes, the door opens and much to my disappointment, Brawler walks out wearing the usual kind of clothes he wears to school. I narrow my gaze at him. "Where'd you get those?"

"I ran home this morning to get a few things."

"So, you're moving in now?"

The look he turns on me lets me know the question I just asked is trouble. Instead of answering, he says, "Your turn."

"I should hope so, it's my shower."

I walk into the steamy room, shutting the door behind me, and tearing my soaked clothes off. Everything is just as neat as I always leave it. It's obvious he's used my shampoo, conditioner, and even body wash, but he hasn't left the bathroom a haphazard mess. Maybe all the shit people say about boys being messy is wrong. I haven't had any experience with that. When I moved in with my aunt and uncle, I had my own bathroom. Hell, I practically had my own wing of the house. I could throw parties there and they would never know. This is my first real experience with a roommate, and it's going good so far.

At the mention of my aunt and uncle, I remind myself that I need to text them to tell them I'm okay. I won't be able to do it in front of Brawler though. Maybe I can do it when I head into my room to change. He won't come in when I'm doing that. Not judging by his response to our compromising position only minutes ago.

I hurry, washing the sweat off me and letting the

hot water massage my tight muscles left over from the workout. I usually love to spend extra time in the shower after a hard workout, but I don't have the luxury this morning. Not only did I have to share my bathroom time with someone else, but now I need to make sure I text my aunt and uncle without getting caught.

As soon as I get out of the shower, I dry off and wrap my hair in the towel to help dry it. I move in front of the sink and look up at the mirror. I'm about to wipe the fog off it but stop.

No way.

No fucking way.

There, in the glass, are two words written out in a quick scrawl.

Fucking beautiful.

My throat starts to close. My mind tries to rationalize it away. There's no way Brawler wrote that. The person who lived here before me must have written that on the mirror and I just hadn't noticed it yet. A sweet message for his girlfriend or wife.

Not for me.

Definitely not for me.

Despite the steam in the room, my body shivers. I grab another towel and wrap up with it, warding off the cold even though I damn well know my body's reactions have nothing to do with this room being cold. It's toasty in here.

It's me. It's my body responding to the words Brawler left for me.

I allow myself a moment to appreciate it, taking in his quick, easy handwriting, and then swipe the message off, leaving my reflection in its wake. I see me. The girl who lost her parents. I see someone who's broken inside in more ways than one. Hell, there's even bruising on my face so my exterior matches my interior.

The last memory I have of someone calling me beautiful is from my mother. That's what parents are supposed to say, right? They're supposed to build their kids up. Make sure they feel loved and special. My aunt and uncle are adequate guardians, but they're not parents.

I take a deep breath and let it out. The heat of my breath threatens to bring the message back, so I wipe the mirror down again. I need to forget that happened, and if Brawler was smart, he'd forget it happened, too.

I make quick work of getting ready for school and then sprint from the bathroom to my bedroom with a towel around myself. There, I lock the door behind me and pull out my stashed cell phone. There's a message there waiting for me today. **Hope you're well. Thinking of you.**

They don't know exactly what I'm doing here. Even adequate guardians would've told me there's no way they'd allow me to take down a gang boss for retribution. Though the message is only two short sentences—six short words—I cling the phone to my chest. It's nice to have a whole other world that's apart from this one. It gives me hope for what my future could be. I just know that unless I sever this tether that's keeping me here, keeping me sad and angry, I'll always be in two places. I need to cut this thread from my life now, so it won't affect me later on.

Miss you both, I text back. **Everything's fine here.**

It's another short and sweet message, but it gets the point across. I hurry up and silence the phone, putting it back in its hiding place before looking at my closet for something to wear. Once again, I'm caught between two worlds. If I wear the baggy clothes again, Rocket will put a stop to that. But how much do I want to show? Not skin-wise, obviously, but do I walk into school like I'm a part of the Heights Crew now?

Nerves roll through me because I have no idea how today is going to go down. Oscar and Brawler seemed to think that word would've gotten out that I'm Rocket's girl already. Hell, there were a shitton of kids from school there yesterday. Maybe they've passed along the gossip.

I pick out a pair of well-worn jeans and an old band t-shirt. Middle ground works best. It's not showing off everything I have, but it looks badass. I figure after the showing I gave last night, this might help with that persona. I sit on my bed and apply a little makeup to even out the bruises marring my skin, and then run my fingers through my hair. A quick check of the alarm clock tells me it's about time to head to school, so I unlock my bedroom door and step out.

Brawler turns, a plate of toast in his hands. There's nothing about him that says he left me that message. In fact, his face is hard, stoic. He holds up the plate to me, an offer, and I take it. He places two more slices in the toaster while I eat.

We eat in silence, but I can't help but wonder if he's asking himself if I saw his message or not. Or if he's wondering if I responded, or what I think about it in general.

I think no one's called me beautiful in a long ass time. I think I love his message.

I'll never tell him though. And as far as I can tell, he's not going to speak of it either.

12

The walk to school is uneventful, but as soon as we step onto school property, it's a different story. People are side eyeing me, sizing me up. The guys are smirking like they know something I don't. The girls look at me like they could pounce, but they don't have the lady balls. At least not now that I'm attached to the Heights Crew.

Is a member of the Crew seriously the best way out of this place? I'm pretty sure that would get them stuck here forever, not the other way around.

"Don't worry about them," Brawler says. "They won't dare touch you."

"So, you noticed, too, huh?"

"It's hard not to."

We pass through security easier than I have yet.

The uniformed security guy doesn't even look into my bag.

I pick it up from the table and hike it up my shoulder. "I just don't understand why."

Brawler looks over at me for the first time since training this morning. "To them, the Heights Crew is a way out."

"But they're just trading one bad scenario for another."

His eyes turn to slits as he tries to make me out. "Aren't you doing the same, Princess? You have to stay here," he challenges me, throwing in my face the fact that I won't leave. "Why are you doing it?"

I lift my chin. *Stupid, stupid me.* I'm getting way too comfortable around him. "None of your damn business."

He shakes his head. "Well, whether you admit it or not, girls only get involved in the Heights Crew for a few reasons. Either you're stupid enough to fall for someone already involved, you're looking for a way out of your own shitty life, or you're doing it for protection. So, which one are you?"

He's wrong. There is another reason. One he'll find out eventually, but I'll never be able to tell him "I told you so" because I'll be long gone by the time they realize I'm the one who put a bullet between Big Daddy K's eyes.

I don't answer him, and he doesn't push me for one either. He just lets the question linger until I walk toward my first period class.

School flies by. Everyone gives me a wide berth physically even though I feel like I'm under a microscope for most of it, which does nothing for my fight-induced headache. Everyone wants to gape at who's caught Rocket's eye, but when I swear someone's looking at me and turn to tell them to fuck off, they're already looking away.

The girls are the worst. The jealousy wafting off most of them is thick and heady. It makes my heart ache. When you think you only have a couple options in this life and one of the better ones was just taken, envy and anger are natural. If they only knew what I have planned though. I won't be around forever, and they can have Rocket when I'm gone. I couldn't care less.

Either Oscar or Brawler stays with me throughout the day. They walk or sit through each class with me whether they're supposed to be in the class or not. Not one teacher even looks at them twice, and that's by design too. They're not interfering with Crew business.

At the end of the day, I don't even bother bringing

books with me. The school really is a joke. I'm not sure what I'm even being graded on yet, and I sure as fuck know my grades won't matter in the long run because I don't know when I'll get my opportunity with Big Daddy K. If it's sooner rather than later, I plan on disappearing from this place anyway. No need to stress about the work I leave behind. Hell, no need to stress anyway. Kyla Samson is made up. She's no one. I could fail and it won't even go on my permanent record.

Brawler walks me out the front of the school, past the eyes of the lingering security detail, and right up to a black car that looks the same as the one who dropped us off at the apartment last night. Everyone who passes it, looks without looking. They're acutely aware of what's going on, but they don't show it. They go on with their business, but I know each one of them has filed this moment in their memory banks for later. Perhaps to talk about with a few trusted friends.

Rocket emerges from the back. He's all smiles for me. "Hello, love."

Brawler stiffens, and I don't know if I'm reacting to him or my own free will, but I follow. My body locks up at the easy way Rocket addresses me. I try to shake it off, but it's harder than I imagined it would be. It's crazy how easy I molded to Brawler, but with Rocket, I can't even pretend.

I have to though.

"Hi," I say nervously. That part isn't even faked.

Rocket leans over, his lips grazing my cheek. He breathes in deep, and instead of it being sexy, it reminds me of a predator sniffing out its prey. Or worse, marking his territory.

He takes my hand and pulls me behind him into the car. Before the door shuts, I take one last look back. Brawler's turning away. Suddenly, I'm freaked out that I'm alone with Rocket, the son of the guy I've grown up loathing. Who I've imagined killing time and time again. So much so that it's almost like a lullaby in my head, lulling me to sleep. The act promises me better days, tranquil nights.

Yes, it's sick that a murder could make me feel better. But it's also true.

Rocket pulls me into his side. "I know it's weird," he says. "In time, you'll get used to me. I'll make sure of it. You've probably heard stories, and even though they're all most likely true, I would never hurt you."

I swallow. His words are supposed to be sweet—at least in his eyes—but they fall far short of hitting that emotion for me. "Sorry," I say, blinking up at him. "I guess we can start by getting to know one another first."

His lips pull back. "Excellent idea. Your name is Kyla Samson. You're a senior at Rawley Heights. You just moved here from the northern most part of the state..." Rocket goes on and on, regurgitating every last piece of my "past" that I compiled. It cost a pretty penny to make up a whole person, and I'm glad I paid as much attention to it as I did. "Your parents are gone. You have new guardians now, but they leave you alone. You don't fight like any other person I've ever seen. Like a beautiful warrior," he says, his voice soft as he trails a finger down my cheek.

I smile at him. "You've done your research."

"It comes with the territory," he says.

I turn into him, propping my knee up on the seat so I can face him. "But none of that really matters, does it? All the facts about where I grew up and what happened to my parents?" My stomach twists just saying that. It's the most important thing that ever happened to me. "That's not really how you get to know a person."

He tilts his head to the side as he appraises me, gaze pausing over the bruising my makeup can't quite cover. "I guess you're right."

"But, let me hear about you. So far, all I know is that you're called Johnny Rocket. That people fear you for your role in the toughest gang around. Fuck, I don't even know your last name."

He threads his fingers through mine. "I want you to

call me Johnny. Rocket's for those who need a reminder of how powerful I can be."

My heart thumps, another reminder that I'm too close to the fire.

He plays with my fingers as the car pulls out of the parking lot. Apprehension builds in my gut. I don't even know where we're going, and the only people who know where I am wouldn't narc on the Heights Crew if they tried selling their own sister as a sex slave.

Johnny's quiet for a while, and I realize I'm going to be the one asking questions. "How old are you?"

"Twenty-one."

"Where do you live?"

"You'll see it eventually."

"Do you fight?" I ask, hoping he'll expand on at least one of the questions I ask him. This isn't helping me get to know him at all.

"Only when I have to."

He gets closer and closer. He traces his lips up my neck, stopping just under my ear. "I kind of want to piss all over my father's rules right now."

"Rules?" I ask, mouth working. I can't help but put my hands on him. He's so close. His presence is heavy. My fingers slide around his forearms, and suddenly I don't know if I'm trying to keep him away or pull him close.

Johnny growls and sits back. "He's decided you're my prize for when I move up beside him." He kicks the seats in front of us lightly.

My skin flushes. I don't like the sound of prize, but I really need to know what the hell he's talking about. It kills me, but I place my hand on his knee and squeeze. "What do you mean?"

His gaze traces over my hand. "He saw how much I liked you. That it's more than the other girls. I don't just want to fuck you," Johnny says, like that's all he's ever wanted. "He's promised you to me as soon as I move up."

His attentive gaze makes heat bloom all over my body. At least I know he won't be trying to seduce me at every chance he gets. I try to steady my heartbeat. "I guess good things are worth the wait."

"I've never been patient."

His eyes grow dark. For a moment, I'm like a caged animal clawing at the bars of her prison. He's not happy about waiting. He loathes that he's waiting, but he doesn't voice any of that because the car comes to a stop. When the door opens behind me, I all but fall out of it, my ass hitting the pavement.

A hand reaches out for me, and I take it. When the owner of the hand helps me up, I stare into Magnum's brown eyes. "You okay?" he asks, gaze feathering over my body like he's looking for anything out of place.

I nod, but it's Johnny who gets right out of the car and pushes Magnum out of his way. "Hey..." he says, his gaze and voice full of concern. He likes to flit between personalities, like there are two different people living inside him. It's scary. He's never been a monster to me, but I've seen glimpses under the surface. Of course, that could be me just putting things on him. I know who his father is. I know what he's done.

Then again, another voice tells me that since Johnny's in practically the same position, he's done the same shit. Maybe he's killed innocent people. Maybe he's ruined a little girl's life for the Heights Crew. Decisions, actions, they have consequences. No one thinks how far those consequences might reach while they're in the thick of it, but it goes far beyond the one action, the one moment in time. One second, I'm just a happy kid without a care in the world. The next, I'm thirsty for vengeance. I uproot my whole life. I worry the fuck out of my aunt and uncle. Those consequences won't just stay in its place either. Every decision I make—and each of those consequences—is now a consequence of Big Daddy K's action.

I place my hand over my stomach to keep from

overreacting even though in my head, I'm already there. I hate being tethered to him in this way. I just want to end it and be done with it.

Johnny runs his hands through my hair and cups the back of my neck as he rights me. For a blissful moment, I close my eyes and pretend he's doing this because he really does care about me. For a second, I close my eyes and pretend it's anyone but him.

Then, his lips touch my forehead, and it's like being doused with cold water after coming out of a coma. "I'm okay," I say, my voice scratchy. "Sorry, I don't know what came over me."

Magnum's brows pull together, but it's Johnny who speaks. "We're heading in here, Mag. Can you make sure someone brings her a glass of water?"

Magnum's jaw ticks. For as much power as Johnny has, it always looks like people don't want to follow his orders. I don't have the lay of the land yet to draw too many conclusions, but just from the little things I've seen. I doubt he has as much power as his father yet. It's possible he hasn't proved himself.

Johnny fits his arm around mine, holding me steady. I glance over at him, wishing I could stare into his soul. Not his heart or his brain. Those can be masked. But his soul. The very center of his being.

Those are as true, as raw, and as open as anything. Is his tarnished? Has he stained it already?

I don't know why, but I hope he's as much of a victim in all this as I am. Maybe everyone tied to the Heights Crew is a victim too. Of their surroundings. Of their circumstances. Of their upbringing.

Oscar's face drifts into my head.

I take a deep breath and face forward again. "Where are we?"

Clothes hang from mannequins in store shop windows. The style is street chic, I guess it could be called. I look up and down the sidewalk we're standing on and am struck by how busy it is. Well, comparatively. Instantly, I know we're not in the Heights. There's too many people walking around in business attire like they've just walked out of their places of employment. People don't dress like that in the Heights. At least not many.

"Pampering my girl," Johnny says. He holds the door to the store open for me. When the workers see him, their eyes round and they come right over, calling him Sir and Mister even though they never say a last name to go along with it. "This is Kyla," he tells them, gripping my shoulders. "She can have whatever she wants."

I blink up at him. "What?"

He takes my face in his palms. "You're my girl now, Kyla." His eyes are bright, almost glittery with excitement. "You can have everything your heart desires."

I swallow as he brings my hand up to place a kiss on my knuckles, then he passes my hand to one of the women waiting. I look behind my shoulder as I'm dragged away. The girl titters next to me. She's practically blushing and tripping over herself. She breathes out dreamily like she just saw her favorite actor and wants to melt into a puddle. In the next instant, she's shaking her head like she needs to clear her mind. "Let's get you started. I'm Lynette. That's Ryn. And that's Glo."

I give a half-hearted wave to them all. This is the last place I thought I'd find myself in today. I look back to find Johnny taking a seat on a pure white couch in the front area, his arms outstretched over the back cushions like he owns the place. Who knows? Maybe he does. Maybe this is another front for the Crew.

There's so much I need to learn.

A bottle of water in hand, Magnum strides through the front door. He brings it over to me, gaze on the floor.

I breathe out. "Thanks."

"God, you must be thrilled," the girl who Lynette

called Glo says. A wishful sigh pushes past her pouty hot pink lips.

"I'm—" I stare at them. I don't know how to react. This is more than anything I thought would happen. Listen, I'm not immune to clothes. I love clothes. I love girly shit. Just because I like to fight doesn't mean I can't do my hair and makeup the next day and still feel as powerful as when I'm slamming someone twice my size into the mats. It's just I've never given into that side of me before. I've always been focused on the plan. "I don't know what to think," I say honestly. I take a drink from the bottle Magnum got me. The crisp, cool water slides down my throat, cooling off my suddenly flush skin. Afterward, I hold the bottle to my head. It was a mistake not to ice my face last night.

The girls giggle all the way to the back corner. When we arrive, they split off, gathering up different outfits for me after asking what my sizes are. I hardly know. When I was at my aunt and uncle's, I had to wear a uniform to school, so I didn't have many other clothes. I had jeans and shirts for lazy days and fancy dresses for when I was forced to attend parties. I've grown up since I've taken control of my life. The clothes I have on were all bought from Walmart, much to my aunt's distaste, but I refused to be even more of an expense for them.

It strikes me then that I've never picked out new clothes I've actually wanted for myself. My parents did it when I was a kid, and after that, my aunt handed over the credit card while I chose whatever was cheapest. I didn't have much of a choice in anything because I declined to take pleasure in it.

With that thought, I go to the closest rack and pull out a couple of things that catch my eye.

After about twenty minutes, I'm taken to the side of the store, the girls still smiling and laughing next to me. They've pulled out many more outfits than I have, some of them gaudy and ridiculous. They take me into a dressing room surrounded by mirrors and hang up all the different outfits. I'm literally in a sea of colorful, revealing, tight-fitting clothes. It blows my mind to see all of them here.

Lynette's gaze looks around the room and then she nods. "We'll be right out there if you need our opinion on anything. Rocket is through that curtain," she says, pointing to a different way out of the room. She winks at me. "If you want him to see anything."

I smile, the feeling awkward, but a warmth worms through me anyway despite knowing who I'm here with. When they leave the room, I stare at my reflection in the mirror and just shake my head at myself. Last night and into today has been a whirlwind. I can't imagine what I would be feeling if I was actually a girl who wanted Johnny. Like one of the three outside the curtain right now who are all whispering and laughing with one another about how hot the gangster is.

Because that's what he is. A gangster. I can't forget that important fact.

I try on a bunch of different outfits. Some of them I put right back on the hangers and move them to the side. They're just not me. They're not anything I would wear in a million years. All the while, I make sure I'm focused on what I can move well in. Or outfits I can hide shit in. In this life, I'll never know what's going to come at me, so I need to be ready for anything. I can't be wearing anything too skimpy that I can barely hide my private parts let alone a weapon.

The more and more I try on, the guiltier I feel. How am I going to pay for this? And I'm not talking money. By accepting these clothes, does that mean I'll have to do something for Johnny? He told me his father ruled I was off-limits for now, but he also said he was an impatient man. I want to be off-limits. I want to have my own say in who I get naked with. Is this just a show? A way for him to get in my good graces, so I don't notice how terrible he is and fall into bed with him?

I sit on the bench in the room, staring at me in a

nice, new outfit. If it comes to it, I'll have to sleep with Johnny. I don't know why the realization's hits me just then, but it hits me hard.

In order to keep up appearances, I'll have to do things I don't want to do. Things I wouldn't do in a million years.

But the outcome will be worth it. Right? I can lose a little bit of myself to save my entire self. That has to be worth it.

In a heartbreaking moment, I wish I could leave. I wish none of this ever had to happen, but that isn't my lot in life. If Johnny demands sex one day, I'll crawl into the sheets and spread my legs because I'm "his girl" and being his girl gives me access to the real prize.

Taking back my life.

13

In the end, I come out of the dressing room with three outfits. I checked the tags on them first to make sure that they weren't super expensive. When I walk out with just the three, Lynette and Glo gape at me. "That's...all you want?" Lynette asks.

My heart clenches when I realize I've offended her, but how can I tell her accepting a bunch of clothes means I'm Johnny's bitch? Hell, I'm already his bitch. I don't need to press my luck. The only reason I'm taking three is because if I walk out of here with no clothes, Johnny will be the one who's offended, and I don't know how that will work out for me.

I'm distracted, so when I walk into the main area, I don't immediately realize it's just Magnum there, standing by the main door like he's making sure no one else comes in. Beside me, the girls blush, but take my garments over to the marble-topped counter to ring them up. I stand in front of them like I know I'm supposed to, but I also have nothing to pay them with. Well, I do, but it's all in an account I'm saving for when I have to escape overseas to get away from the mess I'll be leaving in my wake.

Lynette blushes after she's finished ringing them up and putting them in a bag. Then, we just stare at one another awkwardly. "I'm sure he'll be back in a minute," she says.

There's no reason for her to be as embarrassed as she is. I take another look at her, seeing how red her cheeks are and realize there's something I'm not getting. I place my empty water bottle on the counter and turn on my heel to approach Magnum. "Where's Johnny?"

His face remains stoic. "He's in the back."

"Okay..." I move that way. Something's just not sitting right with me.

Magnum sighs. "Where are you going?"

"To get him," I say. "I'm sure these ladies don't want to be waiting all day."

Magnum grabs my wrist. "You can't do that."

"Can't do what?" I pull out of his grip and keep going.

For his part, he doesn't try very hard to stop me. Either that, or he's slow, which I highly doubt. The guy is fucking built. I move into the back of the store and turn in the opposite direction of where they set me up with a dressing room. If he was that way, I would've seen him.

A muffled noise reaches my ears. I stop. Magnum almost plows into me. My ears perk up when a breathy moan sounds to my left.

Son of a bitch. How many girls were just out there? Just Lynette and Glo. There was another girl, too.

I step forward, but Magnum's voice stops me. "You shouldn't do that."

"Fuck you," I snap.

I follow the noise to another fitting room and move the curtain aside. Johnny is balls deep inside Ryn who was helping me pick clothes out not fifteen minutes ago. She squeals and moves to a standing position, dropping her palms from the wall.

Johnny's dick falls out of her. She covers herself, and if Johnny was half the guy he pretends to be, he'd be helping to cover her himself, but he's not. Instead, he's smirking. He leans casually against the wall, letting *all* of him hang out, and trust me, it's impossible not to see it. "I thought I told you to keep her away," Johnny muses, staring daggers at Magnum.

"You saw her fight. She's squirmy."

I peek at Mag over my shoulder. He lifts his chin in the air. He's fucking lying. A big guy like that could've stopped me if he really wanted to. Hell, he could've tackled and pinned me down, but he didn't. He only made a mediocre attempt to grab my wrist.

He wanted me to see this.

For fuck's sake, it isn't as if I thought Johnny and I were actually going to be a thing. I don't fucking want him. He's the last person in the world I want. But knowing all that, pricks of anger still heat my skin. He just made me look like a fucking dumbass.

He's a liar, a fake. What the fuck did I expect?

Apparently, I expected more. I don't know why. The area behind my eyes heat, and I blink back the threat of tearing up. For a minute, a very short fucking minute, this almost seemed like a fairy tale. I never pegged me as the girl who would get all swoony over a guy who would drop money on me, but I guess I'm not as immune to that as I'd like to be.

I throw the curtain back to hide them both again and turn. I plow through both Lynette and Glo and wonder if they knew all along something like this would happen. I'm sure it's happened a shitton of times before. Everyone probably knew what was going on but me.

Somehow, Magnum beats me to the front entrance. Thoroughly proving he could've stopped me from looking at the scene before. "I can't let you leave, Kyla."

I raise my eyebrows. "Are you shitting me?"

He shakes his head and disappointment riddles his features. Why does everyone act differently than I think they're going to?

He shocks me into a beat of silence, but I can't stay quiet. I need to get the fuck out of here before I do something really stupid: act like I care. "Please," I say, gritting my teeth.

He shakes his head then looks over my head like he doesn't want to look at me anymore.

I turn to Lynette. "Is there a back way out of this building?"

She looks at Magnum like she doesn't know what to say, which tells me already that there is one. I move toward the back of the building again. I'm almost to the dressing room where I found Johnny and Ryn when Ryn comes out. Her eyes widen, and she tries to get out of my way, but I don't let her. I grip her shoulders and shove her into the closest wall. "You should have more fucking respect for yourself." She quivers beneath my touch, matching the anger shaking my whole body. I'm madder at myself than anything else. Getting caught up in this shit was never part of the plan. I lean in close. "You want someone's dick inside you who'd treat you like that? Someone whose girl is just in the other room? Woman up."

I push her into the wall one last time and turn, only to be face-to-face with Johnny. Glitter of excitement shines in his eyes, but it looks far more dangerous than it did earlier. He reaches for me, and I shy away. His jaw ticks. I doubt he ever gets rejected, but fucker can't think I'll just act like everything's fine after cozying up to me in the car and then sinking his dick inside someone else not an hour later. That's not how shit works. I don't care if you are Johnny Rocket of the Heights Crew.

He sinks his fingers into my forearm and pulls me away from our audience. We step out a back door, and just like I did to Ryn, he pushes me against the concrete block exterior. Rank garbage wafts in the air around us. I almost choke on it.

Johnny gets in my face, his lips thin, practically quivering with anger. "Do not ever fucking reject me."

I swallow. There's that rage I would've bet was simmering underneath the surface at all times. My own indignation rises. I want to tell him to get fucked, but I'm caught because I can't do that. I still need to have a way to get to Big Daddy K.

God, I fucking hate this.

Any other guy who would have done this to me could've expected to get his ass kicked. But this asshole? I can't do anything to. I just have to sit back and take it.

I don't have to play the part of hurt girlfriend for the next words to come out of my mouth. "You said I was your girl."

"I also said I can't have you yet," he seethes. "Do you think I'm just going to sit back and wait?"

Actually, yes. Any girl would fucking think that.

"Yes," I hiss, holding back about seventy-five percent of what I really want to say.

He laughs in my face, then takes his hands off me. Until he did that, I didn't realize how much pressure he was putting on me. I'm going to have a bruise on my shoulder from him slamming me into the wall. Asshole.

"Did you think I was going to abstain from sex while waiting for you, Kyla?" He smirks. "That's not going to happen. I'll be discreet. Hell, I was being fucking discreet. No one else would've known if you'd just stayed away. Now, all those women know what happened," he says, pointing back inside. "If you were going to be embarrassed, you shouldn't have made a big deal about it."

"They *knew*, Johnny," I tell him. *Does he think*

they're all fucking idiots? "And you think Ryn would've kept her mouth shut after we left?"

"She would've if she knows what's good for her." He moves toward me again, and my back hits the wall in an effort to stay away from him. "No one disrespects my girl."

I snap my mouth shut. Is he even listening to himself? *He* disrespected me.

He slides his arm around me, pulling me toward him. My hips graze his and his raging erection. "You're the one who made it known what we were doing." He tips my head back, running his hands through my hair and tugging at the ends to expose my neck. He drops a kiss there. "Otherwise, no one would've been the wiser. You could've still had your cred. The bitch still could've had her dignity. I would've gotten off, and we would all be happy. Now I have to go in and fix this. Shut these bitches up before they spread the word to everyone in town, making you look like just another side piece. That's not what I want. I want all these slaves to look up to you. I want them to revere you. I want them to know that if they fuck with you, they're fucking with the Crew. I can't do that if you blow everything for me, do you understand?"

I nod.

I don't know what it says about me that I understand what he's doing. I get the code they all live by. I'm not saying I agree with it. Johnny thinks he wants me, but he doesn't. If he did, he wouldn't fuck around on me, and he wouldn't let his father make some lame ass rule about not touching me until he moved up.

Big Daddy K's rule actually works in my favor, but my pride took a blow today, I guess. That's the only way I can explain the mixture of emotions swirling inside me.

He pulls away, puts his hand through mine, and we walk back into the shop. Everyone is waiting for us near the front. Rocket takes charge, addressing Magnum. "Did anyone leave or make any calls?"

Before Magnum can answer, Lynette says, "Of course not. We would never do that."

Ryn keeps sending me frightened looks. I kind of want to punch her in the goddamned face. It's girls like her who make other girls crazy. What part of understanding another guy is off-limits do some women not understand?

Also, what the hell am I doing still getting caught up in this shit? I shouldn't care he was fucking someone else.

Instead of taking Lynette's word for it, Rocket continues to look at Magnum until he answers in the affirmative. "All clear," he says.

"Excellent. Can you take Kyla out to the car? I'll be out in a minute."

Magnum nods and waits for me by the big front entrance. Outside, everything seems to be passing normally on the street. No one out there is involved in the shit going down in here. Warped senses of responsibility and rules.

So, it's okay for him to fuck around? That's what he's saying. I bet it's not the same for me. I bet if I ever touched someone else, he'd kill me.

Brawler pulling me back into his hard body earlier flits through my head. If Johnny knew that happened, he'd kill us both.

Johnny kisses my hand again, and I keep my chin up as I walk toward Magnum. He opens the door for me, and we step out onto the sidewalk. I pause for a minute as the fresh air and rays of sun hits me. I need to soak as much as I can in because I have a feeling nothing will feel as real as this does while I'm inside the Crew. Magnum moves around me to open the door. I peek up at him. "I could've gotten that."

He grunts in response. He acts all moody, but he wanted me to see what Johnny was doing. Out of all of them in there, he was on my side. The girls were too scared to say anything. Ryn was obviously just looking out for herself. Everyone wants to catch Johnny's eye.

I turn to get into the car, my head about to explode with all the different nuances of everyone's behavior around the Crew, but Magnum's hand on my back stops me. "Shit. You're hurt."

I step back and stand. "What?"

Magnum pulls my shirt away from my skin. The cotton sticks, and he has to peel it away before it finally releases.

"You're bleeding. I didn't notice before because your shirt's black. Why didn't you say anything?"

"I didn't notice," I tell him. Not because I'm trying to be brave because I honestly didn't notice, but if he's looking at the area where Johnny shoved me into the concrete blocks, there's no wonder why I'm injured.

Magnum sighs. "Are you okay?"

"I think so?" I try to look at the wound on my shoulder, but I can't twist far enough. "It hurts, but I can't see it, you know?"

Magnum checks over his shoulder. "I can't go back in there right now to get you anything. Rocket will be pissed if the women find out he hurt you."

I give him a look. *The* look. The kind that says, *Are you fucking kidding me?* That is the most fucked up thing I've ever heard. Their ideas are warped.

"It's better this way," Magnum says. "Get in the car, and I'll tell him when he comes out. In the meantime, there are cocktail napkins next to the alcohol cabinet. Use those to place on it."

"I can't see it," I hiss. What does he want me to do? Grow a third eye on the back of my head?

We stare at one another for about thirty seconds before Magnum says, "You're going to have to deal. I can't touch you."

"That's the most asinine thing I've ever fucking heard. You do know what just happened in there, right? Johnny and Ryn weren't just playing hide and seek. They were fucking. And all you would be doing is patching me up."

"I know," he growls. He runs a hand over his copper scruff.

God, he's really good looking. This close, I can tell his eyes are hazel. I thought they were just brown before, but today, they're amber with green flecks.

"If I touch you, there's the possibility he'll kill you and me. Is that what you want?"

I grind my teeth together. The hypocrisy of all this is pissing me off more than anything else. He can't even touch me to help me? What if I was bleeding out? Would that be a good enough reason for Johnny to allow someone to help me? Do they have to ask permission first?

Hopefully I can persuade Brawler to train with me

again, so I can get out all of this aggression I'm feeling, but for all I know, he'll never want to do that again. After all, he touched me. And it wasn't just because I was injured. He *touched* me. Because he wanted to. Because he felt a connection.

Not because I'm his property.

Magnum's gaze lowers. I can tell he thinks this is nonsense, too, but he's too worried about Johnny's reaction to do anything about it. Maybe I should be too.

I blow out a breath. "Fine. I'll be fine. No one has to worry about it." I crawl into the car, and after a beat, Magnum shuts the door on me.

I keep my injured shoulder away from the nice leather interior but lean my head back against the seat. After I sit there for a while, the injury starts to pound. The adrenaline moving through me must've dulled the pain. That's why I didn't realize sooner that I was this injured. It's probably a scrape. Or a cut. Or both.

Ten minutes later, Johnny exits the shop, the three girls in tow. I sit up. Through the hazy fog of the dimming package in the car, there are a lot more bags coming out than just the one that held my three outfits earlier.

What the actual fuck?

The trunk opens, and minutes later, it slams. The women move back into the shop while Magnum and

Rocket talk outside until the door opens and Rocket scoots in next to me. As soon as the door shuts, he turns, his eyes filled with desperate concern. "I'm so sorry," he says. "Let me see. I didn't mean to hurt you. I would never do that."

Someone needs to explain to Johnny that there's more than one way to hurt people. Not all of it is just physical, it's mental, too. It's a good thing I don't care about him because if some guy I did care about cheated on me like that, I would be devastated beyond reason. I wouldn't listen to any sick sort of excuses thrown at me to try to get me to understand why it was okay for me to be cheated on.

He turns me in the seat until I'm facing away from him and lifts the back of my shirt. The divider between the front and the back starts to slide down. Rocket yanks my shirt back down over me. "Not now, Mag! Take us to Kyla's apartment building."

The divider starts going up before he even gets all his orders. Once we're hidden away again, Johnny lifts my shirt with a gentle touch. He sucks in a breath once he reveals the injury. He stays there for the longest time, not moving, but bearing a hole right into me.

"I wish you would've told me I was hurting you."

I try not to laugh. Like it would've stopped him. He needed to prove a point, and he did.

He reaches over me to grab a stack of napkins next to a bottle of alcohol tucked away in a compartment. He cleans me up, pressing gently against the cut or whatever I have there while I keep my jaw locked down. There's no way I'm showing any sort of emotion while he's doing this.

Finally, he starts to talk. "I know the way I do things can seem confusing. I haven't had a chance to talk to you much after I—"

"Claimed me?" I throw out there.

He snickers like that's such a funny way to see it, but it's true. It's one-hundred percent true. He saw something he wanted and he did the equivalent of a dog marking his territory. That's what this is about.

"Yes, but I hope it's more than that too. The world I grew up in is different from the world everyone else has. We love fiercely. Quickly. If we want something, we take it before someone else claims it." He stops working on my wound and breathes out. His hot breath hitting my bare skin. "The way you fought did something to me, Kyla. I don't know how to explain it, but I had to have you. And I will have you. I could tell we were meant to be together."

In any other world, this might be the sweetest conversation ever. Except, this is the gang world and instead of professing love, Johnny's professing a claiming. A want. A need. A desire he just couldn't hold back.

"I promise to never throw things like what just transpired in your face. Like I explained at the store, you'll have a role fit for a queen. People will fear you. Respect you. Love you," he says, his voice trailing off as his fingers brush my skin. "That's all I want. Respect is everything in the Heights Crew."

His touch passes over my bare back and sneaks around my front. His fingers stretch out, his thumb a centimeter away from my breast. I can tell he wants to touch me. I can tell he wants to move his hand to cup me, but Johnny's a good little soldier. He might not go against his father after all.

He drops his forehead to my spine and breathes in, his hold tightening around my midsection. "I want you to be happy here. To do that, there are only a few rules for you. Don't ever disrespect me like you did in there." His hand tightens again, his nails biting into me. I close my eyes through the pain, focusing on the prize at the end of all this. "You don't disrespect the Crew, and you honor me and my family by doing what we say and knowing that it's for your own good or for the good of others. Do you understand?"

Bile rises up my throat. Johnny will never be

married to anything but the Crew, and that's sad. He doesn't know any other way.

"Kyla?"

I nod.

He sinks his fingers even further into my skin. "I need to hear you say it."

"I understand," I say quickly.

Johnny immediately releases his hold on me. "I'll take care of you. I only ask for a few things in return." He presses his lips against my bare skin like he hasn't just asked me to give up myself for him. I would never be my own person with my own thoughts and feelings. Or at least have any I could act on independently. He doesn't get that. "Hopefully, eventually, you'll fall for me despite all of this."

His words stop me. Just when I was thinking love didn't come into the equation for Johnny at all, he says that. I let out a breath. My back heats at Johnny's proximity. His fingers trail over me almost reverently. He's an enigma. A riddle I bet he himself doesn't even know how to solve.

He moves my shirt back down when the car comes to a stop. My ears ring from all the conflicting thoughts warring in my head, but some part of me understands that we're at my apartment building. Vaguely, I hear Johnny telling me that he has to go to a business meeting. When he opens the door for me, I step out, blinking at the bright sun. I can't even enjoy that I'm free. That the sun is shining. That the fresh air blows on my face. I can't enjoy that I'm out in the real world because his words still bang around inside my head.

A strong, stern voice says, "I called ahead to have Brawler meet us."

Just as Magnum says that, Brawler emerges from the front door of our building.

Johnny takes my hand again, kissing my knuckles. He just loves doing that. I tell myself not to pull away *and* not to get caught up in his gravitational pull again. Then I'm being led up the stairs and into my own apartment like I could never make it there myself.

I get out my key, but Brawler's beat me to it. He has a replica of the key I'm searching for already in the lock and pushing the door open despite the fact that he's also carrying every single bag from the clothing store in his hands. "What the fuck?"

Just how did he get his own key to my place?

Brawler ushers me in and slams the door behind us. He drops the bags of all the clothes Johnny's bought me just inside the door.

The events of today have caught up with me. I'm boiling. I'm madder than mad. I'm fucking furious, and there's nothing around me to take this out on because it's all my own fault. This was my idea. This was my plan.

I was never big on self-loathing though. I scream out in frustration and slam my hands into Brawler. "Fuck you!"

The look he gives me in return could crack marble.

14

*B*rawler staggers back a few steps, surprise lighting his face.

"Fuck this!" I scream again.

I move forward to push him, but he grabs my arms, holding me in place.

"Don't," I say. Everything in me is telling me to lash out. I never wanted to be anyone's property. Hell, that's why I came here in the first place. Big Daddy K owned my thoughts. He owned everything. Day after day was just a running scene of how he took my parents from me. I'm doing this to stop that scene. I'm doing this to take back the narrative. To make my own scenes. I don't know what they'll be, but they have to be better than the two gunshots to the head, ending with my parents lying in a deserted, dank, gross, forgotten alley with blood running toward drains like water. Anything is better than that.

But why doesn't it feel that way right now?

"You got yourself into this mess," Brawler growls. It's like he already knows what I'm thinking. I don't even have to say it.

"Did I even have a choice? Fuck that. He just told me he *claimed* me. Could I have refused? Could I?"

I sound like a fucking crazy person. Maybe I am losing my mind.

"No," Brawler says, his voice a low growl. "But if you were smart, you would've just taken the fall for that fight. You could've just kept on going in the background if that were the case. You didn't have to knock Cherry out. You didn't have to show everyone what you were made of. That's on you."

I had to do all that though. Brawler will never know, but I had to kick Cherry's ass. It was the only way to endear myself to the Crew. In doing so, I just caught Johnny's eye in a way I didn't think I would.

Fuck me.

"You done?" Brawler asks.

I blink and finally see him. His face is flushed. He's holding my wrists with a vise-like grip, which he immediately lets go when he sees me staring.

I take a step back. "I'm sorry."

He takes a step back too. Shit happens when we're next to one another. A pull. I fall back onto the armchair and let the cushions surround me.

"What the fuck happened?" he asks. Other questions simmer in his eyes too. What happened that would make me lash out like that? Why beat on him? Why not take my anger out on the person who deserves it?

Then again, Brawler knows how trapped I am. Whether he knows the reason for it or not.

I'm in, and I'm not getting out.

I eye him up and down. Brawler's been the kindest to me so far, but can I trust him? He's the only one who's not in the Heights Crew, but he's in their pocket. Is there that much of a difference?

"Listen," Brawler says. "We're in a world where you can't trust people for shit, so you probably won't trust a goddamned word that's about to come out of my mouth, but you can trust me. I won't run to Rocket, and I sure as fuck won't run to Big Daddy K."

I close my eyes. My head and my heart telling me Brawler is telling the truth, but if I fuck this up, I won't ever get another chance like this. If they find out why I'm really here, I'll be dead. It's as simple as that.

"Johnny thinks he owns me," I say.

"Did he hurt you?" Brawler growls, his muscles tensing.

I shake my head. Again, people need to understand that physical hurt is not the only way people can suffer. But it's what we always ask. When we say, "Are you hurt?" We're never talking about mental suffering. Never.

I'm about to tell him I caught Johnny fucking someone else, but I know how naïve that sounds. Brawler's just going to stare at me like I should've known that would happen. The truth is, I should have. Their sense of right and wrong is not my sense of right and wrong. Johnny pledging an attraction for me doesn't mean shit. Obviously.

"I need to take a shower," I say, realizing the places where Johnny touched me are like pock marks on my otherwise smooth skin. It's not an imprint I want on my body for any longer than it has to be.

"You can trust me," Brawler says, trying again.

I don't bother answering. I can't trust anyone but myself. And shit, I can't even trust myself. I got caught up in Johnny's world for a second. In his sweet words and actions that had another meaning all together.

I stand from the armchair and move toward the bathroom. The second overdose of adrenaline is leaving, and I'm about to crash. A nap is in order after this, I think.

"What the...?" Brawler follows me, his angry steps stomping behind me. "He did fucking hurt you!"

Brawler's hand clamps around my shoulder. I look over my shoulder, my gaze catching on a bloody spot I left on the tan recliner.

I sigh. "There was an...altercation," I say, for lack of a better term. I don't really know what all that was. Johnny being a dick? But also, Johnny doesn't know any other way to be.

"Why did you tell me he didn't hurt you?"

I turn, knocking his hand off me. "You know in a fight when there's so much hype and energy around you. Sometimes you can get hit straight in the face and not even feel it because you're so focused? I didn't realize."

He nods, understanding written all over his features. "Can I see it?"

From the looks of the blood on the recliner, I don't know if it's just what was on my shirt that seeped through or if I'm bleeding again. I turn so he can get a good view. "Johnny cleaned it up once."

Brawler pauses as he grips my shirt. After what I said sinks in, he pulls the shirt up, placing it in his other hand to leave his other hand free to inspect.

"What's it look like?"

"Looks like you got slammed into something."

"That's about right," I say, humor lacing my voice. I don't know why I think that's funny. It's really not. If anyone else had done that to me in a fight, I would've given it back to them worse. I can't do that where Johnny is concerned though.

He lets the shirt back down. "It's still seeping a little. After you take a shower, I'll put some bandages on it."

"So, *you* can touch me? Magnum seemed to think he'd end up in a ditch somewhere if he tried to help."

"Don't trust anyone that fucking close to them," Brawler grinds out.

I turn, letting my shirt fall naturally. "But I can trust you?"

"Yes," he says, voice firm, like he's never been more sure of something his whole life.

I press my lips together, still not willing to believe it. Turning, I leave Brawler behind me as I make my way into the bathroom to take a shower. The shower stings at first, as does the soap running into the cut, but I let it happen, wanting it to be as clean as it can be before Brawler puts a bandage on it. When I get out, I wrap up in a towel, leaving my upper back bare while covering everything else up. My hair's damp from the shower, clinging to my neck, so I move it over my other shoulder and walk back out into the living room.

An array of first aid materials sits on the counter. Brawler must've run to his own apartment because I don't have much here. I have a tiny First-Aid kit under the bathroom sink but that's it.

"Have a seat," he says, pulling out the stool that sits next to my kitchen bar. The Formica is chipped in some places, but it doesn't look half bad. It's like everything else in this apartment. It's not terrible.

I place my foot on the rung and heave myself up there, making sure to keep my towel closed as I give Brawler my back.

"Take that pill there," he says, motioning toward the glass of water and small white pill next to me on the bar. "Then place that ice pack on your forehead."

Oh look, an actual ice pack. I do as he says and lean over, resting my elbow on the bar while holding the ice pack to my forehead.

"This looks a lot better," he says, voice lowering. "Is it okay if I put some ointment on it?"

"Please," I tell him, my throat suddenly very dry. After what happened this morning, I've realized I'm sitting here in a towel and Brawler's about to touch me again. "Can I reach it myself?" I ask, pulling away.

"Just let me do it," he says.

I try to relax, turn back around, and steel myself for Brawler's hands. When they finally touch me, it's just a grazing like he doesn't want to hurt me. He runs his fingertips over the wound, and I suck in a sharp breath.

He yanks his hands away. "Sorry."

"No, I'm sorry," I say. It had less to do with the fact that he hurt me and more to do with the fact that I liked it. "It's okay."

He places his fingers back on my skin, quickly rubbing the ointment in this time before walking over to wash his hands in the kitchen sink. When he moves back over, he places a pad over my throbbing skin and then uses Band-Aids to make it stick.

When he finishes, his fingers trail down my back for a moment before he pulls away and takes a step back. "Done," he says. "You'll be fine, it's just a few cuts that bled."

I turn to look at the armchair, remembering I have to clean the blood up, but it's already gone. Stepping off the stool, I face Brawler who's packing everything back up. "You cleaned the chair?"

He shrugs.

"Thanks," I mutter. The tension in the room thick like hovering storm clouds. Everything in me is telling me I can trust Brawler, but if I can and I take him up on it, I'll just be sucking him into my story and that's not good either. He doesn't need to go down with me if this all turns south. "I'm taking a nap," I tell him. "If Johnny told you you had to stay with me, you don't. I'll be fine."

"I actually have to go do something," Brawler says. He places the last gauze pad back in the box and stands. "I'll tell whoever comes to stand outside. Okay?"

"Outside outside, right? Meaning outside the apartment?"

He nods.

"Thanks," I tell him.

He turns away, avoiding my gaze. "Don't mention it."

I hesitate for only another moment before I head to my room, closing the door behind me, and flicking the lock in place. If someone else is coming over and it's not Brawler, I don't want them to have access to me.

15

Sometime later, someone knocks on my door. Not my apartment door, but my bedroom door. I'd been staring at the ceiling after taking a nap, going through different scenarios based on what happened today, but never really finding myself a way out except for the way I'd already planned. I know I just have to sit back and play the game.

"Yeah?" I call out, taking the now warm ice pack off my forehead. My voice comes out all raspy like I haven't used it in a while.

"Babe?"

My heart stills. I throw the covers off me and stand from the bed only to stare at the closed door. Johnny's on the other side of that door. Immediately, I will myself to move forward to let him in. I flip the lock back over and peek out.

He smiles when he sees me. His gaze drops, scanning the length of me, making me acutely aware of the thin tank top and booty shorts I threw on right before I laid down a few hours go. "Oscar said he hadn't seen you in a while."

"Oscar?"

Johnny pushes through the open door. "He's been outside."

I run my hands through my hair, trying to make myself a little presentable. "I hadn't realized."

Johnny looks on this side of the door, inspecting my lock. Then, he just lets the door stay open without comment. Out in the apartment, the footrest is being raised on the lone recliner I have in there. Probably Oscar.

"Where are your guardians?" Johnny asks.

"Not around," I tell him. "They never are."

He cocks his head to the side, his gaze still sweeping over me like he can't possibly just look me in the eyes when I'm dressed like this. "They just let you live alone?"

"Is it weird that they don't care?" I ask defensively. "I thought that was normal, especially when you're used to being a ward of the state." Really, I just don't want him snooping around in my background. It's as airtight as I could get it, but I'm sure the Heights Crew has far greater resources than me. That's why I have to get them to trust me.

"I just feel bad for my girl," Johnny says, stepping closer to me. He cups my cheek with one hand and moves the other around my back, hand slipping under my tank top.

I shrug. "I like being alone."

He pulls me toward him possessively. "I hope you don't include me in that."

I raise a smile toward him. "Of course not," I say, heart beating. Confusion grips me. There's only one reality, but I get so lost in the other sometimes.

A groan pours from him. His hand moves lower, squeezing my ass. "I can't believe you were hiding this body away. Fuck me, Kyla." His hand kneads my ass, and I stand completely still. "Your hair has this just-fucked look," he growls.

"It's called just waking up," I tell him, smiling, so he knows I'm teasing. Or, at least, I hope he does. This is my attempt not to poke the beast. I can't fight back when it comes to Johnny, so I don't need to be on the other end of his anger either.

"Whatever it is, it looks amazing on you." He edges his chin down, staring at my cleavage. My skin heats at his attention. "I wonder if I should take just one look..."

I swallow, my tongue sticking to the roof of my mouth. If he looks, I'm afraid he won't be able to come back from it. He's already threading a dangerous line. "Do you want to torture yourself?" I ask, pulling his hands away from me and stepping back. "I bet your father has eyes and ears everywhere," I say, nodding toward the apartment. Yep, I'm throwing Oscar under the bus, but I don't care. "What happens if you have me before your father says you can?"

This gives Johnny pause. Thankfully.

"Plus, I'll be worth the wait."

He takes a deep breath, resigning himself—I hope—that right now is not the time for where his mind was headed. After a few moments, he shakes his head. "I forgot the reason I came over here. Turn around. Let me see how you're doing."

"Oh," I say, a little surprised that he would come over to check on me. I mean, he's the one who put it there. "I put a Band-Aid on it," I say, the lie feeling right on my lips. If Johnny knew Brawler was the one to do it, he wouldn't be happy.

"Well, turn around anyway," he says. "I want to make sure you're taken care of."

I turn and immediately his presence looms over

me. His fingers move around the thin tank top strap and gently guide it down. His heated breath hits my skin first, making it tingle, then the soft pressure of his lips linger over the pad Brawler placed there, and I shiver.

"I'm so sorry I hurt you," he says, and if I didn't know any better, I'd think there was genuine remorse in his voice. Who knows? Maybe there is. Johnny might be a victim of his circumstances just like me. His morality is skewed because of the way he was raised. It's okay to dick around. Respect is everything. He has no empathy or concern for those who aren't in the Heights Crew. I don't know. I can only say that I'm just glad I hadn't grown up like that.

He kisses the area again and then moves my tank top strap back into place, muttering something about marring such a beautiful canvas.

I blink. The guy could be a poet if he wasn't a gangster. No wonder why women flock to him. It's not just because girls think he's their only way out. He's smooth. He's charming. He's got bad boy polish written all over him.

I turn to face him. "I'm glad you stopped by."

"Me too," he says. He looks around the bedroom, and my heart explodes in my chest again, taking off with a sprint. It's not as if anyone could tell I have a hidden compartment in that shelf, but it still makes me nervous he's in the same room with the one thing that could take me down. Then again, there's also a gun in there. I'd use it on him to protect my aunt and uncle. I made a promise to myself long ago that no one else would get mixed up in this. This is my story, and my story alone.

"I'm sorry I had to take off earlier...and that I'm about to do the same again." He smiles hesitantly like he hopes I'm not mad. "Father and I have an important business meeting."

I nod. Tentatively, I reach up and run my fingers down his angular face. "I know you have other commitments."

His jaw tenses, then he moves forward, taking me with him until my back is pressed against the wall. His hips sink into mine, and his hot breath caresses my throat. "God," he groans. "It's not fair that you get me so hot."

I'm thrown by his outburst. All I did was graze my fingertips over his cheek. It's not like he's starved for attention. He fucked someone mere hours ago. I don't get it. It must be the fact that he can't have me. I'm probably the only girl in the Heights who he can't have and it's driving him crazy.

He moans again, the sound filling the room. "Kyla?"

"Yeah?" I choke out. His dick's getting harder by the second, pressing into me. I'm trying to think of anything but, but it's hard.

Ha. Literally.

"Can I kiss you?"

My mouth drops. It's a good thing he's not looking at my face right now. His head's buried in the crook of my shoulder as he wrangles his breath. I didn't take Johnny for the kind who asked if he could kiss. I took him as the kind who would just take what he wanted. Why are all these Crew members so difficult to understand?

"I—"

A knock sounds on the apartment door. "Fuck," Johnny spits. "That's Magnum." A second later, the voices of Magnum and Oscar fill the living room.

I expel the breath I'd been holding in my chest. "He's here to take you to the business meeting?" I guess.

Johnny nods to confirm my suspicions. He moves away, and fresh air winds its way around me. It's hard not to react to Johnny. The attraction is completely physical. He's good looking. He's a charmer. He's good at seducing.

I look away to get a hold of myself. *Jesus Christ. I'm sick.*

"I have to go," Johnny says. "Oscar's staying with you."

"I really don't need anyone to stay with me," I hedge, finding something to fixate on other than the hitch in my breath.

Johnny smiles. "It's just part of being with me, babe. You need protection. Trust me. If you don't want Oscar, just tell me."

I shrug. It's not Oscar at all. I don't like the fact I'm being watched twenty-four-seven. "It's not him."

"Okay," Johnny says, giving me a small smile.

"Rocket?" Magnum calls from the living room.

"Be right there," Johnny says. He takes my hand and turns toward me again. "If any of them bother you, you just let me know. Okay?" he asks, eyebrows raising.

I nod in response. Oddly, it's not Brawler or Oscar I have to worry about. It's the one reminding me to tell him if anything is wrong.

He pulls me to him, placing a soft kiss on my cheek. "I'll call you tonight."

"Okay," I say. He walks out into the apartment, and I wait in the doorframe. Magnum nods at me and then they both leave.

Oscar makes himself comfortable in the recliner as

soon as they exit. He throws his arms behind his head. "Please tell me you have something to fucking eat in here. I'm starving."

"Seriously?"

He shrugs. "What?"

"Were you in my apartment the whole time?"

"Yes," he says, his voice unapologetic. "Rocket got us keys."

"How did Rocket get keys?"

"The super, I imagine." He shrugs again. "It's not like I asked but trust me when I say that pretty much anyone will bend over backward to do whatever the Crew needs."

"Really? Is that how it works? Maybe you can summon some food up here then if you're that hungry."

He laughs exaggeratingly then cuts himself off, glaring my way.

His stare makes me remember I'm barely wearing any clothes. I walk back into my bedroom and change quickly. When I come back out, Oscar's just hanging up the phone. "I hope you like Chinese. There's this bomb Chinese restaurant on the corner. They're going to run some food up for us."

Mildly impressed, I turn the TV on and take a seat

at one of the bar stools since Oscar's occupying the only comfortable chair in the room.

"Ooh, Netflix?" Oscar asks.

"You know it." I flip through the offerings and head toward the series I've been watching about a stalker. When Oscar asks what it's about, I start to explain it to him, but then I decide to start over from episode one since I'm only three episodes deep anyway.

Ten minutes into the first episode, someone knocks on the door and Oscar hops right out of the chair. I fumble with the remote to pause the show, so he doesn't miss anything.

He approaches the door silently, then reaches into the corner and grabs a bat. My eyes round. I hadn't seen it stashed there. He holds it behind the door as he answers it. When he sees who it is, he relaxes and places the bat back in the corner and pulls his wallet out.

After he pays the delivery guy, he sets a few boxes out on the counter. I smirk, wanting to tease him that he actually paid for the food instead of using his status in the Crew, but I actually like that he did that. People shouldn't be using fear to get what they want. That's just sad.

Oscar and I fall into an easy silence as we watch the

show and eat food. In between when the credits are rolling and before the next episode starts, we chat about what we just watched. It all seems so normal; I almost have to pinch myself. It's like I can forget Johnny's probably off doing something illegal with his father. Or that Brawler left me earlier, sexual tension practically ringing off us both. I can even overlook that Oscar brought his bat with him in case he needed to use it to protect us. And, oh, I'm actually forgetting that Oscar's here because I'm Johnny Rocket's girl and apparently, I have to be watched now.

If it weren't for all that, Oscar and I might even be doing this at another place and time. I actually like having him here and watching TV with him. He hasn't had his bad boy gang persona on, he's just been real. And just for thinking that, the itch to scrub off the top layer of my skin hits. It's not Oscar per se. I don't want to become accustomed to this. This is not my life. It was never supposed to be my life for fuck's sake. This is just a means to an end.

Oscar laughs at something on screen. I hadn't even been paying attention for the last five minutes. He peeks at me. "You got quiet."

I shrug. "Just spaced for a second."

He stares at me a while longer then drags his hand down his face. "Listen, I know this life can be crazy. I'm a member of the Crew, don't get me wrong, but if you need someone to talk to about it, I'm here."

I tilt my head at him, trying to make him out. Trusting these guys was not part of the plan either. Brawler's almost there. He's creeping up on me. Then again, he's on the outside of the Heights Crew. Oscar? He isn't. He's right in the thick of things. "What do you do for the Crew?"

Oscar's jaw snaps shut. He's wearing a faded Rawley Heights football shirt that stretches across his muscles. He's lean and tall, but with a muscular build. "Right now, I help watch you. I do whatever they ask me to. Sometimes it's one thing. Sometimes it's another."

"Vague answers. I could've guessed all that."

"I guess I'm just easy to read then." His dark eyes shine with amusement.

"That could be. Or maybe you're just asking me to trust you without giving that trust in return."

Oscar grins easily. "Listen, I know you probably already heard about me. It's everyone's favorite topic where I'm fucking concerned. I bailed on the Heights. I spent a few blissful months in Spring Hill where my mom had a job with a great place to live and look after. A place where I could focus on football."

"You play football?"

"Yeah. You won't hear too much about it because here, the Crew is everything. We have a game tomorrow, and if you notice at school, no one gives a shit."

The hardness in his voice tells me football might just mean a lot more to Oscar than the Crew. "What position do you play?"

"Quarterback." He tries to hide his pride, but it comes out anyway. His chest puffs up. "And I'm fucking good, too."

I smile, a genuine one. Oscar's fucking full of himself. That's for sure. "So, you played football in Spring Hill, too?"

He nods. "Briefly. Their QB was hurt, and I stepped in."

A shadow passes over his features, telling me there's way more to the story than he's telling me, but I won't push.

"Football's a big thing in Spring Hill. Their games are huge. They actually have a cheerleading squad, nice uniforms, and new pads."

"And the Heights has?"

"Decades old pads, uniforms without our last names on them, and I think I saw a Burger King wrapper in the stands last time we played. When we go to away games, we have to drive ourselves."

His eyes grow darker, anger seeping in. I can't

blame him. It would make anyone mad. This piss poor community holds him back. If he's as good as he says he is, he would be better off at another school that actually has money. "It sounds like you really love the game if you're willing to put up with all that just to play."

He blinks at me. Uncertainty crossing his face. He didn't expect that to be my reaction.

"Are you going to go to college to play football?"

The degrading laugh spills from his mouth again. My shoulders lock in annoyance. "What?"

He shakes his head, and I have a feeling I've just told him more about not being from around here than anything I've done yet. "If I get a scholarship, I might be able to go. Even if that, maybe not. I'm a part of the Crew now. They might not let me go."

Understanding fills me, pulling at the string in my stomach. I'm beginning to understand who Oscar is now. "And you joined the Crew because..." I wait a beat for him to tell me the story, but he seems content for me to put the pieces together. "Because when you came back, you had to. It was the only way you had protection."

"Because no one leaves the Heights thinking they can have a better life, Princess. No one."

His words seep into my pores and then sink into my stomach like a dead weight. *No one gets out of the*

Heights. That's about as worse of a threat as you can get. This place isn't for people who want to better themselves. There's no opportunity. Sometimes by force, sometimes by choice. It's not like the kids around here see people succeeding every day. There's no one to look up to.

And even with all that, Oscar tried. And even with him trying, things got a lot worse for him. Now he probably won't ever be able to escape. He'll become a statistic the suburbs hear about on the nightly news. Another gang member gunned down. Or stabbed. They won't tell his whole story. The people listening will sit in their picture-perfect lives shaking their heads at all the youth who can't seem to get their shit together.

16

The next morning, Oscar's still with me. I tell him to take off because he has to attend practice to be eligible to play in his game. He hesitates, but eventually, I push him out the door. If Johnny realizes he left, I'll — Well, we're just going to have to hope he doesn't realize he's left.

As Oscar walks out of the apartment, a genuine smile lighting his face, he looks about as real as I've seen him yet. He's fake when he walks around the school like his shit doesn't stink. He's fake when Nevaeh plastered herself all over him. He doesn't want that. He doesn't want any of that.

It makes my heart hurt to think how trapped he is.

No wonder why I've felt like he's like me. We're

both trapped. The only difference is, I plan on getting the fuck out.

I'm not alone for long. Just enough time to shower and think about how I'm going to spend my Saturday even though I should've known it wasn't mine to plan. The door to my apartment opens, and I peek out of my bedroom to see who it is. A rough looking guy with long hair moves a loveseat into the room. "Hey, whoa," I say, not recognizing the guy who's currently turned away from me. "What are you doing?"

He ignores me, but Brawler pushes through holding the other end. "New furniture," he says in explanation.

"New furniture?" My mind starts to race. I didn't order furniture. What the—?

"Rocket," Brawler says as they place the loveseat down in the area where we trained only yesterday. He bends over to push the loveseat against the wall. Bandages wind around his neck, and I suck in a breath. Before I can ask him about it, he stands and looks to the side of me instead of right at me, and asks, "Is this good?"

I shake my head. "What's going on?"

"Rocket," Brawler says again, turquoise eyes still avoiding me. "He told us to pick up this furniture and to drop it off for you."

The other guy, who'd left, comes back in carrying a short table and plops it in front of the loveseat. Brawler claps him on the back, and the guy leaves. I stare at the stuff in shock. It's clearly a set. A nice one. The coffee table is squat with a beautiful cherry wood. The loveseat is a dark gray microfiber.

"He probably realized you didn't have much," Brawler says, his voice tight.

"Nobody does." I'd picked just the old armchair out because I knew no one would have very much, and I wanted to blend in. Plus, the more money I keep in my getting-out-of-dodge fund, the better.

"He doesn't want you to be like everyone else." After a heavy pause, he says, "It's brand new. We picked it up at the furniture store across town in Pedro's truck."

"It's nice," I mumble, eyeing it and not knowing what to say. I'm not used to this. Whatever Johnny is, I can't say he's not observant...and caring? He must've seen how sparse my furniture was and wanted to give me more.

Brawler glances around the apartment. "Where's Oscar?"

I stand there like a deer in the headlights. It doesn't take Brawler long to figure out he's not here. There really isn't room for me to lie. What could I tell him?

He's in the bathroom? The door's wide open. Clearly, no one else is here with me. "He had to go to a football game," I say, shrugging. "He didn't want to. I made him."

Brawler shakes his head. His eyes turn into that stormy color again. "Fucker would do anything for football."

"Johnny doesn't have to know. Right?" I ask. I'm beginning to think I can count more and more on Brawler, but I'm not sure. Shit's weird between us right now. I'm not sure I'm even thinking clearly.

"Not my place to narc," Brawler responds.

He reaches up like he's going to itch his neck but stops as soon as his fingers brush the bandages around his neck. He sees me looking and flushes. "What are those?" I ask, worried he's been hurt. He isn't acting like he's in pain, but why else would he be swathed in bandages.

He finally looks at me. "I got a new tattoo last night."

"Oh." My voice rings high with surprise. "What did you get?"

He shrugs. "Nothing big." His answer is intentionally vague, and I immediately want to call him out on his bullshit. I have a feeling Brawler just doesn't decide to get a tattoo one day. Especially where he's gotten it.

He won't ever be able to cover it up unless he wants to wear a scarf, so it must mean something to him. He motions toward the furniture with his head. "You should probably call Johnny."

"Right," I say. "Of course." I should've done that already, but Brawler is distracting.

Johnny answers the phone with a smile in his voice. He's definitely pleased with himself. I thank him a few times, telling him I never expected he would do that. He repeats over and over that his girl should have the best. The call doesn't last long because he's needed in another business meeting, so we hang up, and I find myself smiling.

Ridiculous, I know. I'm judging myself, so I can only imagine what those on the outside see.

I school my features, but I turn to find Brawler staring at me. His gaze intense as he watches the smile fall off my face. It's like I'm on display for him, so I immediately turn to place my cell phone on the counter. Then, I head toward the new furniture and sit. The cushions envelop me. It really is a nice couch. The kind I might see sitting in my aunt and uncle's den. "The only downside to this is that there's no room to train now."

"We shouldn't do that again."

My mind flashes to Brawler putting his hands on

me. His arm wrapping around my middle. How good it felt. There's only been two times since moving to the Heights where things felt normal. Watching TV with Oscar last night and training with Brawler.

He's probably right. We shouldn't train together again. It's too much temptation. But I want to. "We should go to a gym," I press.

"We can't."

His attitude pisses me off. "Why can't we?"

He runs a shaking hand through his short-cropped hair. "You know what I don't get? One minute, you're pushing me around because Johnny fucked some other girl and cut your back open. The next, you're giggling into your phone because he bought you furniture."

"I wasn't giggling into the fucking phone." My mouth drops, and I suck in a breath. "How did you know he fucked some other girl?"

He gives me a look of disbelief. "It's not hard to guess. He handed me a bunch of bags filled with clothes. I know exactly where you were. My brother used to date the owner."

I stand, ready to escape to my bedroom. She told him. That Lynette girl is probably the owner, and she told Brawler what happened. Mortification brims at the surface. I'm so embarrassed I could scream.

Brawler moves in front of me, blocking my exit.

"Like what the fuck is it, Kyla? Do you want to be a princess? Is that it?"

"Why don't you man up and tell me what this is really about?" I threaten. He wanted me yesterday. The bulge in his pants clear evidence. His arm around me made the thoughts churning in his brain abundantly apparent. Plus, he fixed me up last night. His gentle fingers made sure I was okay.

That had to mean something, and he just doesn't want to admit it.

Brawler just stares at me. His chest raising and lowering in front of him.

I raise my eyebrows. I'm not saving him from this. He needs to talk.

"I can't," he finally says.

"Then get out of my way."

I try to move around him, but he steps in front of me again. "How's your back?"

I flinch. From all that to how's my back? "Fuck you."

He growls, the low grumble pricking my skin.

"You can't insinuate what you did about me and then ask if I'm okay. I wasn't giggling on the phone, and yes, I was fucking pissed off yesterday. More than you know. I'm not used to being treated like that."

"You shouldn't be treated like that."

"We've already come to the conclusion that I really don't have a choice. But please, throw it in my face if it makes you feel better."

Brawler swears under his breath. "It doesn't. It makes me feel like shit. It makes me furious." His body shakes. His fingers curl into his palms until his knuckles turn white. He's a volcano about to erupt, spewing his shit over anyone close to him.

I'm not afraid of getting a little dirty.

"Good," I say. "Then get your shit together because we're headed to a gym. We can pound the shit out of inanimate objects until there's nothing left inside us."

We lock gazes, and I silently pray I'll be so tired when we've finished that I'll be able to resist the pull to Brawler. Whether he wants to admit it to himself or not, he's jealous of Johnny.

An hour later, two workers at a local gym across town hold pads for us as we obliterate them. The looks on their faces when Brawler walked in was something to behold. I could tell they were regulars at the fights and had probably seen more than a few starring the guy to my left. For never setting foot in a boxing gym, Brawler takes to it easily.

They run us through round after round of focus mitts, then let us punch our aggression out on huge swinging heavy bags that rock forward and backward with the force of our punches. It's like having someone come swinging back at you. At least, it's easier to pretend this way than just hitting a stand-up heavy bag.

During a break, Brawler guzzles down water the workers throw at us, and we sit on a bench to catch our breaths. "I knew you'd like it," I say.

He seems less agitated here. More carefree like the heavy baggage around his neck lifted away. "What's not to like?"

"The fuck if I know."

He grins at me, his smile toothy and downright sexy while sweat drips down his face. Instead of returning it, I'm struck, staring at him, imagining licking the bead of sweat edging down his cheek right now.

The light dies in his eyes, and a low rumble starts in his chest. "Don't."

I bite my lip.

He looks away. "Fuck." He slams his water bottle down and heads back to the swinging heavy bag, beating the ever loving shit out of it. A few times, I'm afraid it's going to come crashing down off the ceiling, but it holds steady.

To cool us down, one of the trainers has us do some stretching while he runs through some mechanics with

Brawler. The guy's a monster as it is. He just needs a little refinement, and he'll be unstoppable. I'm talking UFC level fighter who brings in multi-millions for Pay-Per-View matches. I've never seen anyone who fights quite like him, and I've been around a lot of gyms across several states.

The sad fact is, he might not ever get out of the Heights to see what he's capable of.

We take quick showers at the gym and then catch a city bus to our apartment building. People give Brawler a wide berth which is fine by me. I hide a smirk when I've watched the third person take the empty seat next to him and then change their mind last minute when they see who they're sitting next to. One even changed direction on the descent of butt into chair. I almost drew blood on that one, biting the inside of my cheek so I wouldn't laugh.

When we get to my apartment, the door closed and locked behind us, I ask, "How do the fights work?" I turn, heading into the kitchen to retrieve us both glasses of water.

"The fights?"

I look over my shoulder to find him running his hand through his already dry blond hair. His blue eyes are fucking fierce and sharp right now. Swallowing, I add, "Yeah. Do the fighters get paid?"

Brawler accepts my glass and then sits down on the loveseat, giving me the armchair. "It started out as just the Crew making money off the fights. People needed a structured way of settling conflict. If you had beef with someone, you would call them out. Whoever won, won. You weren't allowed to have beef after that. It was settled in the ring. Then, shit got popular. We started drawing crowds. People started betting on the side, and when Big Daddy saw that, he turned it into what it is now. He was just second-in-command then. It's one of the reasons he got voted into top dog position. When he made it into the fight circuit, they started paying the fighters. Nothing huge, but enough to entice them to fight without settling beef with someone. Now, if you're a good fighter, you can make quite a bit. It depends on how long you've been fighting for us and how many people are betting on your fight."

"You make money on your fights?"

He nods.

Understanding dawns on me. "That's why Johnny was so pissed when you pulled that other guy out last time."

He doesn't have to nod again. It's true. Johnny said as much to me.

I'd wondered how the Heights Crew made money, so this is something. If Johnny can afford to give "his girl" a new loveseat and table, they must be doing okay. I just wonder what else they're into. It can't be just the fights. Not for how big the Crew has gotten. They must have several business ventures by now.

"You're a great fighter," I tell him, thinking back on how well he did today. He definitely fits in there.

His voice drops. "You've barely seen me fight."

"I saw enough. Plus, I've seen you train, so that's more than enough."

I squirm under Brawler's scrutiny. Finally, he asks, "Where did you learn how to fight?"

"Gyms," I tell him.

"Why?"

I swallow. That hits a little too close to home. I can't have that. "Didn't peg you as the anti-feminist type," I deadpan.

He huffs out a short laugh. "I'm not. Just curious."

"Because I fucking like it," I tell him.

He holds his hands up, one still clutching the glass of water, rivulets of sweat dripping from the glass. "It just...it feels like more when you fight. That's all." When I don't say anything in response, he says, "I hope Rocket lets you fight again. People have been asking me about you. They want to see you out there."

"Maybe if you told him that, he'd let me," I say, a spark of hope building inside.

"I already have." He stares at the new coffee table. "I get wanting to fight. The need you feel sometimes. I'll see what I can do, but I won't be able to change his mind if he's already made it up. No one can."

He doesn't look convinced that he can help me, but I won't let that deter my good mood. "When are the next fights?" If I can't be in it, I can at least watch them.

"Tonight."

A burst of energy moves through my tired limbs. "Are you fighting?"

He shakes his head. "Not tonight. Next time."

"I'll help you train," I offer. "I'm a good partner."

His mouth twitches in amusement, and I realize we've had the longest conversation we've ever had. Brawler might actually be opening up to me. And me to him. Maybe we don't just have the crazy physical attraction to one another.

He finishes off his water, and I get up to take both empty glasses to the kitchen sink. When he hands his to me, his fingers slide over mine.

I gasp at the contact. Every cell in my body is focusing on the parts where we touch until it's all I'm aware of. Brawler and I have a connection. One we can't pursue because of who's claimed me. Well, that and because I won't be sticking around the Heights after I've murdered Big Daddy K, so it doesn't matter.

Nothing matters but what I came here to do, I tell myself.

I stand in front of him for a moment then make my feet move. While I'm setting the glasses in the sink, Brawler's cell phone pings. A moment later, he says, "Rocket's on his way up."

I close my eyes, allowing myself a brief moment where I can feel however I want and not have to second guess everything. I underestimated how hard it would be to have to act a certain way and not get caught up in it. The only thing is, with Brawler, I'm not acting. With Oscar, I'm not acting.

With Johnny, I have such conflicting emotions that I can't quite separate them yet.

17

*J*ohnny walks in while I'm still standing at the kitchen sink. I let him and Brawler greet one another and then I walk around the island to the main living room. Johnny's dressed in a suit that hugs his body. He looks like...a man. I know that's odd to say, but I don't usually see guys Johnny's age dressed in suits and looking like they can pull it off. He can. He so can. While I'm taking him in, he turns toward me. His crystal blue eyes catch on me. After a moment, he calls out behind him, "You can leave Brawler. I've got Kyla now."

I meet Brawler's gaze over Johnny's shoulder and hold it. Regret teems at the surface of his sapphire eyes, only getting more intense as he takes Johnny and I in. He swallows then leaves without a word.

I want to go running after him. He has to know we feel something for one another no matter how dumb it is. I can tell myself all day I shouldn't start anything with him, but the pull is too much. It's only a matter of time before I give in.

Johnny continues, oblivious to what's just transpired between me and his fight organizer. "Put on a dress, babe. We're headed to a fancy dinner before we hit the fights tonight."

"Yeah?" I ask, not masking the true excitement bubbling up inside me at the mention of watching the fights tonight. It's where I belong.

"Yeah," he says, tangling his fingers in mine for a moment. "I hope you like steak." I do love steak, but he completely misread which part of his statement made me happy.

I squeeze his hand and then move past him to search the closet in my room, which now brims with the different outfits Johnny bought me. His little bribe for making the shopkeepers keep their mouths shut about his transgression. Though, I'm sure they don't see it as his transgression. I was the one who went looking for them. Girls like me aren't supposed to do that. I'm the prize. I'm the one who gets to enjoy the jealous looks of others because I'm living the "good life" while actually never being free to enjoy that good life.

I'm jealous of them, and they're jealous of me.

I walk out with a midnight blue sequined dress on that barely covers my ass. Seriously, it's the best dress in that closet as far as coverage goes. I tried two on before this that had a dipped neck that reached my belly button. This one, at least, has a high back and long sleeves that cover up the scrape on my back even if it is too short.

Johnny's too busy talking to Magnum when I first appear. I just stand there, waiting for them to notice and also trying to hear the muted words of their conversation. Johnny looks up, and then does a double-take. He captures my gaze, following me appreciatively as I move forward.

Magnum turns to see what's caught Johnny's attention. I try not to focus on him, but his reaction catches my eye. His jaw ticks. His stare captures mine, holding it, and the copper scruff on his face moves as his jaw tightens.

I'm not used to being looked at in this way. Guys at the prep school I went to knew I didn't have any real money, so they never gave me the time of day. I was just a relation to the ones who had money. To them, I begged for scraps off my aunt and uncle, even though I knew my aunt and uncle would do anything for me if I needed it.

Worse than that, I was just my aunt's niece. It was my aunt who married into the wealthy family. His family never got over why he chose my aunt over one of the prim and proper girls attached with a hefty bank account. Apparently, for some people, it's still like we're living in the 1800s

A part of me feels like I belong more in this life. Maybe not the whole gang aspect, but the having to work to get something. Not using the good ol' boy network to make connections. It's all about climbing the ladder here, and I get that. Every day is a fight, and we already know how much I enjoy fighting.

As charming as ever, Johnny moves to pick my hand up and brushes a soft kiss over my knuckles. "You look beautiful."

"Thank you," I tell him, cheeks heating.

Over his shoulder, Magnum blatantly stares at us. Heat envelops me under his inspection. He must think what Brawler thought of me. How can someone treat me like he did at the dress store, and I still stand here in front of him with this dress on as if I'm trying to impress him?

I wiggle my fingers out of Johnny's grip. Doing what I'm doing right now actually goes against everything I believe in, but I'm caught. I have to be here, standing in front of Johnny like this, trying to impress him. I have to stay in his good favor, so I will, no matter what it makes me look like. "There's just one problem," I tell him. "I don't have the right kind of shoes to go with the dress."

A pout pulls his lips into a frown. His stare drags down the length of me until he gets to my bare feet, which I wiggle around, showing off my lack of shoes. He moves forward, and I still. Before I know it, he has me pulled into his arms—one arm in the crook of my knee and the other around my shoulders. He plucks me easily off the ground and turns. "I'll take care of this," he promises.

His cologne fills my nostrils. It's a musky scent that's not all together bad. In fact, it's pleasing. He went all out for tonight. We catch one another's gaze, and I smile up at him as a draft hits my backside when Magnum opens the door for us. "I'm pretty sure everyone can see my ass," I tell him, laughing. "This dress is short."

Johnny cocks a grin. "No one will be looking at your ass. Not unless they want to die."

A heavy mask falls over his face. I blink up at him, but he's deadly serious. He's not messing around. For everyone's sake, I hope we don't run into someone bold enough to check out my ass.

Johnny moves into the open elevator, and we step inside. He adjusts me in his grip, and I say, "You don't have to carry me. I can walk."

"On these shitty floors? Fuck no."

Magnum gets in and immediately faces the other way. With Johnny openly gawking at me and Magnum doing everything in his power not to look at me, I'm feeling the confines of the elevator. The walls push in on us as we descend to the lobby level. When the doors open, the extra room is a relief.

A couple of people mill around in the small lobby when we pass through, and Johnny's right. As soon as they notice it's him, they look the other way. He has a magical gift of repelling people. Or instilling fear in people. Or both.

Magnum holds the door to the car open as we approach. Johnny leans over to set my feet inside first, and then I maneuver in, having to pull my dress down once I get situated. Johnny peeks in. "Give me one second."

I sit there as the driver's side door opens. The

divider between the front and the back is actually open, so I catch Magnum's hard brown eyes in the rearview mirror. He doesn't let up until Johnny slides in next to me.

"Lynette's going to meet us at the restaurant with a pair of shoes."

"Lynette? From the dress store?"

Johnny nods. "What's your size? I need to text her, so she can pick out the perfect pair."

I tell him, and he types it out on his phone and then puts it away. He rests his hand on my leg, his pinky sneaking under the hem of my dress just barely. I may not be looking at it, but it's my entire focus. I close my eyes, hoping he doesn't move it any further up. Hoping he doesn't try anything tonight. I'm entirely too conflicted about him. To distract him, I start a conversation. "Will your dad be at the fights tonight?"

Johnny shrugs. "He hardly goes to the fights anymore. He has other business ventures he's interested in. He lets me take care of this aspect."

Pride lights his eyes, and I look down. So much for thinking I'd have easy access to the guy I'm really here for. "That's cool."

"The fights bring in the most money right now, you know. I've done a lot to grow the business."

I steel myself, then move closer to him. "I bet you have," I say.

He squeezes my leg until it's almost painful, but I don't move. I just sit there with an adoring gaze turned toward him.

It doesn't take us long to get to the restaurant, and when we do, a knock on the door pulls Johnny's attention away from me. He shoves the door open, and Lynette comes into view, two pairs of heels dangling from her fingers. One black and one silver. "I didn't know what color dress you'd chosen, but black or silver go with almost anything." Up front, Magnum turns the lights on in the back so Lynette doesn't have to squint to try to see me any longer. "Ahh, I think the silver pair then," she says.

Johnny grabs both pairs. "We'll take both." As soon as she steps back, he closes the door on her.

Magnum gets out of the car, closing the front door behind him, leaving us alone.

"Let me see," Johnny says, motioning for me to put my foot in his lap.

I turn in the seat, pulling my foot up to place on his thigh. His hand starts at my thigh, smoothing over my knee and down my calf to the arch of my foot. He then picks up the silver shoe and places it on my foot. He does the same with the other leg until I wiggle my feet, admiring the heels I'm wearing. I've never worn anything but sensible half inch heels that went with my private school uniform.

"Maybe he was right," Johnny says, voice throaty and full of want.

"About?"

"Waiting," he says. "I can't think of anyone I've wanted more than you." He spreads my legs, moving his hands up my leg until he gets to my mid-thigh.

My heart stammers as his thumbs press into my skin there. He's got a full view of my panties because my dress rolled up when he moved my legs apart. He edges a little closer until I snap my knees shut and move my legs off him, putting them firmly on the ground with my dress back down over my thighs. I draw in a shaky breath.

I'm turned on. And I'm mad that I'm turned on.

"You're right," Johnny says. "Bad idea. My balls are so fucking blue right now."

I know what he means.

But unlike me, he'll just fuck someone else.

He arranges himself in his pants and then throws the door open. A strong hand grips it, opening it farther. Johnny gets out, and I scoot over after him, the leather of the seats rubbing against my bare thighs. Before I emerge, I take a deep breath.

We walk through the crowded restaurant. Johnny turns heads. How he got all the power *and* good looks isn't fair. A lot of evil things are wrapped up in pretty paper. The sky before a storm is beautiful, but it brings wreckage and destruction. That's what Johnny Rocket does.

Johnny orders food for me like I'm incapable of doing it myself and then we settle in. I try to talk to him about what he does, but he keeps getting distracted by his phone. If I were really his girlfriend, I'd be chucking that thing in the fucking corner. You don't bring a girl out on a fancy date and then not talk to her. Not appreciate the way she dressed up for you.

Instead, I keep my mouth shut and eat while he does business. He was right about the steak. It's delicious. It almost melts in my mouth. It's been a while since I've had food this fancy. Truth be told, I never used to enjoy it all that much when it was surrounded by my aunt and uncle's polished friends. But because I'm being ignored right now, I just eat whatever and however I want.

Eventually, Johnny does put the cell phone down. "I'm sorry," he says, cringing. "I'm not being a very good date, am I?" He lowers his voice. "Something's going down tonight, and I'm being kept in the loop."

I try to smile, but I'm doing a piss-poor job of

pretending. I'm too lost in my own head tonight. I'm wondering when I'm going to meet Big Daddy K. I'm wondering how the fuck much longer this is going to take. Tonight's just one of those nights where I don't see the bright light at the end. Only darkness. It's like I'm being pulled under with all of them. I thought it would be easy to go through the motions. It's not. This world can be overwhelming. And if it's not the world, it's the people. Brawler, Oscar, and I—and yes, even Johnny—we're drowning in the absence of light, in this underworld society where power and money talk. Well, power and money talk everywhere, but this shit is shady and dark and dangerous. Power had by any means necessary, and the same goes for money.

"You've got the cutest frown on your face right now," Johnny says, quickly wiping his face with his napkin. "Are you not enjoying your meal?"

"I am," I tell him, trying to smile once more.

"Good," he says.

He misses the fact that my thoughts are pulling me under. They pull me into a dark space every now and then. Not dark like the Heights Crew, but dark like the absence of feelings. Depression. Anxiety. The feeling that I'll never be able to escape this.

The waiter comes over to fill my water glass. Instead of placing his hand on the back of my chair, he places it on my shoulder. I jump. The waiter spills the water over my plate. "I'm so sorry," he says, placing the metallic pitcher on the table and grabbing a napkin to start wiping it up.

Johnny stands. The waiter apologizes profusely for spilling the water, but Johnny doesn't give a shit. His stare bores a hole into my shoulder where the young man touched me. Johnny drops his napkin on the table, anger pulsating from him.

My stomach clenches. "It's okay," I say automatically. I recognize the look in Johnny's gaze.

Of course, he ignores me. "Did you just touch her?"

The waiter slowly turns toward Johnny, only now noticing how angry he is. "Did I?"

"It's fine," I say, but it's hard to cover it up. Johnny notices everything. He saw my reaction.

Johnny shoots me a silencing stare. "Magnum," he says.

From out of nowhere, Magnum approaches the table. I had no idea he was even in the room with us.

"Please take Kyla away from the table."

Other guests start staring at our table now. The countdown is on. Johnny is seconds from exploding, and nothing can be done to stop it. If I say something,

I'll just get shot down, so instead, I take Magnum's offered hand.

As he drags me away, I look back. Johnny has his hands around the waiter's neck, pulling him closer, so he can spit words into his face. People look on in horror, but they also don't interfere. I don't know where exactly we are, but Johnny's reputation is alive and well here. Or maybe it's just the Heights Crew's in general.

When we get outside, I mutter, "He didn't mean to."

Magnum laughs. "Are you kidding me? The guy's been eyeing you all night."

"What?" I glance at Magnum. "No way."

"It was only a matter of time before something happened."

"That's ridiculous. How would Johnny even notice? His eyes were trained on his cell phone all fucking dinner."

"He sees everything," Magnum says. The way he says it sounds less like an off-hand comment and more like a warning.

"Whatever. This is fucking ridiculous. That poor guy."

"It's not the real world here, Kyla," Magnum warns. "If you're going to claim territory, you have to protect it. The minute he stops doing that, you know there's a problem."

His words silence me. They're like a riddle I have to figure out, and even though it doesn't take me long, I still stop and internalize them, realizing the myriad of scenarios this could apply to.

A few seconds later, Johnny comes out with another well-dressed man in tow. He pushes him toward me, and the man stumbles. "Miss, I am so sorry for your intrusion tonight. My employee has been dealt with, and I do hope you'll deign to dine here again."

The gentleman's eyes look so hopeful. I'd love to tell him it wasn't his employee's fault that Johnny turns into a caveman, but I don't know what will happen if I do. Instead, I turn to Johnny to look for instruction like I can't even think for myself. He gives me a slight nod, so I press my lips together before responding. "If you've rectified the situation, perhaps we might come again," I say, feeling a solid weight drop to the bottom of my stomach.

The owner nods, giving me a shy grin before he apologizes to Johnny and heads back into the restaurant.

"Are you okay?" Johnny asks, slipping his hand around me and pressing his palm into the small of my back.

"Yeah," I tell him, trying my best not to shy away from his touch.

The truth is, I'm not okay. He ignores me most of the night and then freaks out when a guy accidentally touches me?

He's deranged.

18

I'm not used to wearing heels. In fact, I think they suck. I like the way they look on me, but they're just not practical. Especially because if I have to defend myself in them, I'd never be able to. I'd die for sure. With the predicament I find myself in, I never know when I'm going to have to defend myself. So, note for next outing: no fucking heels.

Magnum appraises me, and I wonder if he's figured me out, if he knows who I actually am. So much so that I avoid his gaze for the rest of the night, even though we're stuck in the same warehouse room as before, high above the fights happening below.

At least Johnny is distracted through most of the fights. He's antsy. Jumpy. I don't want to know what happened in that restaurant after I left. With the wattage coming off him, it doesn't bode well for the waiter. At least, he doesn't see me as I watch Brawler from afar while he masters the crowd, getting them hyped up for the fights. Oscar's here, too. He has his game face on, though. So unlike the one day we watched TV together. He sits in the opposite corner of the room, and I catch him glaring at me every once in a while.

The fights are half over when Johnny finally turns toward me. "You really like this, don't you?"

I've been fiending to fight all night. Muscles straining while I picture what I would do in every position below. The blocks I would make. The shots I would take. I thought I'd be fighting in the fights, not watching them up here. I gaze up at Johnny, wetting my lips as I try to figure out if right now is the time to ask him if I can fight again. "I love it, actually."

He grins, and this time, it isn't forced. "I like that about you," he says, reaching over and running a hand over my hair. "You're not afraid to get your hands dirty. It makes me think you're going to be a great addition to the Crew."

I lean over and give him a peck on the cheek. Earlier, I spied a speck of blood on his collar. Another piece of evidence that what transpired between the waiter and him when I left did not end well. "I've been meaning to ask you," I start, taking a deep breath to gather the courage. I don't know why I'm so nervous. If he says no, it's a no. There's nothing I'm going to be able to do about it. "I'd love to fight again."

His brows pull up. "Yeah?"

I remember how he stood in Cherry's corner and hope spreads through my chest. Training and fighting is a good way for the edges of my dark mind to brighten. It sounds sick, and it probably is, but that's me.

"Brawler's been saying people are asking for you to fight again."

"Really?" I ask, like I haven't already heard that part. The excitement is real though. Brawler said he was going to do it, and he did. It's nice to have someone in my corner.

However, my good mood doesn't last long. Johnny's eyes darken over. "I don't like the idea of you fighting. If you lose, not only will I be pissed off you got hurt, but it won't look good for me...or for the Crew in general."

My initial reaction is to get defensive, but I see his point. I'm getting more and more used to the way the Heights Crew sees things. That doesn't mean I have to like it, though.

He watches me deflate and frowns. "I'll see what I

can do, Kyla." He reaches up to run his knuckle over my cheek. "Just know if we do put you out there and you lose, there's nothing I can do for you." His gaze flickers, holding back a suppressed emotion. He's saying that, but I wonder if he really means it.

Before I can delve deeper into that, Oscar stands in the corner of the room. He's glaring down at his phone. "There's a guy downstairs, Rocket. Says he wants to fight you."

This makes me sit up straighter. Rocket doesn't fight. The same rule applies to him that applies to me. If he fought and lost, there goes his reputation. On the other hand, no one would be stupid enough to challenge Rocket. Does this guy have a fucking death wish?

Johnny laughs, the corners of his eyes crinkle. When Oscar doesn't immediately start laughing, the mirth dies on his lips. "Wait. Seriously?"

Oscar shrugs. Glancing down at the screen again, he reads off it. "Says you kicked his ass earlier, and he wants a chance to avenge himself. Also, if he wins, he wants a kiss from your girl."

"The fuck..." Who the instigator is dawns on Johnny before it dawns on me. "Bring the fucker up."

Oscar looks from me to Johnny, but eventually turns and pads down the stairs. He leaves the door open, so we can hear the crowd below, rooting for their favorite fighters. The sound sends goosebumps over my body. I wish I was down there with all of them instead of up here. There're no girls up here tonight, just Johnny, Magnum, and myself. Magnum is keeping himself scarce behind the bar, only glancing up when Oscar informed us about the intruder downstairs. Now that there's someone making their way up the stairs, Magnum moves closer to us, standing guard.

Just as I suspected, Oscar shoves the waiter from the restaurant into the room. He catches himself easily on solid legs. Here, he looks older than I pegged him before. He's even older than Johnny. His gaze moves around the room, first on Magnum, then on Oscar before stopping on me. His lips curl up in a flirtatious grin. "Hello again."

Before I can answer, Magnum steps in front of me and Oscar cuffs him upside the head.

Johnny cracks his knuckles. "What's this about you wanting a kiss from my girl?"

The waiter crosses his arms over his chest, slowly, deliberately. He's really trying to antagonize my friends.

My friends? What am I saying?

"I figure if she saw how a woman should be treated, she might leave you. A woman like that doesn't deserve to be ignored all night over dinner."

I can't see Johnny's face, but his back bristles.

"Isn't that right, pretty lady?" the waiter tries to ask me. A crop of hair comes into view, but Johnny immediately moves over to block me again. There's now a wall of two muscled backs in front of me.

To be fair, they're very nice backs.

"What makes you think she'd even want to kiss you?" Johnny asks. In his question, jealousy, anger, and uncertainty mix into one.

"Because she looked like she was dying of boredom, asshole."

My eyes widen. I have no idea who this guy thinks he is. His voice is lilted in a slight accent, and I wonder if he's truly from a different country, so he doesn't understand who Johnny is. Maybe he saw just what he said he did. A man ignoring his date all night and wanted to step in. If that's the case, what does he think he's doing here? Whose place does he think this is? Maybe he is just dumb.

"Kyla, come here, Beautiful," Johnny says, summoning me.

I move to stand, kicking my discarded heels out of the way. Magnum moves over to allow me space to walk in beside him. Johnny turns toward me, and I do the same, staring into his dark eyes. They're brimming with heat *and* hate tonight, and I'm not sure which emotion is going to win.

He cups my face. "Do you want to kiss the degenerate?"

I shake my head. "Of course not."

The newcomer growls. "You would allow him to treat you like that?"

I turn my head to answer, but Johnny's on me. He presses his lips to mine. They're hungry and bruising, claiming me right there in front of everyone. He forces my lips open and my head back, taking my mouth for his. He dives his tongue inside, pushing it against my own, moving against me until he abruptly pulls away, and I'm left reeling.

"Answer the man again. Do you want to kiss him?"

Angry tears form in the corners of my eye. I didn't kiss him back, but I doubted anyone noticed. He just *stole* a kiss from me. To prove a fucking point. "No," I growl.

Johnny tucks me into his side and turns toward the man. "Do you still want to fight me? Because you won't even get the prize you desire." His hand moves over my dress, skittering across my rib. I worry for a moment he's going to palm me in front of everybody.

The guy sneers at me. "You're a whore," he postulates. "A stupid whore."

I flinch.

Oscar swings first. Surprisingly. He knocks the guy to the side, but Magnum jumps into action, getting in a good left cross before pulling the waiter's arms behind his body and holding him for Johnny. Instead of hitting him, Johnny spits in his face. Saliva hits his cheek and starts to run, coating his skin. "I'll let Kyla do the honors."

I'm reeling so hard, I can barely see. His words hit me, scarring the surface like a tattoo, except those weren't pretty words or images. It's nothing I'd ever want written over my body. Nothing like the canvas Brawler has created for himself.

Disgust rolls through me. Johnny took something from me I didn't want to give. "He's not worth my time," I say, trying to wrangle myself under control.

My arms itch with the need to take my aggression out on something, but not with this guy. I refuse to stoop to his level.

"I guess it's on us, boys," Johnny says, delight in his voice. "He doesn't deserve the spotlight, let's take him out back. Oscar, stay with Kyla."

Magnum drags the waiter out the door. His feet thunk on every step as Johnny follows casually. They don't even draw the attention of the crowd.

"Are you okay?" Oscar asks, moving forward, his arm outstretched.

I move out of his way. "Don't touch me."

I'm trying to stop the emotion from showing on my face, but I can't. It keeps teeming there, threatening to spill over. Worse yet, Oscar keeps looking at me as if he knows what I'm feeling.

He backs off when I tell him to, though. I turn toward the fight, immediately finding Brawler in the crowd. He's not hard to miss. He's bigger than most everyone out there. Unlike everyone else, he, however, doesn't miss the scene with Magnum dragging someone out the side door. He gazes up to meet my eyes, and I look away.

Not Brawler. Not right now.

"Are you okay?" Oscar asks, concern threading through every word.

"I'm not fine china," I seethe.

"Duh," Oscar says plainly. The word is so out of place in this conversation that it makes me want to laugh, but all I have to do is call up what that guy just called me, and my stomach sinks again. "Sometimes other shit can hurt worse than a punch to the face."

I press my lips together and try not to look at him. I'm always saying that. Physical shit hurts far less than grief, anger, and depression, emotions that well up that you don't have an outlet for.

When he doesn't say anything else, I look over at him. He's got a faraway look on his face like he's remembering something. Or going through something. "Looks like you know about that," I say, tentatively.

He nods. "Yeah, I do. Don't we all?"

"I guess."

I wonder if this has anything to do with his time in Spring Hill. Or maybe it's that he can't play football like he wants to. Then again, I'm probably far off. Maybe it's family shit like mine. Or the fact that he thought he had an out, but now he's stuck here again, not knowing if he'll ever get a chance to leave again.

To change the subject, I ask, "Did you win your football game?"

His dark eyes shutter, then blaze while he answers. "Kicked ass actually."

"Congratulations."

I have a feeling he still wants to ask me who I am, but instead, he asks, "You like football?"

"It's okay," I tell him, more comfortable with this line of questioning. "I like fighting. I like competition. I like the idea of winners and losers."

"So, you like things black and white? That rarely happens."

"In sports it does."

"In the game itself, maybe, unless you have corrupt referees or unfair rules. Directly outside the competition itself, there can be so much gray. I've done some dirty shit in the name of football." He jams his hands into his pockets.

"For football? Or for you?"

"For me, I guess."

Footsteps sound on the stairs. Glancing over, I find Johnny stomping up them, taking his suit jacket off and throwing it on the railing. Blood is spattered all over his crisp white shirt.

I don't know how to feel about this. I'm not going to lie. A sick satisfaction rolls through me that Johnny kicked the guy's ass for calling me a whore. If that's why he did it.

It's like the same question I asked Oscar. Was it for football? Or for you? I have a feeling Johnny didn't kick the waiter's ass because he insulted me or even because he wanted me. It was all about his own ego.

Johnny walks in finally, unbuttoning his soiled white shirt. Some of the blood has even seeped through to his wife beater underneath, which he chucks off next until he's standing there in just his crisp linen pants, leaving a trail of clothes in his wake. He comes up to me. "Are you okay?"

"I'm fine," I say, glancing away.

"Don't worry," Johnny says, voice softening. "He's been dealt with now."

My stomach turns over. I don't want to know the extent to which Johnny "took care" of the situation. But if it wasn't me standing here, it would be someone else. This is just another day in the life for them.

"I have to help Magnum with this," he says, motioning back toward the door they took the waiter through earlier. "Brawler will take you home." Johnny glances over at Oscar to make sure he's gotten the message.

Oscar nods. "I'll call you later."

With that, Johnny disappears into a side room to retrieve another white shirt and then leaves Oscar and I alone again. Downstairs, the crowd breaks up. I watch from up top as Brawler pulls his cell phone out of his pocket. Beside me, Oscar is just putting his away, so I know he's sent the message to him.

"I can go home by myself," I try feebly, knowing it'll never work. Especially not tonight.

"You're too cute," Oscar says, his playful personality back again. "Not going to work." After a beat of silence, Oscar presses his lips together. "Johnny realizes what he has."

My face heats, then all the warmth drops to my

stomach the longer Oscar just stares at me. My mind is screaming to tell him that Johnny doesn't *have* me. That's not how I work. That's not what I want Oscar to think. But at the same time, Oscar's a part of the Crew. Anything I say here could be used against me.

I close my eyes, making myself change the subject. "What did they do to him?"

Oscar breathes out, his dark eyes returning. He searches my face, and I think he finds the answer to what I really want to hear, but he surprises me with what comes out of his mouth. "You don't want to know."

Oscar and I wait in tense silence together. Neither one of us is willing to look away from the other, but we also don't step across a line. It's like we're toeing a boundary line, each one of us placing it somewhere between us. I don't know about Oscar's, but mine keeps moving closer to him, allowing me a little freedom. I'm just not willing to step over it.

After Brawler finishes downstairs, he comes up to tell us he's ready. I'm relieved because the tension between Oscar and me was getting a little too much. But instead of Brawler breaking it, he makes it worse. His stare stops on me, snagging there like he wants to look away, but can't. Eventually, he forces himself to, and all three of us stand there awkwardly.

Oscar catches my eye, jaw ticking. I don't know if it's because he just witnessed what happened between me and Brawler or if he's still drawing his own line. "I've got to go."

When he passes Brawler, he whispers something to him that's just out of earshot. I don't bother asking them what they're saying because I know they'll never tell me, so instead, I follow him down the stairs. The two groups part ways once we're outside, Oscar striding toward the bus stop while Brawler and I stop in front of a sleek, black car.

I just stare at it. Even when I'm not around Johnny, he's everywhere I go. He's got his "goons" watching me. I can't leave the apartment unless I'm with one of them. He's a part of every aspect of my life, even how I get home at the end of the night right down to the shoes I wear.

I yank the car door open and slide inside. My anger's returning, so is the feeling of being trapped and called out. Of having to kiss Johnny when he wants, whether I want to or not.

Brawler watches me on the way home as I fume, but he doesn't say anything. Johnny's watching him, too. This car is not the time and place to trust if I was going to put my faith in him. It's too risky.

The car slows. Once again, I throw the door open

and immediately start for my apartment, leaving Brawler to catch up with me. I take the stairs, stomping up them. When we get to my apartment door, I wait for Brawler to open it because there was no place to put a key or cell phone in this dress, and I don't carry a purse. I laugh, but it's not a real laugh. It's not a kind one or to denote that I'm happy. It's the kind of laugh that means I'm going out of my mind. I can't even open up my own fucking apartment door.

As soon as we get inside and Brawler locks the door behind us, he says, "What happened?" His voice is dark. Just another guy pulling an alpha male. His fists clench and unclench at his sides.

"Nothing."

I try to escape to my room, but he gets in front of me. "Don't do that. What happened?"

For a moment, a glimmer of hope rises inside of me. Maybe I can trust Brawler. Truly. Look at him. He's concerned. He's asking. He's fucking asking because he really wants to know.

But that's ridiculous. I shake my head and try to move around him, but he grabs my arm. "Don't do that." He sucks in a breath. "Fuck. You know I'm the most real thing in your life right now. Talk to me."

My jaw locks. I turn toward him. His eyes are practically begging me, and it's too much to try to keep inside anymore. "Johnny kissed me."

Brawler blinks, unable to keep the surprise from his face. Then, he cocks his head. "Hasn't he kissed you already?"

Internally, I scream in frustration. Of course everyone just assumes we're fucking because I'm his girl, right? Because that's what I would do. "Forget it."

"No," Brawler says. "Make me understand."

I yank my hand out of his grip. My skin crawls with agitation. "He. Kissed. Me. He did it in front of that asshole waiter so he could show him he controls me. So he could prove I'm his, that he fucking owns me. He forced his tongue down my throat to show someone he mattered and the other guy didn't, and neither of them asked what I wanted." I shake my head. "One of them wanted to claim me as his prize for winning a fight, the other thinks I'm already his."

Brawler's eyes are like roaring thunder. "No one owns you if you don't want to be owned," he says.

"It's too late. You said that already. You said that from the very beginning."

"I was wrong," Brawler bites out. "Look at you. Christ. You're...unbelievable. Beautiful. Strong." He says it in awe, like he's never seen anything like me. I think back on the message he left me on my bathroom mirror. He's been trying to tell me these things all along.

He goes to turn away, but I catch his arm, making him stop. "Don't. Please. I want to hear it."

"You're a fighter, Kyla," he says eventually, emotion flickering in his sapphire eyes. "You're strong. I can already see that no matter how much he pushes, he won't have you. Not all of you. I don't get why you want to stay. I don't need to. We've all done shit because we felt we had to. I get it. That doesn't mean you're weak. That means you're fucking unbelievably strong."

The tension between us crackles with electricity. I want to jump him. I want to tell him to kiss me, not to wash away the memories of Johnny's kiss, but because I *want* to kiss Brawler.

Damn being "Kyla" right now. Damn the plan. I want what I want. I need him.

19

The moment we both give in is like a hiccup in time and space, where he's just waiting for me to say the words.

They're threatening to spill out, but I don't know what it'll do to me. What it'll do to us going forward. I can't tell Brawler why I'm here. I can't. If I care about him as much as I think I do, it'll only put him in danger.

"It's okay," he says, understanding the conflict I'm having.

I drop my head to his chest and breathe in deep. The collar of the dress cuts into me. The sequins make my neck burn with agitation. "Can you help me take this dress off?"

For a moment, he stops breathing. "I see. You want to torture us both."

"I just don't want to be in Johnny's dress anymore. Not when you're here."

He lifts my chin. "It's not Johnny's dress. Trust me. You own that. You owned the whole warehouse tonight. It's not what you want to hear, but I'm not surprised he beat the piss out of that waiter. I wanted to lay everyone out who looked at you tonight."

"No one looked at me."

"You're blind." His hands move around me, trailing up my spine. "But I'll take it off if you want. If it means something different to you."

His fingers fondle the zipper. I bend my head so he can get a better purchase. The sound of the zipper lowering fills the room. It's like when a video buffers. Time stills, just waiting for what we'll do next.

"I want to be me," I say. He'll never know this, but I want to be *me*, not Kyla. Not the name I made up to come here, but I want to be the girl all grown up in the life she was supposed to have. Someone who's in charge of her own destiny. Someone who would've seen Brawler in a gym and would've been interested right away. Someone who would've had the choice to go up to him.

I pull at the cropped sleeves of my dress until I can

maneuver my arms out without agitating the scrape on my shoulder. Then, I drop the front, wiggling out of it until it's around my ankles. Brawler's gaze never leaves my eyes. Even though I'm standing here in my bra and panties, he never peeks. I want him to, but I can't come up with the words. Saying the words will mean I'm giving in to the temptation of leaving all this behind. Don't get me wrong, I want Big Daddy K to pay. But not getting my revenge? That would have been much easier. So much easier.

"I've already seen the real you," Brawler says.

His words make me wince. He hasn't seen me. Not at all. I'm pretending to be someone else.

"I need to wash my mouth out with bleach."

"You need to let yourself feel how you want to feel."

"We'd be fucked."

"We're already fucked."

Brawler moves closer. He's only inches away now, standing over me, practically vibrating. "Tell me I can kiss you. Tell me I can touch you."

He has no idea how much I want him to, but I can't. I just can't. For me, giving in doesn't just mean that if Johnny finds out, he'll most likely kill us. Giving in means I'm saying Brawler's more important than what I came here for.

He drops his head when I don't say the words. "You know what I see? Someone who's scared. I see an unbelievably strong person, but when it comes to shit like this?" he says, motioning between the two of us. "You're scared. You'd rather hole up with Johnny because that's easier than feeling anything real."

"You're right," I tell him, nodding. Disappointment lapping at my heels. "That's exactly what this is. I'm so glad you figured me out." I bend over to pick up my dress and then push past him to shut myself away in my bedroom. Leaning back against the door, I breathe in deep, trying to settle my nerves. I've never wanted to tell someone something more in my whole life. If I could split myself open, so Brawler could see the things inside me, I would.

"Don't run away," Brawler says. His voice rings clear as if he's just on the other side of the door.

"There are things I can't tell you right now."

"That's everybody. All of us hide dark shit inside."

I close my eyes, trying to put up an invisible wall between us. "Maybe you should get Oscar to stay with me tonight." Though Oscar's not that much better of a choice. Something's brimming there, too. It's just that where Brawler and I are concerned, we're about to overflow.

"Oscar?" Brawler hums until his voice turns

gravely. "Oscar's watching his mom. She got back on crack a couple of weeks ago."

My lips thin. I press a hand to my chest, trying to regain control. There's so much sadness here.

"Just let me in," Brawler coaxes. "I won't try anything. I won't push. Just let me be near you. I won't even make it about you. *I* want to be near you. Okay? Me. Put it all on me."

I step away from the door and reach back to turn the knob before retreating to the small chest of drawers in the corner. There, I find a nightshirt and pull it over my head. The skin on my shoulder stretches with the movement, and I bury a hiss of pain.

As I make my way to the bed, Brawler says, "You don't have to tell me everything. Hell, you don't have to tell me anything."

"I like that fucking idea," I say, getting comfy on the bed. I sit cross-legged, pulling the sheets up over my lap.

He shakes his head, but an amused smile lifts his lips. "I want to know more about how you started fighting," he says.

Now this is a comfortable conversation. I move up the bed, resting my back carefully against the wall and motion for Brawler to take the foot. He sits, the bed compressing under his weight. "I found fighting as a way to get out my aggression." For once, this isn't a lie. Honest to God, a counselor I used to see after my parents' death told my aunt and uncle it might be a good idea. From then on, I was hooked. At first, it worked because I was tiring myself out. It felt good to direct my anger in a good way. Then, when I made the pact with myself that I would take on Big Daddy K, it became bigger than just healing. I knew I would have to be strong. I knew I would have to have a certain skill set. When I heard about the underground fighting, it made this all the better. "How about you?" I ask. "What are the Brawler's origins?"

A shadow creeps over his face, like it's a stalker he can't get rid of, never too far behind. "I just wanted to be like my big brother," he says. "That's what started it for me."

"Your brother was in the Heights Crew," I guess. He mentioned to me once the Crew killed him, so it fits.

Brawler fiddles with the dressing that's still around his neck. "Yes."

"Are you going to join, too?" I know I've already asked him this before, but this time, I'm hoping for a more genuine answer.

He lifts his gaze to mine. "It depends."

His stare is heavy, like he's putting his answer on

me. I'm used to a certain amount of weight being on my shoulders, but this is pushing me over the edge. "On?"

"If you would've asked me a week ago, I would've said 'fuck no'. Not if I could help it. Not that I ever told anyone that. I like doing what I do for the Crew. I like the fighting aspect. It's the only way I'll be able to do it."

"You're wrong. You need to go to a real gym, Brawler. You need to train, get with people who can put you into some amateur fights."

"You should be saying the same thing to yourself," Brawler challenges.

"I can't do that...yet. Or ever. We're not talking about me," I snap.

He lifts his hand, conceding. "I can't do that either," he says after a while. "I'm pretty sure these gyms will want money. Don't have much of that."

"But you get paid for the fights, right? And for running it?"

Brawler nods. "Yeah, I do. And if it was just me, I might be okay, but I have to take care of my mom. She can't work, so it's all on me."

I see Brawler in a whole different light. He's the only one who makes money for his family? It's just so... sad. I wish I could change that for him. But like with

Oscar and Johnny and any of the rest of them, do they even really have a way out of this?

Brawler reaches out his hand, placing it on my calf. I suck in a breath. Every time he touches me, the pull gets stronger. "You know we can't," I say. "He'll kill us."

In any other scenario, I might be exaggerating, but not this one. I don't know what he did to the waiter, but I have a feeling if he's not dead, he wishes he was at the current moment.

"I'm trying to figure out if I care or not."

I pull my leg back and out of his reach. "I'll care for the both of us. You saw what he did to that waiter."

"I've been waiting to fight Johnny for a long time, so maybe I don't give a fuck."

My mouth slams shut. What Brawler's just said is akin to treason. If anyone else were here and overheard what he said, he'd be dragged in front of Johnny and his father to be taken care of.

"Don't act so surprised, Princess. You don't like him either. You didn't want him. You didn't ask for this. He took you, remember? He just decided that you were his one day and now you have to live with the consequences. He forced his lips on you today." He shudders. "Not because he wanted to, but to prove a point. You don't want to be anyone's point, do you?"

My hands fists the sheets at my waist. "Are you trying to piss me off?"

"Actually, yes."

"Well, good, it's fucking working."

"Then leave."

I shake my head. I can't believe we're going through this again. "I'm not leaving."

"You need to. You need to get the fuck out of here. It's dangerous. I know you're a kick ass fighter, but you're too close to the top now. It's not safe for you. You're a target."

"What do you know?" I ask.

Brawler stands from the bed, his hands diving through his blond hair. "I know what happens to people close to the fucking top!" He turns his back to me, walks a few paces away, and then starts again. His shoulders drop. "You asked if my brother was in the Crew, and I said yes. I already told you he's dead." He turns back toward me. His face twisted. "He's dead because of them, and that's not even the worst part. My sister's gone too. She died as a bystander."

Horror rips through me, and I'm not doing a very good job of acting like it's not. The Crew killed his brother and sister. "Your sister? Was she—?"

"Fuck no," he breathes. "Caught in the crossfire when one person is aiming for another and accidentally takes someone else out. That's what happens in the Crew." He reaches his hands up to his neck, pulling at the bandages there. He reveals part of a wing, drawn on skin that's still red and raw. He keeps pulling at the bandage until his whole tattoo is revealed.

I suck in a breath at how beautiful it is.

I drop my feet off the side of the bed and stand, already making my own conclusions on what the tattoo means to him. When I get to him, I reach my fingers out to graze along the crisp edges. Under his left ear is a large, black wing, like an angel of death. It starts in the middle of his throat where his Adam's apple bobs and reaches all the fleshy dip under his ear, the tip of the wing disappearing there. Under his right ear is a polar opposite tattoo, shadowed in a gold color, but filled in with white like a wing from an angel itself.

Brawler catches my hand. He moves my palm over the black wing. "This is for my brother." He takes my other hand and places it over the white wing. "This is for my sister. Together, they're like two parts of me. Some days I feel like this is the only life I'll know," he says, squeezing the hand that's over the black wing. "Other days, I want to be this," he says, squeezing my hand that's over the tattoo for his sister. "Most days I'm afraid I won't live up to either one."

My breath catches. I haven't heard such honesty before unless it's in my own head. "It's okay to be both," I say. "A little dark. A little light."

As I talk, I draw closer and closer, like I'm called there. My lips brush his, and the whole world tilts on its axis. I've never met someone so much like me before. What does it say about me that I feel more at home here than I ever did at my aunt and uncle's house? That I see some of these souls as kindred spirits. Like we were cut from the same cloth. His pain is a Siren's song to me. I want nothing more than to bathe in it, free my own dark thoughts, so we can emerge from the water free together.

I press my lips more greedily against his. A brush isn't enough. This is why I was totally against it. This is why I wanted nothing to do with it. Because I knew once it started, it would never be enough.

He winds his arms around me like two thick tree trunks of muscle, pulling me toward him. My chest brushes his, sending delicious sensations to my core.

We start out greedy. Touching each other everywhere, delving into deep kisses like we'll never do this again. Eventually, he calms us both, stringing his fingers through my hair, slowing the kiss until he's kissing me slowly, passionately. Taking his time, making sure I'm loved in a way I want to be.

"Fucking Christ," he breathes, breaking the kiss. He pulls my shirt up and presses a palm to my belly, his fingers teasing the top of my panties. "I want to touch you, Kyla."

My mind's already obliterated. Sense and better judgement don't have a place here, right now. I grab his wrist and move him down. "God, yes."

His fingers dip inside my panties one second, but the next Brawler rips his lips and his hands from me. I'm so stunned that when he moves into the other room, I start to follow him, but then Johnny's voice permeates my lust-induced brain. I stand there for half a second, unable to move, but then I scramble to the bed and pull the covers up over me.

In the other room, they greet one another. I listen for any indication that Johnny knows what was about to happen between Brawler and I, but I don't hear anything. Brawler definitely had a hard-on, a stiff cock I was dying to explore.

If Johnny figures it out, I already know I won't hesitate to run out there to defend him. I'd throw myself, my plan, and everything else under the bus just to save him.

A moment later, footsteps approach the bed. Fingers tentatively touch my hair and work their way through the strands. The touch is soft, but from the musk he brought with him, I know who it is. I open my eyes, and Johnny smiles. On the heels of Brawler's story, it's a little harder to pretend right now. How much did Johnny have to do with Brawler's brother and sister's death? "I missed you," he whispers.

"Yeah?" I ask, my voice cracking. At least it sounds like he woke me up. He won't suspect I was just about to get off on Brawler's fingers.

Johnny leans over me, getting into bed. My heart races, pumping painfully against my chest. My eyes widen with panic until he settles in behind me, lifting the covers to spoon me. He curls his arm under my head and places his other on my hip, squeezing me gently before dropping his head to the pillow. "Good night, Kyla."

In the other room, the door closes, leaving the apartment empty aside from Johnny and me. I'm still as a stone, but Johnny's breaths fill the room.

My core is aching. I'm dying to find Brawler again to make sure he knows I'm not doing this by choice. I bite my lip, but the longer I lay there, the more comfortable it is. In his sleep, Johnny pulls me closer, wrapping me in his warmth. By some miracle, it doesn't take long for me to fall asleep after that.

20

For the next week, Brawler makes himself scarce. I can't blame him. Johnny is always around, and he's getting more touchy feely since we slept in the same bed together.

Brawler doesn't walk me to school like usual. Johnny's car takes me. If he sees me in the hall, he doesn't acknowledge me. It's for the best, I guess. What did we think we were doing anyway? Starting a forbidden romance that could only piss off one of the most influential people in this town?

Not that I don't think about that moment. The power behind even just the barest touches. In fact, I think about it all the time.

Friday morning, I'm called out of my second period class. The teacher answers a phone hanging on the wall that looks like it's from the 1990s. "Kyla Samson?" There's a question in her words, and then she looks around the room like she's lost.

I roll my eyes, holding my hand up. Bitch didn't even know I was in her class.

"Oh yes, she's here," the teacher says.

For fuck's sake. Could they at least act like they care even a little?

"She'll be right down."

Most people miss the exchange because they're too busy having their own conversations. The teacher, Miss Frida, was just lecturing from the front of the classroom asking herself questions no one else bothered to answer.

"The principal's office," she says as I get up.

If I were in my last school, everyone would be staring, making snide comments and wondering what the hell I did to get myself called to the principal's office. No one gives a fuck here. Least of all me. I have no idea what this is about, but I'm not that concerned either. For all I know, Johnny could've bribed his admin fuck buddy to get me out of school. Not that he'd have to do that. I'd just walk the fuck out if I wanted to. But being here at least gives me some semblance of the real world. All across America, other students are doing this same exact thing. This is normal. And I don't want to get too far away from normal that I can never go back.

I open the nondescript office door and walk right in. Surprisingly, there are actually people in here right now. Workers. To my right is the woman who gave Johnny a blow job. I give her the middle finger for fun. Johnny came to pick me up from school a couple of days ago, and she tried to get him to come into her office, but instead, he swung his arm around me, taking me out to the car. Regardless of who Johnny is, that woman is a child predator. Fuck her.

"In here, Miss Samson."

I follow the gruff voice. I've never even met the principal. There aren't announcements in the morning like at every other school I've ever been to. I don't see anyone official ever walking the halls. For all I know, no one in charge is around while we're here during the day. Hell, I even wonder why a lot of these people bother. Maybe they just want to feel normal too.

I walk into the principal's office and immediately come to a halt. There's a gentleman inside with a cheap suit and tie. He has police written all over him. "What's this about?"

"This is Detective Reynolds. He wants to ask you a few questions." The principal immediately gets up and leaves the room, closing the door behind him and leaving the two of us in here.

I glare at the closed door. Seriously? "I'm pretty sure this is illegal. I'm a minor," I say, even though I'm not. I'm eighteen.

"We couldn't get a hold of your guardians who are on file or else they would be here."

I snap my mouth shut. I guess I can't really push this considering the guardians on file here are made up. They don't exist. Just like Kyla Samson. "Working, I'm sure. You probably know about that," I say, dragging the lone chair left in the room and moving it a few feet away.

He gives me a fleeting smile that's more forced than anything. I'm sure he deals with a bunch of damaged, disgruntled kids all fucking day. I'm no one to him. "As your principal said, I'm Detective Reynolds. I work for the Rawley Heights Police, and I want to ask you a few questions."

"About?" My attitude tells him I don't give a fuck, but inside, I'm trying to figure out how to play this. This has got to be about the Heights Crew. It has to be.

"Word on the street is that Johnny Rocket has a new girlfriend."

"Yeah?"

He smiles, for real now. "Is that you?"

"Is that really what you brought me down here to ask? Surely there's something more important than who's getting Johnny off every night?"

The police officer shifts in his seat. "Alright, I won't beat around the bush then. I hear you're a fighter in one of Johnny Rocket's underground rings."

"I wouldn't know anything about that," I say. Johnny doesn't get to have underground fighting rings without the police turning a blind eye, but that doesn't mean they want it thrown in their faces.

He eyes the soft bruising on my face. "I had a feeling you'd say that."

I stop myself from squirming. My injuries don't even hurt anymore. The slight discoloration on my face is the only remnant of what's transpired. "Then why'd you ask?"

"Glutton for punishment, I guess. Comes with the job description."

I shrug. "Can't help you there."

Detective Reynolds leans back in his seat. He places one of his legs over his thigh, tapping his fingers against his shoe. "Well, let me tell you a few things I can help you with. Big Daddy K and Johnny Rocket—I'm sure those are names you've heard of—well, they aren't the only thugs on the street. They aren't the only thugs with an underground fighting ring either.

They've had some territorial fights about it recently. Had one guy show up charred in a dumpster fire. You might recognize him." He takes out a picture from his pocket, glances at it a moment, and then hands it to me.

I take it from him. Immediately, I know who it is. It's the fucking waiter from the restaurant. The one who accidentally touched me then showed up at the warehouse the very same night calling me a whore. I hand it back, face stoic. "Sorry, I don't."

Detective Reynolds gives me a tight smile like he expected me to say that. "That dead guy's from Roza Fonz's underground ring. She sent him to scope you out. Sounds like you put on a show when you fought."

"Sounds like you don't know what you're talking about," I say, even though my stomach twists. For being on the outside, he knows a lot about what happens on the inside.

"You're new here, so I'm going to tell you some things you don't know, Kyla. Roza Fonz had the fights first. She had that 'territory', if you will, here in the Heights before the Crew was even a thing. Then one day, Big Daddy K took it over and moved her out. They've been fighting about it ever since. If you're on Roza's radar, it's not good. I'm here because I care. I doubt anyone's explained to you how deep you're in. Not Johnny, Big Daddy K, or any of his henchmen.

Roza aims to take the underground fighting ring back. If you're in her way, she'll take you out."

My stomach roils. He's wrong about one thing though. I've been warned about the Crew. Three people have told me just about the same thing Detective Reynolds just did.

The door bursts open, making me jump. I spin in my seat to find Oscar standing there, chest heaving in front of him.

"Goddamn principal fucker," Detective Reynolds curses, his face growing beet red.

I get it now. The principal's in tight with the Heights Crew. Of course he is.

Oscar holds his hand out to me, and I take it. He helps me to my feet. "You're done here," he spits over my shoulder. "They won't be happy about this."

"Ahh, Drego," Detective Reynolds says, recovering quickly. His stare drops to my hand in Oscar's. "Just in time. I was telling our friend Kyla here about Roza Fonz."

"Kyla doesn't have anything to do with that." He squeezes my hand like he wants to protect me from this.

"I hear Roza's not too pleased about the hype going on about her."

"Always nice to see you, Reynolds. As usual, get fucked."

Oscar drags me away. I glance over my shoulder to find Detective Reynolds smiling our way. He tucks the picture of the waiter back into his inside pocket, and I swallow. Magnum told me it was more than just an accidental touch. I didn't believe him. I thought they were being paranoid. I thought Johnny was being overbearing. Criminal.

What if they were right?

"Rocket's so fucking pissed right now," Oscar growls. He's still dragging me down the hallway, so I tear my arm away from him. He looks back. "Sorry," he says. "Word got out that the cops were here and then someone mentioned you being asked to go to the office. I came right away. Johnny'll be here soon to come get you."

"I'm fine," I tell him, rubbing my wrists. "I can stay."

Oscar shakes his head. "For the love of God, don't do anything to piss him the fuck off even more. Just go with him. He was trying to keep you safe, but now that Reynolds has outed some shit, he'll have to explain things."

Was he trying to keep me safe? He murdered that waiter for me. Or I guess he might not have been a waiter at all. Come to think of it, he kind of sucked. Was Roza trying to do something to me there by sending someone undercover in a public place?

"I only fought once," I say, disbelieving.

"And people around here love a fucking underdog. Our last two fight nights have been filled up, just hoping you'll fight. There's been so much fucking buzz. Of course it got back to her. Goddamnit," Oscar growls.

Dark shadows sit like sentinels under his eyes. I wonder how much he's been having to take care of since Brawler said his mom's back on crack. Couple that with football and having to watch me, I would guess he isn't getting much sleep. "Are you okay?" I ask.

He blinks. My heart goes out to him. Both he and Brawler should have a better life than this. Worse yet, it sounds like both of them have a way out that they just can't make work.

"Are you going to be ready for your game tonight? You look exhausted."

"You know I have a game tonight?"

I shrug. "I may have overheard someone talking about it. I wanted to go, but with this shit happening now, I doubt I'll be able to." Football sounded like a nice distraction from everything else going on. Just like going to school every day, it's normal. It's what teenagers are supposed to do.

Maybe that's the downside of what touching Brawler did to me. It made me yearn for normal. For a time where I can just kiss someone because I want to.

Oscar grabs my hand and pulls me down a side hallway. He licks his lips, his expression dark as he leans me carefully against a bay of lockers. "Are you even real?"

I blink at him. It's nice being ensconced in his embrace.

He reaches up, dragging his thumb over my bottom lip until I bite it, savoring the taste of him there.

My body must be going haywire because at this moment, I'd swear I had feelings for two guys. Two hot, forbidden bad boys.

"You want to come to my game?" Oscar asks. In that moment, he's not Bat or the Oscar Drego who everyone in school is afraid of. I imagine he's more like the guy he was when he went to Spring Hill. The guy who wanted more and was going after it.

Tires burning rubber in the parking lot knock us both into reality. He jumps away, shaking his head like he'd been entranced under a spell. But trying to shake it away doesn't work for either one of us. He reaches for my hand again, squeezing me before guiding me toward the front doors. When we get there, he drops my hand, casting me a sorrowful look before opening the door to usher me out.

Ahead, the car has barely come to a stop in front of the school entrance and Johnny is already climbing out. "Motherfucker!" he screams.

For a second, I'm so paranoid that he knows what's just transpired between Oscar and me that my heart drops into my stomach. It takes me a moment to realize he's not looking at me. He's not even looking at Oscar. He's glaring past us toward the school.

He holds his arms out to me, and I go into them. He presses me tightly against him, almost rocking me.

Is it sick that I enjoy this? It most definitely is.

The past six years fucked me up. My aunt and uncle were there, but not like this. I wasn't theirs. How could they hold me like this? How could they tell me how much they loved me when I wasn't even theirs?

I press my cheek into his chest, not even caring when Oscar gives me an indecipherable look.

Magnum calls out, a hint of urgency to his voice. "Come on, Rocket. We got to go."

"I want to kill that motherfucker." Johnny moves me toward Magnum. "Watch her. I'm going in there."

"No," Mag says, voice stern. "I know you want to. That's why I'm getting you the fuck out of here."

I break away from Johnny to look at Mag. He sighs in relief at the sight of me then pleads with his eyes. Taking the hint, I grab Johnny's hand. "Come on, let's go. School was boring today anyway."

The light-hearted comment doesn't get any reaction from the gangster's son. He was disrespected, and he doesn't like it.

"Come on," I try again. I'm well aware both Magnum and Oscar are staring. "Hey," I say, taking Johnny's face in my hands. "Come on. We're going." Reluctantly, he follows me into the back of the car. Magnum closes the door on us, and a few seconds later, he's in the front seat and pulling away.

"Did he touch you?" Johnny asks, looking me all over like he can find some invisible injury on me.

"No," I say, incredulously. "He's the police."

Johnny's gaze darkens. "You can't trust anybody. I don't care if they are the fucking police."

"Right," I say, shaking my head. My origins just showed. I doubt anyone who lives in the Heights trusts cops. "It's just he did a good job of sounding concerned."

"Did you tell him anything?" Johnny asks.

"Fuck no."

He closes his eyes, a sigh of relief passing through his lips. He's jittery, like he's hyped up on adrenaline.

I steel my shoulders. "I don't even know anything to tell him," I say. "Who's Roza? Why does she want to take me out? And why didn't you tell me the waiter was sent by her?"

Magnum lifts his gaze to glance at me in the rearview mirror. His eyes are hard, but he immediately looks away again while I focus on Johnny. "I thought you'd be better off not knowing all the danger you're in. Why do you think I have one of my guys with you at all times? Why do you think I'm with you whenever I can?"

I shake my head. "That's not how I want to live. I want to know the things that are out there trying to get me. You understand that, right? You're the same way."

Johnny growls. "Nothing's going to get you." He places his palms on my cheeks and moves forward, lips pressing into mine. He kisses me like a man being dragged under by a tidal wave. His lips scorch mine. This time, it's easy to fall into him. I open for him voluntarily, letting him in until he's making my head spin.

Before I know it, he's pulled me onto his lap and grinding into me.

"Oh shit." I break away.

Johnny stills. He lets out a breath and presses his forehead against mine, closing his eyes as if he's drinking me in. He tips his hips up, pressing his hard cock between my legs.

Magnum clears his throat. "We should take her to Big Daddy. Don't you think?"

I scramble off Johnny's lap despite his attempts to try to hold me there. My cheeks burn. My stomach churns with bile. Tears gather in the corners of my eyes.

What the fuck is wrong with me?

21

Talk about taking a bath in ice water and then crawling around naked in a snowbank after a blizzard.

What the fuck am I doing? Like, literally, what in the actual fuck am I doing? What is it about Johnny that appeals to me? I can hate him one minute but crush my crotch against his the next.

I need to have my head examined.

I know. It's all Brawler's fault. I've been on edge ever since we had that moment in the apartment. I've been jittery, fucking horny, actually. Oscar didn't make it any better. He only intensified the feelings.

That's all it has to be.

Johnny adjusts his pants and then scowls into the

front of the car. "Yes, we probably should take her to see Big Daddy."

I blink. The conversation in the last half a minute is coming back to me without all the hot and botheredness. "Big Daddy?"

"My dad," Johnny says, his voice low and hard.

I almost roll my eyes because who doesn't fucking know that? Instead, I take a deep breath, my stomach bottoming out. The ice age that consumed my body is melting until my limbs are hot, pulling against me like I'm dead weight. I'm so anchored in this moment. "I'm going to meet him?" I ask like I'm some sort of ditzy brunette with an ultra-low IQ.

"He said he'd meet you when the time was right and considering you had a conversation with Detective Reynolds today, this is probably the time."

Ever since the night my parents died, I've been wondering what this man looked like. This man who took everything from me. In my head, he always looks dark and dangerous. He looks like the kind of guy who would murder people for no fucking reason.

But when I check out Johnny's profile, I wonder if he's not like that at all. What if he's handsome like Johnny? What if he looks like a normal person? We always tend to think of evil people as being able to spot easily. It's one of those things that make us feel better about walking down the sidewalk at night. Or sending our kids off to their friends' houses. That guy? That girl? No, they look normal. You know who looked normal? Ted Bundy. They even got Zac Efron to play him in a movie, like what the fuck? If that doesn't tell you that terrible people can come in all different bodies, I don't know what does.

Magnum's gaze flicks to mine in the rearview mirror. I glance up to find the corners of his eyes creased in concentration as he stares at me. My stomach twists. If they know I'm not who I say I am, I'm dead tonight. I'm one hundred percent gone. In a blink of an eye, I could cease to exist just like my parents.

Except, I willingly walked into this. That's the difference.

Even though my stomach is still roiling with the news, I steel myself. This is when shit gets hard. In a matter of minutes, I'm going to have to face the guy who killed my parents and not react. It will be the worst kind of torture. One I hope I'm ready for because everything is counting on this. This is what I came here for. If I can't gain the leader of the Heights Crew's trust, then I won't be able to do what I set out to do. Sure, I might be able to walk in there now and somehow get in a lucky shot on Big Daddy K. Maybe even steal Magnum's gun, go for the unexpected nature of it all. Pop off a shot that would hit him right where I need to. But, the odds of that are slim.

Besides, I don't just want to kill him. I want to get away with it. Killing him will mean nothing if I don't get away with it. I don't want to go down too. Then I'll have sacrificed my own life just to take his, and that's not what I promise my parents when I talk to them at night. I promise them I'll make my life better. That this is the means to a beautiful end.

"No need to be nervous," Johnny says, inching closer. "I've already talked you up."

I can imagine that conversation.

Yeah, Dad, I want to fuck this girl.

That's good, Son, but you can't fuck her until I say so.

Oh okay. Sure.

Maybe the conversation was lengthier than that, but that was the bones of it.

Johnny reaches over and tangles his fingers with mine. In the moment, it's comforting. I don't want to analyze it and tell myself that it's disgusting what I'm doing. He's offering me comfort, and I'm taking it. That's it.

Within ten minutes, we're pulling up to a modern building on the outskirts of the inner city in the

Heights. Magnum takes a right, the road slanting down until we're at a lower parking level. It's an expansive parking area, but very few cars are parked inside it. "Who all lives here?" I ask.

"Dad, me, a few of the other guys at the top. Magnum," Johnny finishes like his bodyguard is an afterthought.

I avoid the gaze that's burning into the side of my face right now. Magnum sure is doing a good job of being intimidating. He doesn't like that they're bringing me here. I doubt he sees me as that much of a threat, but the fact that I'm going to be so close to Big Daddy K has him on high alert.

"Do you have your own place?" I ask. It comes out sounding like I want to know what my boyfriend's living situation is, for *reasons*, but I actually need to know for recon. And you know, maybe *reasons*. After I figure out what the fuck is wrong with me, I'll worry about my traitorous body.

Johnny's fingers tighten in mine. "We live on the same floor, but I have my own place," he says, his voice oozing sex. That incident earlier really got him ramped up. I'm going to have to avoid him until I straighten shit out in my head. Then again, he could be leaving me in a moment to go find someone else to fuck. Big Daddy K's orders are still in place.

My skin crawls with that thought, but I rub my arms to ease it because that shouldn't be my focus right now. Even if it was, I might actually think Johnny hasn't done that again. He certainly blew off the lady at school for me.

Magnum parks the car near a nondescript door with a glass side panel. Johnny pushes the back door open and gets out, reaching back for my hand once he's standing. I get out next to him, my heart thumping in my chest like the furious beat of hooves during a horse race. He touches my cheek. "You'll be fine."

Magnum moves ahead of us, opening the door which reveals an elevator. Once we're all inside, he presses the button for P, which I'm assuming stands for Penthouse. Other than that, there are two other floors. He's literally surrounded by other higher-ups in the Crew. If I decide to take him out here, escaping will be tricky. Then again, I might not have a choice. I haven't seen Big Daddy K out anywhere. When Johnny says he's going to meetings, I'm pretty sure they're held right here.

The elevator moves us up briskly. When it stops, Magnum steps out first and then turns to face us in a bare, but high-ceilinged hallway. There are two doorways. One to the left and one to the right.

"Hands up," Magnum says as I step out.

"Um, what?"

He reaches for a black metal detection wand that sits on a table—the only piece of furniture in the hallway.

"It's just a precaution," Johnny says before moving to stand next to Magnum.

They both face me, and I bite down on my lip, but widen my stance and hold my arms out to the side. Magnum waves the wand over me. It goes off over my chest. "Underwire in my bra," I say. I cock an eyebrow. "Should I take my shirt off?"

"No," Johnny grunts.

Magnum keeps the same fierce look of concentration as he finishes up. The detector doesn't go off again, but already I'm pleased with what I'm finding out. I'll probably have this same treatment every time I come up here, unless I somehow put myself on the other side with Johnny. If they trust me enough, I just might someday not get the wand treatment. Otherwise, I have no option. I'll need a weapon to take down Big Daddy K, and right now, their security is on top of things to make sure that doesn't happen. I suppose I could always hide it in my bra. Especially if I'm with Johnny. He won't let them make me take my shirt off.

"All good," Magnum says as he places the wand back down.

"No shit," I deadpan.

My words don't faze Mag though. He's just doing his job, and he probably doesn't care if a teenager gets salty about it.

Magnum turns toward the door on the right and opens it. Johnny follows him, and I take up the rear. Now that the metal detection part is over, the nerves are back. My palms sweat. Overall, there's a sickening feeling twisting my stomach. This is like meeting your real-life boogeyman. The guy who's haunted your dreams and terrorized you for years. Sure, I may be older now and able to comprehend that he probably won't do anything to me, but that doesn't mean there's not a bunch of turmoil going on underneath the surface.

The worst part, I don't know how I'm going to react when I see him.

We walk into a posh suite. Everything is modern with sleek lines. Brushed silver and grays seem to be the color of choice of Big Daddy. The king of the Heights Crew obviously lives in opulence, which I highly doubt the same can be said for a lot of his members. Oscar, for one, who's living with a junkie mother. He told me he wanted to get out of the Heights to make a better life for him and his mom, and this guy, who has the nicest place I've seen since coming to the Heights, holds him back.

I scan the room, taking in everything I can as we work our way through it. Voices rise from a different room, and my stomach fills with dread. The world around me fades away, and I fixate on a voice I'm sure has to be owned by the man I hate. Soon, I'll be putting a face to a name. Everyone knows who Big Daddy K is, but not everyone has seen him. Despite how difficult it's been being "claimed" by Johnny emotionally, it really has been the best thing for my plan. Not everyone gets this access.

We walk toward a section of couches facing each other in the main living area. There's a man facing away from us, sitting on the edge of the couch. I bore a hole into the back of his head, but then another voice sounds.

It's Oscar. I blink, surprised to see him here. He has a fucking football game tonight. He should be at school, making sure he's at practice. Instead, he's here. And how exactly? I just left him at the front entrance.

When the man facing away from us sees Johnny round the couches, he looks back, like he's expecting to see someone new following him in. For all I know, Johnny or Magnum contacted him ahead of time to say we were coming. Then again, Johnny was a little preoccupied.

The man stands. His body is clad in a slimming gray suit. He has dark hair, gelled back like a scene from Goodfellas, though he doesn't have the Italian coloring. In fact, he looks like an older version of Johnny. His face is more refined. He has more taut lines and a bit of crow's feet around his eyes. He's aged in a way Johnny isn't. In his looks, there's a wisdom there. A look that tells me he's seen some things. He knows things. He's done things. And he sure as fuck doesn't put up with shit.

Under all that, I see him for the monster he is. For the guy who killed two innocent people because it suited him.

I hate him.

I loathe him.

I want to chop his dick off and feed it to his dying body.

"This must be Kyla?" he says, that strong tenor I heard when I first walked in filling the room like he's used to being listened to.

Johnny steps up. "Yes, this is Kyla Samson. Kyla, this is Big Daddy."

For some reason, him being called Big Daddy makes me want to laugh. I half expected an overweight guy with bulging pants and a double chin. "Nice to meet you," I say, as he puts his hand in mine, gripping my palm with a firm handshake.

I bite the inside of my cheek. My stomach upheaves. It feels like his murderous germs are crawling up my arms and infecting me. When he lets go, I use everything in me not to wipe my hand against my jeans.

"Oscar was just telling me what went down in the shithole of a school today."

I glance at Oscar. He's all dark and dangerous right now. He has his gang member mask firmly in place. You'd never know by looking at him that he has any aspirations other than to be Big Daddy K's lapdog. You wouldn't know about his mother. Or the shit he endured when he came back to the Heights. He was forced to join the Heights Crew out of self-preservation, but all that is gone when I look at him now.

"Something's got to be done about Reynolds," Johnny says. His face is red. I don't know if I missed all the tension in him before, but he looks like he's all fired up again. "He can't be doing shit like that to our people."

Big Daddy K gives me a once over. I stand up straight. His gaze is inspecting, like he's trying to pick apart my flaws so he can exploit them. It definitely doesn't feel like a look a father would give his son's new girlfriend. But I already know what I have planned will go far deeper than that.

"Aww yes, to poor Kyla." Big Daddy's gaze stays on me. "My son's choice."

Johnny looks over at me affectionately. I, on the other hand, have no idea how to fucking react.

"I think I'd like to talk to Kyla alone, boys."

My pulse picks up. Blood thumps in my neck and at my wrists.

"But—" Johnny interjects.

His father holds up a hand to stop whatever excuse is about to come out of his son's mouth. "Give us a few minutes."

I swallow and glance at Johnny. The look he gives me says even he's a little scared of what's about to happen.

Fuck me.

One-by-one, the guys leave the room. Oscar is the last, nodding at me as he leaves. It feels like he's trying to tell me something, but I have no idea what that might be.

"Have a seat," Big Daddy K says, motioning toward the couch behind me.

I walk calmly over to the space Oscar just vacated

and sit. I lift a nonchalant expression and meet his eyes.

"My son's enamored with you."

He lets the statement hang in the air. I don't know how to respond to it, so I don't. I figure wrong words can crucify me right now, so I'll just let him talk, see what he has to say.

"Haven't seen him like this in...ever," he smiles lightly, but I don't trust it. I feel like Big Daddy K is the type who can turn on a dime. He nods to himself like he's figured something out. "If you would, I'd like to hear the entire conversation you had with Reynolds. Don't leave anything out. You never know what might be important."

I recount the entirety of the conversation the detective and I shared. I don't exaggerate. I don't downplay it. I say it word-for-word with a sure voice because I want him to know I'm not intimidated by him or his gang. He doesn't want a girl like Johnny would usually bring home. He doesn't want a girl who would just nod and laugh at everything that's being said.

Unless I've read him wrong.

"You know what's interesting, Kyla?" Big Daddy K asks, the last vowel in my name dragging out a few seconds, lingering in the air like a threat.

"What's that?"

My heartbeat gets so loud I can hear it in my ears.

"I had you vetted, of course. You understand. I have to with anyone who is brought near me or my son or into the Crew. It's for our safety."

"Understood," I say. I press my hands into my thigh as they start to shake. Maybe my background isn't as tight as I wanted it to be. I'm almost expecting him to bring in my aunt and uncle, murder them in front of me because he saw right through the mask I placed over my real life.

He gazes at me, eyes intense. "I think... Well, there's just something odd about you."

He leans back in his seat and crosses his arms.

Well, fuck.

22

Big Daddy K tilts his head to the side, inspecting me like he wishes he could slice me open. As if doing that would give away all my secrets.

The fear rising inside me makes me want to lash out. Get defensive. But guys like Big Daddy K don't abide by that. I force myself to wait to see what he has to say. He'll get it out eventually, but I assume he loves making people sweat it out. I have to seem as unaffected as I can.

Mirroring him, I also drop back into the cushions of the sofa like I belong there. I smile at him, encouraging him to keep talking.

A smirk pulls his lips up higher. "It's just it's so sparse," he says. "Your background."

"What do you want to know?" I ask, stomach unsettling. "I can fill in some blanks if need be."

"Your guardians?"

"Losers," I tell him. "I keep my distance from them. They don't care about me, and I don't care about them."

"Parents?"

"Dead." I swallow, my voice dark even to my own ears.

He nods. "I get a lot of the same stories around here. No one comes to the Heights if they can help it."

"So you're probably used to people having sparse backgrounds then?" I ask boldly. "Not much to say about a shit life."

His jaw ticks. "I'm told you fought with a lot of skill."

"I like fighting," I say, using the words I always use. "It helps me get out some of the aggression I hold inside."

The more answers I give him, the more relaxed he gets. I don't think I've gained the man's trust by any means. I'm sure that's hard to come by. Like with anyone who has a lot of power, you have to earn trust. You have to earn someone's respect. You can't just get it on the fly.

"I have an idea," Big Daddy K muses. "Johnny won't like it."

My stomach squeezes, once again threatening to expel the breakfast I had this morning. It's taking everything in me to sit in the presence of my parents' killer calmly. I have a feeling once I get out of this place, it's going to be a shit show. I can only pretend for so long.

Without waiting for an answer, he calls out, telling everyone he sent away a few minutes ago that they can come back.

Johnny sits next to me on the couch, putting his hand on my thigh. "It wasn't so bad, was it?" His question starts out as a remark but turns into a question. He doesn't relax until I smile in reassurance.

The more I see out of Johnny, the more I think he actually does care about me. Except, he only has so much capacity for caring.

Once everyone is settled, Big Daddy K says, "Reynolds is right about one thing. We've been having this territory fight with Fonz for too long. We're each undercutting the other. It's time we settle this for good."

Johnny smirks. He's excited about the prospect. Obviously.

It's Oscar who asks, "How do you propose we do

that? We try to get her shit shut down and then she retaliates."

Big Daddy K's gaze lands on me. He licks his lips, and an unsettling feeling falls on my shoulders. "I'm wondering if Fonz will settle this with a good old-fashioned fight. If she wins, we give up the fight ring in the Heights."

"What?" Johnny explodes. "We built that business."

Big Daddy K holds up a hand. "If we win, we keep the rights to the Heights' ring, and she has to move to another city."

Johnny swallows. Indecision marking his face. "It's a lot to lose. We built the Crew on that fight ring."

"We have other ventures that can sustain us if we lose it," Big Daddy K says. "But the point is to win, too. If we win, she's out of our hair for good."

"So, a fight?" Oscar says, musing. "Our best against her best?"

Big Daddy K nods, crossing his legs. There's an air of mischief underneath all his actions though, making me feel like this is bigger than what he's just said. Also, he keeps staring at me which is unnerving as fuck.

"Who will fight for us? Brawler?" Johnny asks. I can tell by the look in his eyes that he's already two steps ahead. He may be Big Daddy K's son, but he's earned the spot he has. He shakes his head. "He's not even a part of the Crew though."

"I had someone else in mind," Big Daddy K says. He turns his gaze to me and understanding punctures the brief oblivious bubble I was living in. Of course. This is his way of vetting me.

"I'll do it," I say automatically.

"What? Fuck no," Johnny says.

At the same time, Oscar says, "That's not a good idea."

I can't see Magnum, but Big Daddy K glances over my head, lips thinning. "I was actually thinking exactly that. Kyla up against whoever Fonz chooses."

Johnny gets to his feet. "Fuck no. Have you seen her fighters? They're huge. They'll fucking destroy her. Dad..." he begs.

I gaze at him, eyebrows pulling in. *Jeez. Thanks for the fucking vote of confidence.*

"I'm with Johnny," Oscar says.

I turn to glare at him. "Fuck you."

Big Daddy K smirks.

Johnny turns away from him and addresses me. "Hey. I'm just worried about you. I don't want you to get hurt."

"Didn't you tell me she was the best fighter you'd

ever seen?" Big Daddy K interjects, a small smile over his lips. He's enjoying this.

"She is."

"So, what's the problem? In the Crew, we use everyone and everything at our disposal."

"The problem is, she's mine!" Johnny growls.

Big Daddy K's eyes narrow. "If she's yours, she's a part of the Crew which means she can be used for Crew business. This is Crew business. She has a chance to do something for us we've wanted desperately for a long time."

This is my chance. I have to do this. I stand next to Johnny. "I'd be happy to fight."

I should feel nervous as fuck because I have no idea who Fonz will choose to put me up against, but I'm also getting exactly what I wanted. I'm a fighter first. It's in my blood. Plus, this is the way to get the leader of the Heights Crew to trust me. I know it.

"I think we should bet on someone we've seen fight more than once," Oscar says. He's avoiding my gaze now, but I know what he's trying to do. He's trying to save me. "I say Brawler," he says nonchalantly. "Rascal, even."

"Rascal uses his strength," Magnum says, speaking up for the first time. "He's not skilled. He's just big."

"I *want* to fight," I say again.

Johnny takes my arm, squeezing it hard to the point of pain. "Shut up," he grits out.

Big Daddy glances at his hand on me, so I can't do anything about it. I just stand there. "Obviously, I'll go with whatever is decided," I say, staring right at the most important person in the room. It's up to Big Daddy K. He has the final decision in everything. "But know that if I'm chosen, I will win. I don't care who I'm up against."

Johnny squeezes harder. The bones in my wrist rub against one another.

"Thank you," Big Daddy K says. "Oscar, take Kyla home." He gestures our way like he's shooing us out the door. "Make sure she gets some ice for her wrist since my son doesn't know how to treat a woman who's his. We'll decide what's happening."

Johnny immediately drops my arm like it's a scalding hot pan he's just burned himself on.

I don't make a move to even inspect what he's done. Johnny tries to catch my eye, but I don't give him the satisfaction. I walk toward the door we came in, and Oscar follows me.

As soon as we get outside, I spin on him. "What the fuck?"

"What?" he growls back.

His mask slips. He's back to being Oscar Drego,

the guy who was forced to join the Crew.

"What the fuck was that back there?"

He ignores me, and we get into the elevator. I have no idea if there are cameras in here or not, so maybe I shouldn't even be talking right now, but motherfucker. His opinion could've swayed Big Daddy K away from me and then what advantage would I have?

"I'm not allowed to have an opinion?" He glances up to the corner of the elevator, and I'm wondering if he means to tell me to wait to have this conversation.

Even though that's the last thing I want to do, I keep my mouth shut.

The elevator opens in the underground garage and Oscar turns the opposite direction from the car I arrived in. His taut muscles don't make his lithe movements more jumbled. Instead, he looks like a predator ready to strike. Whatever was said up in that suite affected him as much as me. He strides up next to a motorcycle. "This is what I brought with me. It'll have to do."

I stare at it. My jaw unhinges. "You don't have a car?"

"I used to, but it went to shit. A fellow member of the Crew was getting rid of this, so he sold it to me for cheap."

It looks cheap too. Well, it looks like it used to be a

damn nice motorcycle when it was first built, but now it's showing its age. It looks like a goddamn death trap. "I'm not riding on that."

Oscar drops his head back in annoyance. "Don't give me shit about this. I have to take you home, head back to school because I have a fucking game tonight I don't want to miss."

Fuck. I'd already forgotten about Oscar's game. I swallow back the selfish feelings rising inside me and sigh. "Fine. But don't fucking kill me."

"Are you kidding? You get hurt and Johnny will fucking kill me." He makes sure I'm staring straight into the abyss of his eyes. "He'll also give me shit because those beautiful legs of yours will be wrapped around me." My heart kicks up. He's trying to bait me.

He winks, and a flush of heat hits my cheeks. In another place, another town, Oscar would be the shit. I bet the girls swamped him when he went to Spring Hill. Who doesn't want to date the quarterback? Especially if he's as good as Oscar makes himself out to be.

"Are you seriously flirting with me after you told them you didn't think I should fight?"

A scowl crosses his face, and he stalks toward me. "Did you ever think Johnny's not the only one who doesn't want to see you get hurt? Don't be so fucking dense, Princess."

"Don't call me fucking Princess."

His lips quirk up. "I like calling you Princess. I like the angry heat it brings to your cheeks and the mouth it gives you. That's like crack to me, Pretty Girl. Pretty, Pretty Princess," he tacks on, like shoving the knife that much deeper.

He returns to his bike and hops on. He revs it up, and it surprisingly roars to life without hiccups. In fact, it thunders, dangerous and sexy. And Oscar most certainly has sex appeal while he's on it.

"Careful when you get on," he calls back to me.

I bite my lip and step forward. He points out where to put my feet, and I straddle the seat, then end up having to move closer to him as the bike vibrates beneath us.

"Hold on," he says, his voice loud enough to hear just over the purring engine.

I stare at his back. His shirt hugs his torso, so I can imagine the athletic body underneath. I move my arms around him, but it's Oscar who pulls them tighter, overlapping my hands until I grip one in the other. He pats me as if saying, "Good girl," and I grit my teeth.

"Don't enjoy this too much, Princess. I'm sure there are eyes all over us right now. Wouldn't want someone seeing how much you enjoy being pressed against me."

If they're watching the look on my face right now, there's nothing I have to worry about.

But when Oscar hits the gas, I squeeze him. Try as I might not to, a skitter of fear runs through me. I've never been on a motorcycle before. The guys I went to school with had Porsches and Mustangs, not bikes like this. Not that any one of them ever asked me out for a drive anyway.

Oscar drives the city streets, muscles tensing and moving beneath my touch. There's no doubt about the fact that he has a six-pack hiding under his shirt. The hard ridges of his abs bite into my wrists.

Once we get going, the fear of the ride floats away. My hair blows in the wind, and a sense of freedom flows through me. I wish escaping was this easy.

The feeling of being free doesn't last long though. After a while, my mind retreats, catching and dragging on all the things that just happened. Now that I'm out of the moment, my body locks up. Oscar must feel the change in me because he pats my hand again, then smooths his fingers over the tiny bones in my wrist to comfort me. Without even seeing my face, he knows I need it.

I met the guy who killed my parents.

Fuck.

I touched him. I sat in the same room with him. Hell, I fucking strategized with the asshole.

Oscar pulls up in front of my building. I stumble off the bike and make it to the cement wall. I lean my forearm against it as my stomach revolts. The hand that touched that dirty fucker dangles at my side, my fingers outstretched. I stare down at it, and my stomach twists again with the threat of losing its contents.

Behind me, the engine cuts off, and Oscar runs up to me. He puts a hand on the small of my back, rubbing there. "It's okay."

I swallow, my eyes closing on their own free will. It's not okay. Not at all. It's not okay that I have to make nice with that asshole and his friends. He should be able to hear what I really have to say. He might've, in court. But that day has long passed. The fucking corrupt cops and the Heights Crew's reach made sure of that. I never got the chance to stand up and tell that fucker exactly what he did to me and my family. And even then, at twelve, I wouldn't have known the extent. All I knew was grief. Now, I know the extent. Now, I could tear that fucker down.

Then again, since he doesn't have a soul, he won't care. He has no feelings left inside him.

This is the guy I have to appease.

I know what I have to do, but for just this moment,

I'm going to rage against it all.

"Let's get you upstairs," Oscar says, his voice gentle. All the teasing and flirting from earlier is gone. In its place is true concern.

Since it doesn't look like I'm actually going to throw up, I take his hand and we both move up to my apartment.

Oscar opens the door for me, and this time it doesn't even faze me that everyone else seems to have a key to my apartment too. I'm used to it. It no longer bothers me that certain people do. I'm not used to having friends. People who care about me.

Oscar guides me to the chair. "Have a seat. I'll get you some water...and some ice," he tacks on.

I stare blankly ahead, my elbows on my knees as soon as I'm sat in the chair. The faucet runs, and a few seconds later, Oscar thrusts a glass in my face. I take it with shaking hands and then press my wrist onto the icepack Oscar sets on the coffee table in front of me.

I swallow down a few mouthfuls and then put the glass down.

It's a few more minutes before Oscar even says anything. "You want to tell me what that was about because I know it wasn't about the bike. You liked that."

"You wish," I say.

"You have to open up to someone," he says, trying again. "You know my background with the Crew. You can talk to me. I won't say a goddamned word. Promise." He puts up the scout's honor sign.

"You were a scout?"

"Fuck no," he says, his lips teasing into a smile.

I laugh at that. The easy banter makes everything that just happened feel even further away. Even with that reprieve, I try not to trust these boys. Especially not Oscar. He's in the Heights Crew, and that's all that matters.

"Fuck me," he says, pacing around the room, hands diving into his thick head of dark hair. "I'm such a fucking sucker," he mutters. He blows out a breath then turns toward me. His dark eyes light with passion. "Sometimes I fucking hate those guys." He glowers. "You're pissed off because I said I didn't want you to fight. Do you know why I don't want you to fight? Because I don't want you to get hurt. You don't belong in the Heights, Princess. That much was clear from day one. Yes, you're badass. Yes, you're strong. I'm not talking about any of that shit. I'm not even saying I can put my finger on why you don't fucking belong here, it's just a feeling I have in my gut." He places his hand around his midsection, pulling it into him. "It's a feeling I can't fucking get away from, and I've learned to listen to my feelings. That's why I don't want you fighting. Because once you fight and win, you don't have a fucking chance of ever getting out of here."

His stormy eyes draw me in. Oscar isn't what you see on the surface. Not at all. "What makes you think I want to get out?"

"I don't think you want to. That much is clear. You want in or else you wouldn't have said you'd take the fight. I don't even need to know the fucking reasons, but what I'm saying is there are certain people who should be in the Crew and certain people who shouldn't. *You* shouldn't."

My mouth goes dry. "And you should?"

His exterior starts to crack. "You already know the answer to that."

"You don't," I say. "You don't belong here either."

"Some decisions are borne from desperation."

"And you hate being fucking desperate."

"More than anything in the fucking world," he says, voice sure. "But I've been living in this arena since day fucking one on this Earth, and I don't expect to get out of it now. There's no fucking hope for me."

Hope. There's that word. Or in the Heights, it's the lack of that word that's like a shroud over the entire city. It's fucking depressing.

"You're better than this. Than them."

"I'm not sure I agree with you, but I know you are."

I shake my head. Ever since being here, I've felt exactly like them. I'm caught up in their business. I'm attached to Johnny at the hip, and some-fucking-times, I actually like it. I actually want to be next to him like some sick, fucked up kid with that syndrome that makes you want to be with the person who treats you like shit. "You don't know a thing about me," I tell him, my finger trailing over the bruising that's just starting to appear on my wrists from Johnny's tight hold.

"I get that, but there's one thing people who grow up around here know right off the bat. Whether someone is worth their time or not. I knew you were worth my time as soon as you walked into school."

Oscar steps forward. My chest tightens the closer he gets. He reaches out, placing a strand of hair around my ear. It's like we're back at the school all over again, hiding down an empty hallway, warring with our emotions.

"That makes me sound crazy, but I'm used to sounding fucking crazy. Did you hear the conversation we all had earlier?" His voice lowers to a low hum. "Fighting for a fighting territory. Sending an innocent girl into the ring to win our right to fight. Hell, K didn't even ask you. He already had his heart set on you. We all fucking know that."

"I'm not innocent," I tell him, not sure why I'm choosing to comment on that part of his speech and not something else.

His lips tip up. "Just because you said that... it means you are."

Oscar tracks his gaze across my face before pausing on my lips. His presence is commanding. The broken parts of him call to me just like Brawler's do. My heart thunders in my chest as he moves closer.

"What are you doing?"

Oscar blinks, but he doesn't pull away. He slides his other hand around me. "Showing you that just because I'm a part of the Crew, doesn't mean I'm like the rest of them." He swallows. "Or maybe I'm showing myself."

His lips graze mine—a brush that calls up every surge of emotion inside me to the surface. He clings to me like I'm his anchor in a storm. He doesn't deepen the kiss, he just leaves his lips there as we breathe each other in, holding one another in place.

"I forgot that I could still feel things," Oscar says, his words seeping out of him like a secret he didn't know he kept inside.

That's when I realize how fucked I am. No wonder why these guys call to me. I'm *exactly* like them.

23

The doorknob rattles. Oscar and I break away from each other like we're both on fire and we don't want to get burnt. Actually, that should've been the reason we shouldn't touch. We're both playing with fire, and we know it.

Brawler stomps into the room. His face is pure viciousness, but it falls when he sees the both of us there. "Hey," I say, my voice rising several octaves.

Brawler glances between the two of us. Confusion riddles his features, but then it's like he has a moment of clarity before the clouds roll in again.

My heart thumps like mad. It's beating a rhythm of *Why? Why? Why?* Somehow, Brawler and Oscar have bored a hole into my skin. They're both lost, sad, angry.

They're both stuck in a place they shouldn't be, whether they know it or not.

"I take it you heard?" Oscar asks.

A fierce look crawls over Brawler's face again. His muscles pull taut. "All I know is I got a call from Johnny asking me to train Princess."

Oscar snickers. "Let's not pretend anymore, dude. You fucking like her. It's obvious. You may have even done shit." Oscar glances at me for confirmation.

I swear I stop breathing. Irrationally, I wonder if Johnny has this place bugged. Or is that irrational? It sounds exactly like something he'd do in an effort to keep me safe. Then again, the guys he chose to keep me safe have been doing more than that. They've been working their way into my life.

Brawler strides forward. It's like watching two boulders collide. He runs into Oscar and pushes him against the wall. "Do not fucking joke about this, Drego. I swear to fucking God."

Oscar looks away, bored. He catches my eye and winks.

My nerves tear apart even if I do think he's downright sexy winking at me in the middle of a fight. "Stop," I shout.

Brawler looks over at me. He must mistake my gaze

because he steps away, shaking his head. "You *like* him?" His disbelief is written all over his face.

"Hey," Oscar says. "I'm not so bad. Never had any complaints before, actually."

My brain feels like it's buzzing with flies. I have so many things to concentrate on, but I can't pick one and stay with it. Just overall, there's a sense of foreboding lingering everywhere. Can I confess to this? It seems like it would be so easy.

Brawler's hands turn to fists. I want to walk away. To escape. I don't want to have this conversation, and I definitely don't want to be having this conversation right now. Not just after I met my parents' murderer and found out that in order to get on his good side, I'm going to have to fight a rival gang member for overall territory.

Both of them stare at me. Like a spotlight has been turned toward me, heat creeps over my skin, prickly and uncomfortable.

"Let's not talk about this right now."

"Fuck that," Brawler says. He's seething. "I want to talk about this now."

Oscar shoves him out of the way. "Can't you see she's upset? Something about meeting K today threw her off."

"It's probably the fact she has to fight one of Fonz's fighters. What the fuck? Did no one stick up for her?"

"We all did, fucker," Oscar grits out. "Even Johnny. For whatever reason, K was dead set on having her do it. I don't fucking know why."

Oscar twists behind him, looking at the clock. His shoulders deflate. "I have to go," he says. His gaze searches mine as if he's wondering if I'll be pissed if he goes.

I wave him away. Never. He loves football, and I would never stand in the way of it. Not like the Crew has. It'll actually be nice if I can be alone, too. Even though it'll never happen now. I need time to think. "Go. Good luck. Make lots of...plays," I say, unsure of myself. I've never had feelings for a quarterback before.

Oscar moves over to me, dropping a chaste kiss on my cheek. Even for how short it is, it makes my breath catch.

"Where the fuck are you going?" Brawler demands. His voice has kept that same perturbed inflection since he walked in.

"My game." Oscar moves to the door and starts to open it. Before he leaves, he turns back. "Don't get so fucking pissy, Brawler. I'll be around to help. Don't worry. I won't let you have all the fun with our Kyla."

Brawler growls, which just pushes Oscar that

much more.

"Love the new tat, by the way."

"Eat a bag of dicks."

Oscar's laugh lingers in the room after he's gone. Or maybe the sound just keeps ringing in my head. It was nice to hear it, especially confronted with a very pissed off Brawler.

"So you can officially help me train now," I say, trying for light-hearted.

It doesn't work. The wings of his light and dark angel tattoos move with the rapid beat of his pulse.

"What the fuck is going on?" Brawler asks. The anger drains from him and all that's left is someone withering under uncertainty. "I like you. A lot. It takes a-fucking-lot to say that, and I know you're off limits and I shouldn't be pissed that just when I needed you, fucking Johnny swooped in. He slept with you, didn't he? He stayed the night in your bed while I'm down the fucking hall thinking of a thousand different ways we can leave this fucking place. Of all the fucking things I want to do to you when we leave this place." He runs a hand down his face. "Oscar?" He shakes his head like he just can't believe it. "I know you can't help Johnny, but Oscar? I thought—" He clears his throat. "At the risk of sounding like a whiny bitch, I thought you liked *me*, Kyla. Me."

The words start to bubble up from my chest, but I push them down. What good will admitting that I like any of these guys do me in the end? This is why I didn't want to get mixed up in this.

"I think we should just focus on training."

"Why? Because you want Oscar?" Every time he says it, his voice sounds so incredulous. Like how could I possibly want Oscar more than him.

"No!" I finally blurt out. I stand there wide-eyed. There are so many things I want to say to him. Like how, for the first time, there's someone who cares about me for me. Not just because I'm the offspring of a relative. But someone who truly sees me and likes me for who they see. Someone that when I meant enough to them, they didn't force what they wanted on me.

"I didn't *sleep* sleep with Johnny." I sigh for all the beating around the bush I'm doing. "I didn't fuck him," I say, making it plainly clear what I'm talking about.

"I know. You're not allowed to."

"I just wanted you to know."

"Oscar?"

"I didn't fuck him either. Why is this what we're talking about?" I ask honestly. "Shouldn't we be discussing fighting? Shouldn't you be telling me the best way to beat Fonz's people? Who do you think she'll put me up against?"

He shakes his head. "I'll talk about all that with you, but Christ, Kyla, I've been like a fucking zombie the past week. I can't get it out of my head that you were lying next to him when I'm not allowed to, and I'm fucking sorry, but I'm not moving past this until I get answers."

He's got me trapped. My hands strain into fists at my sides. "What do you want from me then? You want to hear that I like you? You already fucking know the answer to that, Brawler. You also know we're fucked if we do anything about it, so I don't know why this is what we're choosing to talk about."

"Because through all the bullshit, this is what fucking matters!" Brawler roars. "Because if you tell me right now there's something here, we're leaving. We won't have to worry about the fight, Kyla, because I'm not going through Crew shit if I don't have to. They took everything from me. My brother, my sister, my mom just sits around the apartment. It's only me." He shakes his head. "This shit isn't happening to me again. I came over here to tell you we're leaving. I just need you to say the word."

My heart cracks in two. "I can't leave. I can't."

"Johnny?"

"Fuck Johnny," I cry. I wipe my hands down my face, knowing I'm not entirely being honest either. "It's not that. I can't leave, and I can't tell you why right now." Leaving the Crew is one thing but telling someone I want to take out Big Daddy K is another. I can't put that on them.

Hurt splinters Brawler's deep blue eyes. "You don't trust me. After all I've just said…"

"I do," I say. "It's just I can't leave. I want to," I tell him, pleading him with my heart, my body. "I just can't right now. Please don't ask me why. The less you know the better."

Brawler's silent. I've hurt him. I've cut him open and tossed his promises aside. I sound like a cold-hearted bitch, but that's not it at all. At least, that's not my intention.

He looks around like he doesn't know what to do with himself. He keeps looking toward the door time and time again. Eventually, he'll leave through it, and I won't know if the same Brawler who just said all that will come back to me.

"I have to go," he says, despair draping over his words. "Lock the door behind me. If you leave, call me or Oscar. Or Johnny," he adds like he's reconciled the fact that Johnny's a part of my life now.

"Yeah," I choke out. "Sure."

He takes one last look at me then strides to the door. His heavy footsteps stop just outside, waiting for me to put the locks on. I do, and as soon as the last one is in place, his muffled footsteps shuffle down the hall back toward his place.

As soon as he leaves, I do him one better. I go into my room and put the lock on that door in place, too. Now, no one can get to me.

I throw myself on the bed and start to feel sorry for myself over everything that's just happened, but then my gaze locks onto my secret hiding place. I sigh. It's been a while since I've had the chance to contact my aunt and uncle.

I stand, go to the shelf, and take it out. When I power it on, I find more than a few unanswered texts. Each newer one more worried than the last. Instead of sending a text in response, I call. My aunt's phone rings and rings until it eventually goes to voicemail. "Hey... I'm okay," I say. "Everything's fine here. Just school and stuff. I hope you guys are doing well." I take the phone away from my mouth and breathe out. I wish I could tell her everything. Why does the closest person to me still feel like they're miles away? "Talk to you later. Bye."

Everything I just said is a lie. I'm not okay. School's a joke. Everything's not fine.

I don't expect anyone to sympathize with me though. I came here alone. I'll do this on my own.

24

I don't stay in the apartment for long. I can't stand being cooped up by myself anymore. If Oscar or Brawler were with me, I'd be fine, but not by myself. Not now, anyway.

I send Johnny a text, telling him I'm going to the school football game and that I'm alone for the moment. I do it to cover Brawler's ass. He doesn't need to get in trouble because I left without him. I'm pretty sure he doesn't want to see me right now anyway.

A response pings through immediately after. **I'll send Magnum.**

I stop in the stairwell of the building to type out: **You don't have to. I kind of want to do this by myself. Plus, Oscar will be there.**

My phone rings in my hand as I'm slipping it into my pocket after sending the last text. Johnny sounds agitated. "I don't want you to be alone right now. It's dangerous."

I bite back a groan and lower my voice as I cross the street away from my building. "Hey, I'll be okay," I say. "I mean, I'm tough enough to fight, right?"

"Fists don't stop bullets, babe."

His term of endearment makes a short smile flicker across my lips. "I don't want to be cooped up in my apartment forever, Johnny. You can see that, right?"

"I've been thinking about that," he says. "What do you think about moving into the tower with me?"

I swallow. "The tower?"

"You know, my place."

The back of my neck bristles. I can't move in with him. Even if that will put me in a prime place to see K. Actually, fuck that. I *can* move in with him, can't I? My mind wanders to Oscar and Brawler. If I can kill Big Daddy K sooner rather than later, would they come with me?

Jesus. What the hell am I thinking? They both have lives here. I'm the only one who doesn't.

"My dad will probably want us to wait until after the fight at least. I don't know. It's just a thought."

"What would that change for me?" I ask, biting my lip. Johnny wants me to live with him. It's so stupid but tears come to my eyes. This is the first time someone's expressed it like that to me. I settle my beating heart and return to the conversation. "If I move in, I'll just have to stay in your place instead of mine."

"I'll get you your own bodyguard."

"No," I say right away. That has done nothing but make things more fucking difficult for me. I don't need another guy I'll be staying with, trust me. I don't want to keep my hands to myself on the two I have.

"Kyla..."

"So, I am really fighting, right?"

"Yes," he says, his tone clipped. He still doesn't sound very happy about it, but it's his father's decision, and he knows it. "I'm sending Magnum. Bye, Kyla."

He ends the call. I pull the cell phone away from my ear and stare at the screen before shoving it into my back pocket as I approach the school. Whatever. I don't know why I thought he would let me get away with this.

There are fewer cars in the parking lot than normal. I follow the sparse crowd to the back of the school as a sharp whistle pierces the air.

The field is small, and the crowd doesn't even fill the few seats the bleachers have. I guess there's way more important things for people to do than go to a football game on Friday night. Hell, there are more people crowded in the old, abandoned warehouse when the fights are taking place than there are here right now.

This whole fucking city is backwards.

I walk right up to the chain-link fence that separates the crowd from the players. Scanning the uniformed athletes, I look for someone who looks like he's as important as the quarterback should be. I've missed a little of the game. A quick check of the scoreboard tells me it's the second quarter. In front of me, the Rawley Heights players are just coming off the field. I've never been a big sports person unless it's fighting, so I don't even know if it's the offense or the defense coming off until a guy takes his helmet off, and I clearly see Oscar.

My heart skips a beat. I stick my hand in the air and wave. I catch his attention, and his eyes round. He searches my vicinity, and when he doesn't see anyone, he jogs up to the fence. Behind him, his coach is calling his name, but he ignores him.

"What are you doing here?" he asks. Sweat beads over his upper lip. His usual pristine hair is matted to his head.

"I told you I wanted to come."

"Where's Brawler?" Then, his eyes round in understanding. "He's pissed at you."

My stomach dips. I'm pretty sure he is pissed at me and who knows if he'll ever get over it.

As if reading my thoughts, Oscar says, "He'll get over it."

I shake my head. "I just wanted to see you play."

His already reddened cheeks seem to glow like I've just given him the best compliment in the world. "No one's with you though," he says, lowering his voice.

"Johnny's sending Magnum to meet me."

Oscar groans, his lips tipping up at the corners. "He's a lively one. I'm sure you'll have a lot of fun."

He moves in closer. My body remembers what it felt like earlier, and every nerve comes to attention. He'd be stupid to do anything here, but sometimes I think Oscar's brazen enough to do just that. He's reckless, and damnit if I don't want to be reckless with him.

Behind him, Oscar's coach gets more insistent. He gives a dark look over his shoulder but turns disappointed eyes back to me. "Got to go. Feel free to look at my ass in these pants. I'm sure you'll like what you see."

A laugh bubbles up my throat.

He winks before turning around, and I do like what I see. I understand why people like watching football now. As he jogs away, he gives himself a tap on his ass, which makes me bite my lip. When he gets to his coach, he peeks at me and grins when he sees the dumb, sexed-up look on my face.

I stay where I am until halftime. I look around, surprised Magnum hasn't made an appearance yet. It's not like he wouldn't be able to see me even if he stayed in the background. The place isn't crowded, and I'm almost the only one clutching the fence. Maybe that's what he's doing. Giving me space.

Rawley Heights is winning. Or should I say Oscar is winning? He's good. He wasn't exaggerating, and even though I love to watch him play, it makes me sad too. His abilities are lost here. No one gives a fuck. No one, besides what looks like a few football parents or girlfriends of players, sit in the stands. I can't see any of the administration. There's no concession stand. No cheerleaders. There's nothing.

And Oscar's stuck. It's bullshit is what it is.

I pull out my cell phone to see if I've heard back from Johnny. Surprisingly, there is a text there, but not from a phone number I recognize until I bring it up. **It's Mag. I'm giving you some time. If Johnny asks, I was with you the whole game. Don't fuck this up.**

I don't know how to answer, so after deleting the

text, I just put my phone back in my pocket. I figure if he really is being nice and wants me to have a little time, I'm not going to rat him out, so I'm certainly not going to leave evidence of what he's doing on my phone.

"Kyla."

I glance up. It's Oscar. He cocks his head toward a small building on the side of the field then disappears behind it. I look around, everyone else is talking amongst themselves. The coach, in particular, is giving one kid the riot act about some dropped pass. I have to admit, I don't remember what he's talking about. I watched Oscar the whole time.

I make myself move toward the small building even though every fiber in my being is telling me it's a bad idea.

When I come around the corner, Oscar is leaning against the back wall much like when I saw him the first time. Those initial feelings sprout up again. He's so handsome. So dangerously sexy with his dark looks and badass attitude.

Except now, he's in a hot as fuck jersey with tight ass pants on.

"Yeah?" I ask. Looking up at the building behind him, so I don't have to look at his face. "What's this building?"

"We keep equipment in here."

For whatever reason, the area seems to block us from the rest of the world. We don't hear the sounds on the field or the people watching. It's just us.

"I thought you might want to makeout with the quarterback of a football team."

My lips slide into a smile. "You just want to get lucky during halftime. Something to check off a to-do list."

He shakes his head. "No. I've been noticing the way you've been looking at me. You're practically salivating."

"What can I say? I have a thing for athletes."

He pulls me toward him. His pads hard against my chest. "We didn't get to finish what we started earlier."

My heart rate amps up. As much as I want to keep flirting with him, we're treading the line of disaster. "This is a terrible idea, Oscar. Someone's going to see us."

"I don't care. I've been looking from afar for too long."

His skilled hand slides up my hip and just under my shirt. He presses his palm into my lower back and maneuvers his knee between my legs. "Oscar," I warn.

Dark eyes devour me. "One taste," he pleads.

We reach for each other at the same time, our lips

colliding. He slides his knee higher and presses me down until a delicious friction starts in my core. I gasp between his lips, and he smiles. "I knew you'd like it on the bad side."

"This is stupid," I mumble against his lips.

"Very." A moan breaks him off. "Fuck, Kyla. I can't think straight." His fingers trail under the waistband of my jeans.

He changes our position, gently pushing me against the side of the building.

"You know how much it sucks having a hard-on in a fucking cup?"

I grin. "This was your idea."

"I just don't know when we're ever going to have time alone."

"We're not alone, Oscar. Your fans are in the stands."

He looks bemused. "Hardly." He pulls his hand out of the back of my jeans and passes it over my stomach until he's inches away from my chest. "You're hard for me."

I take a quick peek, knowing full well what Oscar's getting at. My nipples are pebbled, pushing against my shirt. Aching.

"I want to take them in my mouth, slide my tongue over them," he groans.

I bite down on my lip. "Jesus, Oscar." I drop my head back against the wall. My core is throbbing. I'm wired for electricity at this point.

I push his knee out from in between my legs and create some distance between us. "This can't happen right now."

"What if I dropped to my knees and kissed you here?" he asks, trailing a hand up my inseam to the vee of my legs.

I brush his hand away after my panties soak through. "You want to make both of us crazy."

"It's fun this way," he says. "Now you'll be watching me, wishing my tongue was inside you."

"And you'll be getting tackled with an erection. How does that help either one of us?"

His lips tip up. "You're my kind of girl, Princess."

I don't take the bait this time. I'm already going to be watching the rest of this game wondering what Oscar's like in bed. I don't need to torture myself any further. "You better take a cold shower after your game."

"Only if you're in it with me."

A whistle pierces the air. Oscar's face hardens. I take a step away from him. "You better get back out there."

His lips thin. He lifts his hand to place his fingertips on my cheek. "After the game," he says. There's no question in his voice. It's more like a command. He turns, running back to the field while the voices around us start to pick up again. I don't leave the back of the wall until several minutes pass. I'm pretty sure the team is already playing judging by the sounds of pads colliding with pads and the occasional argument on the field.

When enough time has gone by, I push off the wall and take my place by the fence again. Watching Oscar is a different experience now, and I was right about one thing. I'm wondering if he moves in bed like he moves on the field. He's lithe, smooth, with the right amount of power.

"Hey," a voice says behind me.

I practically jump out of my skin. Turning, I find Magnum breathing down my neck. "Fuck," I breathe.

He takes me in, and I feel like I have sex on the brain, and he can tell. "I need you to come with me. Something's come up."

I look longingly back over at the field. "What?"

"Just come on," he says. "I'll explain it to you in the car."

I want to protest, to tell him I should let Oscar know where I'm going, but I don't think that would go over well if it got back to Johnny. Instead of doing any of that, I fall into step behind Magnum and just hope Oscar happens to be looking my way, so he doesn't think I deserted him.

That's the last thing I want to do right now.

25

Magnum and I get into the car. The divider is down, and it's just the two of us.

"So, what is it?" I ask as he pulls away. This car always looks so strange in this parking lot. It's by far the best one compared to any other.

"Big Daddy K and Johnny are meeting with Roza Fonz. They're arranging the fight. She won't agree until she meets you first."

My stomach pitches, but at the same time, excitement fills me. This I can do. This is what I came here to do. What I can't do is navigate three guys. Actually, just two. There is no third. The third is a puppet on a string who thinks about his own pleasures before anyone else's.

Right? Right.

"Let's do it," I say, leaning back casually.

Magnum glares at me through the rearview mirror. For all the time I find him staring at me, it's a wonder we haven't gotten into an accident yet. "You seem so blasé about all of this. Aren't you worried?"

"I know fighting. It's the one thing in my life I can control right now, so no, I'm not worried...especially."

Magnum shakes his head. "There's a bulletproof vest in the back there. Johnny wants you to put it on. In case," he says snidely.

His words are so cocky it makes me narrow my gaze at him. He must think I'm a complete idiot. "I understand there are other factors, Mag," I say, drawing his name out like it's a tease instead of the badass name it really is.

Fuck him for having such a cool name.

I pull my shirt off and inspect the bulletproof vest. It's not as if I've put one on before. I get it around my shoulders like a vest, but I can't quite figure out how to fasten it. When the fasteners won't go, I lean back in the seat, sighing. "I hope someone thought to bring me another shirt because that fucking thing is not going to stretch over this."

"There should be a hoodie to your left."

I look over, finding an oversized hoodie. Bringing it

to me, it smells musky like Johnny. I put it back without breathing it in.

A few short minutes later, Magnum is pulling to a stop. The windows are so tinted I can't tell where we are. He shoves his door open, and I catch him before he gets out. "I'm going to need some help with this."

"I noticed," he says.

He shuts that door and then opens up the one to my left, sliding in next to me. As soon as he's in, he turns toward me, his copper hair darker in the low light.

"Only speak when spoken to when we're in there," he says. He looks down at the fasteners and the cleavage underneath before tightening the vest across my chest, making quick work of getting it all set up for me. "This is in Fonz's neck of the woods, so be on high alert. Stick with us. Don't do anything stupid. Wait for Big Daddy's orders."

His list of things to do sounds like a bunch of "duh." I roll my eyes to tell him what I think about it. His jaw tenses, the coppery stubble of his beard sticking straight out in some parts now that he's agitated with me.

"I won't do anything stupid," I promise.

Those sound like famous last words, but I'm going with it.

Magnum holds the hoodie out to me and then gets out of the car. I work it over my chest. Despite the fact that it's big for me, it just barely conceals the fact that I'm wearing a bullet stopping vest. I hope I won't need it, but the brick in my stomach tells me I'm not sure either.

I step out, and Magnum slams the door to the car behind me. Much like where K lives, we're in an underground parking lot. This area of the city is a lot less dingy however. We take the elevator up to the highest level and step out. Magnum steps forward first, standing there in his tactical black pants and tight-fitting black shirt. He has bodyguard written all over him.

Unlike where K and Johnny live, though, we've come right out into Fonz's ... place of business? It's definitely not homey like a house. There are glass walls everywhere that lead into different rooms with large tables like usually meetings are held behind the closed doors.

Johnny steps out of a room down the hall, his face grim. He nods when he sees me, and for some inexplicable reason, the fact that he's here calms me.

A guy, dressed much like Magnum, moves forward. He has a metal detector wand in his hand accompanied by a cocky grin. "You understand?" he says to Magnum.

Magnum shrugs, taking the usual position. The wand goes off by his belt where he keeps his gun.

"You can just take that out and set it on the table," Fonz's guard says. "You can get it back after the meeting."

Magnum does what he's told and then moves to stand next to Johnny. I'm next. Nerves prick, making their way to the very tips of my fingers until it's painful. The guard just stares at me for a moment until Johnny shifts on his feet.

"Eyes to yourself," Magnum finally says.

The guard smirks. "Nothing I want. Just wondering what the big fuss is about."

"Appearances aren't everything," I say. "Your ugly ass should know."

The guy's jaw ticks, but I smile up at him. *What did he expect me to do? Stand quietly?* Then again, Magnum did warn me to keep my mouth shut.

He waves the wand over me, and when he bends down to start at my feet, Johnny smirks at me. He winks, and I smile back. The wand goes off on my back pocket. He reaches inside to grab my phone, but that's not all he grabs. He takes a fistful of my ass in his palm.

I don't think. I react.

Fuck this asshole.

I wind my arm around his until I'm gripping his upper shoulder, then I pull him toward me, connecting his gut with my knee. He groans, his breath leaving him as I whisper into his ear. "You shouldn't touch something that isn't yours."

"Bitch!"

Before he can lunge at me, Magnum puts his hand on his other shoulder, gripping him hard. "I wouldn't if I were you. I'm sure your boss wouldn't like the fact that you took your liberties with one of ours. You want to die on that sword? You fuck with her, you fuck with the rest of us."

My mouth dries. To the side of Magnum, Johnny is fucking furious, and I don't even think he knows why I did what I did. Magnum either for that matter.

"Just get the bitch away from me," the guard seethes.

Magnum pulls the guy up and looks at me, telling me to remove my hold on him. When I don't do it right away, his expression becomes stonier, the look telling me I better fucking comply right now.

I ease up on the pressure, and the guy pulls his hand from my back pocket and steps back. Johnny throws him to the side so he can come to me, and all the guy can do is sneer at us.

"Is there a problem?" another guard asks, peeking his head out from the mouth of the room at the end of the hall.

We all wait for what the guy's going to say. I doubt he'll say anything because if he does, he'll have to admit I bested him with a knee to the gut, which never fucking feels good.

"You okay?" Johnny whispers into my ear.

I nod. "He grabbed my ass," I say, feeling like I need to explain myself to them since I've completely went against everything Magnum told me not to do while we were in the car.

Johnny growls under his breath, eyeing the fucker like he would take his head off if he could.

I swallow, knowing I'm still playing with fire. If Johnny finds out about Brawler and Oscar, I can imagine what he'll do since he won't be worried about starting a gang war then. He'll relish in taking them out for disobeying him.

Especially Oscar. Brawler doesn't have the ties Oscar does. Oscar would get decimated. He could kiss his football career goodbye even though he doesn't think he has one anyway. If he's alive to worry about it, he'll have to go back to the life he had when he got back from Spring Hill.

Johnny leans over to feather a kiss across my cheek

as we follow Magnum and Fonz's guard to the end of the hall. The space opens up to a room with floor to ceiling windows. The building we're in is one of the tallest in this shitty city, and from this height, you can't see all the disadvantage below. The dirty streets are farther away. The drug dealers on every corner are just people having friendly conversation with others. The room itself is dark though. The furniture, the adornments are all black with the walls a light gray color.

When we walk in, I notice Big Daddy K first, sitting stiffly on a black leather couch, one of our guards behind him. I vaguely recognize him from K's house the other day, but the major thing that sets him off as one of ours is the fact that he's dressed exactly like Magnum. I wonder how many guards Big Daddy K has.

Fonz's guard stops next to her side while Johnny escorts me to stand next to his father. My stomach revolts standing this close to him, and I wonder which person in this room I should fear most. The man who killed my parents? Or the woman across from us, pulling on a cigar, embers blazing on the end?

Roza Fonz's hair is done up in hundreds of braids that fall well past her shoulders. She has ebony skin, contrasted by a red slash of lipstick across her lips. She has on a red pantsuit that hugs her curves while she sits cross-legged on a couch that matches Big Daddy K's.

"This is her?" she asks. She blows out a plume of smoke that wafts toward the ceiling in a haze. I can tell from her inspection and the telling twinkling in her eye that she has the same assumption of me as the guard who cupped my ass did. "This does not seem like a fair fight," she says, finally turning her gaze over to Big Daddy.

"You let her worry about that," he says. His voice is edgy, as is the barely tethered tension stiffening his body. He looks nothing like the guy I met earlier in the comfort of his own home. He's on high alert though he's doing a good job of masking it. If I hadn't met him before I wouldn't have noticed anything was amiss.

"It seems like any of my fighters I put her up against would throttle her. How much experience does she have?"

Big Daddy K chuckles. "What does it matter? Now that you've seen her, are you taking the deal or not?"

Roza sets her cigar down in an ashtray. "You may be willing to sacrifice young women, K, but I'm not. Women aren't allowed to fight in my rings. I help them get off the street, not help them stay there."

Big Daddy K glances over at me. The whole side of my face burns. He grabs my hand, and I flinch. He places it on the arm of the sofa, covering it with his own. My face loses all emotion. It drains, and I have no doubt the pallor of a ghost stares back at Roza. He chuckles, patting my hand. "Kyla wants to fight. I hear she's been named Uppercut Princess to my clients."

Uppercut Princess? I like the sound of that.

As soon as he lets my hand go, I drop it to my side and vow I really will just set my hand on fire this time to get his vile germs off me.

Johnny snickers into my ear. "Uppercut Princess," he breathes.

I don't mind the sound of that at all. I could even get used to Princess as long as Uppercut was in front of it.

"You don't need to know her background to agree to the arrangements."

Fonz pushes back into the plush leather couch. "Her against one of my fighters." She flicks a hand toward me. "She represents you. Mine representing me. Whichever one wins will mean the winner for one of us. When that happens, the loser agrees to back off the fighting circuit. Am I understanding correctly?"

Big Daddy K nods once. His eyes dance. It's clear he's getting a thrill out of this. It makes a skitter of fear race up my spine and settle in the back of my neck like a bad seed.

"Why would you agree to this?" she asks, gaze narrowing on him cautiously. "Why her? You could choose any one of your male fighters. Big, brute strength."

"Family business," he says, lips thinning. It's obvious he's over this conversation and just wants an answer out of her, not the third degree.

Since I'm also curious about this question, I'd love to hear the answer. Other than the fact that it affords me the opportunity to prove myself to him, I'm not sure what's in it for him. As far as I can tell, there's nothing in it for him.

"Either accept or don't, Roza. The way I see it, this is how we figure out where the line is drawn."

"I drew the line years ago. You stepped over it," Roza snaps. She flicks her long braids over her shoulders.

"Here's a way to decide once and for all without widespread bloodshed," he says, ignoring her remark.

Roza is shaking. Not out of fear, but out of anger. I can tell she doesn't like him at all, and not just because he's the leader of a rival gang and a contending business owner. It's because he looks down on her like she doesn't mean a damn thing to him.

Her guards keep checking on her. The one I kneed

in the gut smirks at me like he can't wait to see me get my ass kicked.

I've got news for him. I don't intend to be the one who gets my ass kicked. I need to prove to Big Daddy K that I'm worthy to stand next to his son. I'm worthy of his trust. Winning this business exploit for him is how I'm going to do it. I don't care how much I have to train or how many tough blows I have to take, I'll come out the victor.

If I lose this fight, I lose everything.

"You," Roza says, nodding at me. "Why do you want to fight?"

As Magnum instructed, I wait until Big Daddy K tells me it's okay to answer. When he nods, I gaze over the black coffee table at her, a woman who must've risen over these men she surrounds herself with. A woman who commands their respect. By the way they look at her, I know if one of us started something, they'd stand in front of her in a heartbeat.

"Respect," I tell her. "Not just for this fight, any fight."

I stare at her, gaze narrowing. I'm hoping she sees something inside me that's inside her. From her point of view, I can understand why she won't agree right away. Anyone has to admit it looks like Big Daddy K is throwing the fight.

"I'm good," I tell her. "Skilled. Practiced. I don't care who you put me up against, the fight will be a good one."

"Just ask your guard," Johnny says, nodding toward the piece of shit who's probably still nursing a stomachache.

Roza turns her head to glance at the guard to her right. He nods, and it dawns on me then that his little show of overt affection might not have been an accident at all. She would've wanted to test me. To see if I was just a decoy Big Daddy K was sending in.

"If he touches me again, he'll get worse," I say, driving the point home.

Roza stands, and Big Daddy K follows. She extends her hand and Big Daddy K shakes it. "I accept your terms," Roza says. "The fight will take place next Saturday. Neutral grounds. The back parking lot of the abandoned mall should be sufficient."

Big Daddy K agrees. "We'll expect to hear your choice in fighter tomorrow."

"No need," Roza says. "The girl will fight Evan."

And like that, Evan steps forward. I hadn't been looking around at anything other than what was in front of my face, but I don't know how I missed this guy. He's a little smaller than Brawler, but that doesn't mean a thing. He's tall with long arms that reach past his hips. His reach is going to be a bitch to handle. He's also muscular, but the kind of muscles that come with functional training instead of lifting. In other words, the guy's a beast, and I would've gladly fought anyone else in the room but him, including Magnum.

I nod at him, and he nods back at me. A show of mutual respect that I like, but it doesn't last. He licks his lips, then presses them together in a mock kiss in my direction.

Johnny stiffens next to me, but I play along. I wave my fingers at him like a southern belle. "See you next week," I say.

As we're walking out to the car, I'm already in fight mode. My mind races with ideas of attack, the coming hours of training I'm going to have to fit in.

If I lose this fight, I'm done. I'm not dumb enough to think that if I lose, Big Daddy K will forget all this. It isn't as if he'll just punch me playfully in the arm and say, "Aw shucks. That's too bad."

If I lose this for him, not only do I lose his trust, but I'm dead.

26

Johnny and Magnum drop me off at my apartment building at the orders of Big Daddy K. It was decided Magnum will be my Evan stand in since they have similar builds. I don't doubt they have similar skill sets, too. He'll be a tough sparring partner; one I'll need to get me in shape for this.

Johnny walks me up the stairs, his hand in mine. It's odd seeing him here in this shithole of an apartment now that I've seen him in places of luxury. Now that I look at him, he does look a little out of place here, like he doesn't quite fit.

He's been tense on the car ride home, even while coming up with a plan. It isn't until we're outside my door, away from prying ears, that I have the courage to ask him what's wrong. I'm supposed to be his girl, right? That's a question girls can ask, and I have a feeling no one ever asks Johnny how he feels.

The tension leaves him, his shoulders falling. "It should be me fighting, not you."

My first reaction is to laugh. There's no way Big Daddy K would put up his own son. That's just asinine. Johnny's stoic though. He truly means what he's saying. The thought pulls me up short. "That's admirable," I say. I shake my head because that couldn't sound even less romantic than if I tried, so I try again. "We all have our roles to play in this," I tell him, leaning down to catch his eye. "This time, it's me who's fighting."

His jaw locks, and a fury crosses his face I haven't seen before. "If he hurts you, I'll kill him."

The conflicting thoughts in my head all jumble together. Instead of expressing any of that, I say, "You know you can't do that. A fight's a fight. Whoever wins, wins fair and square." The look Johnny shares with me next tells me he's also figured out that if I don't win, I won't be around either. For whatever else he is, it does seem like he has at least some feelings for me. He may not understand them all, and he certainly doesn't express them in the right way, but they're there. "Tell you what," I say to him. "When I win, I'll let you nurse me back to health."

Johnny's lips twist. Hunger flashes in his eyes. "I like the sound of that."

I'm not stupid enough to think that if I were to lose, Johnny wouldn't just find another girl the next day, claim her, and be having this same conversation with her somewhere down the line.

It makes my heart ache for him. Being caught up in all of this, he doesn't know what true feelings are. He doesn't know the pure bliss of having someone care about you, or the heartache when it gets taken away. I guess that's one thing that can be said for losing someone. At least you know how much it meant when you still had it. At least it tells you you loved someone with so much energy that it makes you die inside when they go. I have a feeling Johnny will never feel that.

This time, I initiate a kiss. His poor, confused soul. I press my lips into him like I'm trying to resuscitate him. I'm trying to infuse his soul. I'm trying to make him feel, not just at the surface, but bone deep. To the depths of his core. In every cell. I don't know why I just haven't given up on him yet. The pretty words he's said are just regurgitation from thinking that's what he's supposed to say.

I want to light a fire in him. I want to help him like I want to help Oscar and Brawler. Maybe I see something in him, something that tells me even though he has evil DNA running through his veins, that this isn't the life for him. He shouldn't be going to meetings with talk of territories and fighting and murder and death. He should be going to college for crying out loud. It's obvious he's smart. You have to be to survive in this business, but his energy is going in the wrong direction.

That's what I try to say with the press of my lips to his and the sweep of my tongue. He kisses me back with the same passion, but it's short lived.

He backs away. "I have to go."

He has to go scheme with his father. He hasn't heard me at all.

"Yeah," I say.

"Hey." He cups my cheek. "Don't be sad."

I shake my head. "Just a long day."

He kisses my forehead, his lips a soft press against skin but nothing more. At least not yet. "Get some rest. Tomorrow you'll start training."

He's right about one thing. I don't know one guy who would let his girl fight his battles for him if there was anything he could do about it. His words make me think he's halfway to caring, but on the other hand, I don't know if he'll ever get there. If he'll ever see he can have a better life.

He squeezes my hand. "Brawler should be inside."

I press my lips together. *Fucking wonderful. This day is about to get worse.*

Just when I think he's going to leave, he stays while I open the door, sending a warmth through me. Brawler stands from the recliner, his gaze staring holes straight through me. Johnny presses a hand at my back, ushering me in when the last thing I want to do is confront Brawler. "Bye, babe."

I don't answer. I'm too caught up in Brawler's stare. As soon as Johnny's footsteps fade away, I shut the door behind me. Everything I want Johnny to feel is seeping out of Brawler. From his every pore, from his eyes, from his chest heaving, he's telling me he cares. "You aren't fighting Evan."

"I don't have a choice."

"We all have choices."

"Then my choice is to stay here."

I turn, clicking all the locks into place. The heat of Brawler's gaze makes my movements hurried. It's amazing how rapid the feelings grew between us. Then again, it's not all that difficult to understand. When you live a life here, you never know which day will be your last. Brawler knows that more than most.

The two tattoos gracing his neck tell his story, but they also tell a cautionary tale. You don't even have to be directly involved in shit to become a victim of hate. When you never know what might happen, you find that the world opens up to you. You find beauty in strange things. You find feelings in the tiniest of moments. In that, him and I are the same.

The heat from his body washes over me before his fingertips graze down my arm and back up, circling where he patched me up from the day Johnny slammed me against a wall. His fingers trail down my arm, across my wrist, until they tangle with my fingers.

He kisses my neck, and I drop my head to the side, allowing him space. "I asked for you," he breathes. "I asked for someone to give me a reprieve from all this fucking pain. You're the first person to draw me out, to make me stop. You, Kyla." His soft lips trail to the spot behind my ear, and my body shakes as the sensations roll through me.

He grips my hand before moving them both to my stomach, splaying our fingers there, pushing me back into him until his hard cock presses into my lower back. He takes my cell phone out of my back pocket and tosses it onto the recliner before fitting himself behind me again, making delicious waves of pleasure tighten my core.

"I know I can't. I know I'm just sentencing myself by even touching you like this, but when you've lived in the dark for so long and only one thing brings you out, that's not the time to go running scared. I don't care, Kyla. There was never much hope for me anyway, and I'd rather die at your altar than turn away."

I breathe in a shaky breath, letting my head fall back onto his shoulder. He presses more soft kisses to my skin, making my body come alive under his touch.

He's right. I came here to the Heights so I could have moments like this *after* I took my life back. Taking Big Daddy K out means taking control of my life. It means having moments like this, a reprieve from the thoughts that have haunted me.

"I asked you once if I could touch you, if I could kiss you. Please tell me yes."

My body aches. It can't hold back anymore. "You're already kissing me, aren't you? You're already touching me."

His fingers tighten on my stomach. He breathes out, his hot breath teasing my already sensitive skin. "I need to hear you say it."

Growing some lady balls, I turn in his arms, facing him. I want him to see how much I mean it when the words come out of my mouth. I lift my hand and press my palm into his cheek. His blue eyes light with desire. "I want you to touch me. I want you to kiss me until I can't breathe anymore and then kiss me again to fill me back up."

He doesn't need any other invitation than that. His lips slam into mine, moving us back several paces before he steadies us. He kisses me like a man starved, his hands capturing the back of my head to hold me in place. He devours me. Attraction radiates through every lick, nip, and stroke.

One arm bands around my back and lifts. I bend my legs, pressing my thighs into his hips as he walks me into the bedroom. We stand there, each devouring one another until he breaks the kiss, pressing his lips down my neck and collarbone. I breathe out, biting my lip as shivers overtake my body. I start to rock into him, and he pauses, moaning against my skin. "Fuck me."

"I intend to," I say, smiling.

He pulls back, caught off guard. He presses a chaste kiss to my collarbone. "One day, but not now."

I pout, and he grins.

He presses a finger into my lip, effectively stopping me from asking why. "Today, I want to taste. You told me I can kiss and touch, and I'm taking full advantage of that fact, Princess."

He lowers me to the bed, my back landing on the soft sheets while he stands between my legs. He places one knee between my thighs and leans over, kissing the base of my throat, and then trailing his nose down my body, making a flush of heat follow him wherever he goes. When he gets to the tops of my jeans, he leans back, using his hands to make quick work of the button and zipper. I lift my ass as he pulls them down, taking his time, trailing his fingers down my legs as he frees one foot first then the other.

Leaning over me again, he kisses a trail across my abdomen, then moves up, moving my shirt with him. When he gets to my bra, he uses his hands to move it up and over my breasts until he's helping me pull the shirt off. He tosses it to the side and stares down at me. His gaze lingers. I don't have anything he hasn't seen before, but the way he stares at me makes me feel like I do. He makes me feel special, wanted.

First, he trails his finger along the curve of my bra, lips chasing his soft stroke until he's pushed the cup aside and captured my nipple in his mouth.

I buck off the bed. "Fuck."

He presses me back down, trailing his lips down my front until he hovers over my drenched panties. He slides them off with the same care he did my pants.

My heart lurches in my chest. I'm not a virgin. I'm

not a stranger to sex, but this is different. I've always been a in-the-heat-of-the-moment-I-just-want-that-release kind of girl. I want the high of breaking apart, and my partners were only too willing to give that to me.

This is something much different. His heart is in every move he makes. He's not just chasing his own release, he's making this about me.

He traces his hands up my thighs, then pushes down until I'm bared to him. Even though everything I have is just waiting for him to ogle, he stares into my face. He keeps my gaze as he leans down, his hot breath hitting my core. My hips arch off the bed. "Oh God."

He smooths his hand along my stomach, fingers spreading wide over my skin, and when he finally darts his tongue out, he closes his eyes as if he's taken his first breath of fresh air in years. "Mmm," he murmurs.

Fuck. This is too much.

He slides his other hand under my ass, propping me up to him like I'm his last meal. He sweeps his tongue over my clit, and my whole body trembles. He nuzzles me, taking his time in deciding where to taste next. Where to devour me. The anticipation is almost too much. He presses a soft kiss to my fold and then licks a drop of pleasure seeping out of me. "God, Kyla."

My toes curl. I press my knees to the bed, moving closer to him, silently telling him I want more of what he's giving me. At this point, I might just come apart with any of his tastes that last longer than a second. Fuck, I might just cream before he does anything.

I whimper, a sound I'm not used to hearing from me during sex, but it's well deserved. Brawler opens his eyes to watch me. His gaze turns darker, like a dark fire has lit him from within. "You want me," he says, not a hint of question in his gaze or words.

I can truthfully say I've wanted him to touch me more than anyone else I've ever met. Which makes me think he's done all this on purpose. The fuck if I care. "I do."

This time, he locks gazes with me as he gives me exactly what I want: him. If it's not his tongue devouring me, it's his blue gaze, heightening the pleasure coursing through me. He's skilled, his tongue sweeping over me in expert strokes as I cling to the bed for support. He laps at me, hungrily, enjoying this as much as I am. Just when I think I can't take anymore, he flicks his tongue over my clit.

It doesn't take him long to make me cry out. I clutch his shoulders as he barrages my core with more until my limbs relax like useless putty, waiting to be molded into something new.

After I come back down, he slips in beside me, holding me to him. I try to ask him what he wants me to do for him, but he tells me to stop and kisses my temple as he holds me, molding his body around me until neither one of us can tell where one of us begins and the other ends.

27

The next week, we barely bother with school. For me, that's never been the point of being here other than the fact that I needed to be where the Crew was. Since they're always around me now, and we have more important things to worry about than our grade in English, we don't even pretend to care we're missing out on it.

Oscar is the only one who goes just enough to stay on the football team. Not even the administration of Rawley Heights will look the other way in that regard, but it doesn't have anything to do with enforcing the rule. It has everything to do with the fact that if they enforce the rule, they're hoping they can use it as a way to shut the sport down. It's one of the few ones still being funded by the shitty money the school gets every year, and I half suspect that the team isn't getting all the money they're supposed to be allocated anyway.

But that's a fight for another time.

Brawler hasn't left my side. Oscar, when he's not taking care of his mother or at practice, is with me, too. They seem to have come to a sort of truce. For now. Each one eyes the other when they're with me. And when Johnny is around, each of them stalk to the sidelines like Johnny's kicked their puppy.

Magnum is all business. I have to hand it to him. He's taken a lot while we've trained. Don't get me wrong. He's given a lot too. I had to stop an argument between him and Johnny because Johnny thought he was giving it to me too rough. When I explained that Evan will be trying to kill me, and I need Magnum to do as much if not more, so that I can come out on top, he stopped, begrudgingly. The rest of the night he eyed Magnum like he was plotting his demise.

Magnum, Oscar, Johnny, and I have been going for morning runs. Magnum drives us to a park in Johnny's nice car where we get out and run like we're a running club instead of four people worried about winning the rights to continue an illegal underground fight ring. We pass other morning joggers every day who I'm sure aren't happy about seeing the newcomers on the trail. They eye us warily. The guys I'm with are badass looking, and every one of them exudes trouble. If Brawler jogged with us, I'm sure the other runners would stop coming once they spotted his tattoos. Little would they know what they represent. To them, he'd just be a thug with a neck tattoo who has ruined his chance for any real employment. To me, he's a hell of a lot more.

Whenever Johnny isn't around, we sneak kisses, words of affection, and come together to plan the fight with words hanging heavy between us. In each other, we have more reasons for me to come out on top. For us, it's more than just getting the win for the Heights Crew, it's needing to win so neither of us have to lose again.

Oscar helps where he can, but I'm adamant about not sparring with him because he can't get hurt while football is still ongoing. He let it slip that he's up for a major scholarship. One that could give him the money for college. Knowing Oscar, he could give a fuck about college, but it's the opportunity to keep playing that makes him tick. It's the possibility that he could move on from that and play professionally even. It makes me sad to think I was only able to watch part of his game before. Even in those few short minutes, I saw the caliber of player he was, but I would've loved to have seen more. Seeing Oscar play football is like seeing into his soul. When we're anywhere near the

Heights Crew, Oscar's in a disguise he has to wear to stay alive.

Two days before the fight, Johnny takes my hand in his. "I'm claiming you for tonight."

My flirtatious banter with him comes easily now. It's almost like I'm not pretending. I seriously worry for my sanity. "You already claimed me."

His mouth pulls into a smirk. "I mean I told my dad to clear my schedule. It's just us two."

"Us two and your favorite guard?" I ask, motioning toward Magnum.

He's in the corner of the warehouse, sucking down water. I'm still trying to get my breath under control from our last sparring session. Sweat has slicked my hair back until it's matted to my face. I'm in desperate need of a shower and a massage. Something Oscar's been happy to oblige me with lately. As long as no one else is around, of course.

"Some things just have to be," Johnny says. "You can just ignore him when we're together."

I'd love to be able to, but the truth is, Magnum is always staring at me. So much so that I'm surprised Johnny hasn't noticed. "Right," I say, taking a bottle of water and cracking the top, so I can chug it down. Its icy cool temperature does wonders to cool me off. "And what will we be doing tonight?"

"Something...normal," he says.

My brows pull together. Normal? Johnny is so abnormal I'm not sure he knows what normal is. Does he realize training for a fight against a guy that could probably snap me in half isn't normal? Does he realize having a guy follow us around all the time isn't normal?

He lowers his voice. "I just want to show you that we can still be normal," he says again, his voice trailing off. "I feel like you need that, like you've been missing out on that."

Honestly, this conversation is probably the most surprising one I've ever had. But the fact that Johnny recognizes it is even more of a surprise. "What's your idea of normal, Johnny Rocket?" I tease.

He opened up to me just yesterday, explaining to me why his Heights Crew nickname is Rocket. Apparently, the guy has a penchant for explosives, which is scary as fuck. A silent killer. You can take out anybody with an explosive and not even be anywhere near them to have to clean up the mess. Ever since he's told me, I can't seem to stop asking myself how many people he's killed. Or if he's done it at all. Does Big Daddy K even allow his son to get his hands dirty?

I can't make myself form the words to ask him. I'd rather not know.

"Dinner and a movie. And I think I can help with your Magnum problem."

Magnum looks our way, no doubt hearing his name. The back of my neck burns.

"We'll just do everything in my apartment."

"Oh," I say, nerves reaching up to bite me. Being alone with Johnny still isn't on my to-do list. I don't know how he'll act. He says dinner and a movie, but does he really mean foreplay before hitting the sheets?

"Come on," he says, oblivious to the war I'm having with myself. He stands from the bench first and offers me his hand. "You can take a shower at my place."

Brawler, Oscar, and Magnum glare at us. Their heated gazes chip away at my armor. I can't even look back at them because I'm afraid all the feelings I have will show on my face and all Johnny has to do is look.

Brawler speaks up. "Didn't you want to get your wrist checked out?" he throws out there.

"What happened to your wrist?" Johnny asks, concern twisting his features.

I lick my lips, still avoiding the gazes of the other guys in the room. "I may have bruised it, that's all."

"I'll make sure you ice it."

"I thought we were going over last-minute shit," Oscar says, agitation lacing his voice.

They're trying their damndest to get me out of this.

Johnny stills. Oscar's question makes the soft, approachable Johnny leave. In its place stands the guy who's not to be second-guessed. "Big Daddy K prepped me earlier, Bat." He spits out Oscar's nickname like it's a curse.

I don't dare look, but whatever motion Oscar makes seems to appease Johnny for the moment. He puts his hand around me and guides me toward the side entrance.

"Mag," he calls out, his voice slicing through the tension in the air. But Magnum already understood what was happening. He reaches the exit door before us and holds it open. He goes from sparring partner to guard at the drop of a hat.

Johnny draws lines over my fingers and knuckles the whole time we're in the car. Drenched in my own sweat, I'm acutely aware of what I must look and feel like, but I don't move away. Training again has me feeling on top of the world. Like I can conquer anything. This is why I love to fight. It's having power within yourself. Faith in yourself that you could protect yourself if it came right down to it.

There were so many times I wished my parents had taken a self-defense class or *something*. Maybe things would've ended differently if they had. Bullets win over fists every time, and you can't stop madness, but at least you can try. At least there might be a flicker of hope.

"What are you thinking about?" Johnny asks.

My parents. The ones your father killed.

For a moment, I imagine what would happen if I actually said that. Johnny can be so sweet. At first, I see him caring and loving, but the second he puts two and two together, that I'm not here to worship his father like everyone else but to take him out, I'm done for. For Johnny, it's the Crew all the way.

"The fight," I lie. I turn in my seat to face him. "Do you think I can win?"

Uncertainty crosses his features, but his stare is steadfast. It's such a mixed message that I don't know how to take it.

I start to pull away from him, but he stops me with a steady grip on my fingers. "I do," he says.

"Good," I tell him, still trying to get a gauge on his reaction. It's not what I expected. "Because I'm going to."

"I don't want to talk about the fight tonight." Johnny leans back in the seat to look out the window. "I just want this to be about you and me."

"Dinner and a movie?"

He nods tightly, and it's obvious something has

affected him. Whether it was my question or if he's distracted about something, I'm not sure.

Magnum pulls the car into the lower parking level and parks near the same door we did last time. I don't like being here. As soon as I get out of the car, my stomach tightens. I place my palm over it, worried I'm going to be sick the whole time.

Johnny puts his hand on my back and steers me toward the elevator. We get in with Magnum who turns the other way to give us privacy. The sweat marks on his back dip low and a feeling of pride washes over me. I'm glad I can give someone like Magnum a workout.

"Do *you* think I can win?" I ask Magnum.

Magnum's shoulders bunch. He peeks over at us, gaze hard. He reaches up to scratch his scruff, but whatever he was going to say is cut off by Johnny.

"I told you I don't want to talk about the damn fight."

His fingers cut into my wrist. I pull it away, yanking it to my chest. Magnum turns fully now, watching us both. His gaze keeps flicking between Johnny and me, like he's waiting for the former to explode.

"So, I can't talk now? Is that what you're saying?"

Johnny's lips thin.

"I wasn't making you talk about it. I was asking Mag."

"It doesn't matter what Magnum thinks. He's here for one reason and one reason only: make sure no one gets killed. We don't care what he thinks."

I don't know what's crawled up Johnny's ass, but he sounds like a petulant child. Magnum makes no reaction. He just keeps staring ahead, his glare settling above mine and Johnny's heads now. He doesn't even act as if he heard Johnny's cutting remarks.

I turn away from the Rocket. Not for the first time, I wonder why I get so confused around him. He'll always come back to this guy. This one who thinks he's better than everyone else because of who his dad is. Someone who's used to getting their own way.

Johnny curses under his breath. He tries to move closer to me, but in a moment of serendipity, the elevator doors open, and I walk quickly out, avoiding him. I'm not sure what I'm going to do when we're in his place alone together, but for right now, at least he knows that shit isn't going to fly with me. He really shouldn't have been a dick just after I got done training. I'm never in the mood to put up with shit after beating the shit out of things.

Magnum stops me in the hallway. He goes over to

the table to pick up the wand, and I stand there, arms and legs wide so he can run it over me.

Johnny stands to the side, head shaking the whole time.

"She's good," Magnum says.

"I should hope so," I tell him. "You've been training with me for the past few hours. I think you'd be able to tell if I had a weapon on me."

Johnny turns, moving toward the door on the left. Magnum's upper lip quirks up as I walk past him. Johnny opens the door into a suite that is much like his father's, only smaller. Everyone in this city would be drooling over this place. It's three times the size of mine with new furniture, sleek lines, and that feeling when something is just clean. It's barely lived in.

As soon as the door closes behind me, Johnny whirls. "Don't talk back to me in front of anyone," he spits. He's in my face, nose-to-nose. "Don't fucking back talk me at all. Who the fuck do you think you are?"

I blink at him, swallowing. This is the moment where I don't know if I should push Johnny or not. I sure as fuck don't want to be his punching bag—verbally or otherwise—but what kind of options do I have? The thing is, Johnny can be better than this. He just doesn't know any better.

I move in closer, the tips of our noses touching. "You claimed me because of the way I fight. It's not just in the ring that I'm feisty," I tell him, making it clear I will not fucking take shit from him either. "I get who you are, and I've accepted that. But that doesn't mean you disrespect me in front of other people either. It was a simple goddamn question."

"I told you I didn't want to talk about it."

"Well, I do. Your wants aren't any more important than mine. Deal with it."

I move past him. I search the room for a bathroom. Only a couple of doors lead off from the main living area, so I choose the one to the left, only it opens up into a bedroom, the sheets a pile at the foot of the bed. Luckily, there's a door ajar inside Johnny's room, a towel lying on the floor, so I know it must be a bathroom.

Johnny grabs for me. "You are infuriating."

"Me? Try dealing with you."

His pale blue eyes flash. It's sexy as hell, not going to lie. But hot or not, I won't put up with this. Not when I'm going to fight for his Crew. There's no way he should be treating me the way he is. Even he should realize that.

He backs me up. I walk backward until my legs hit the side of the bed. "You think so, huh?"

I nod.

He pushes my shoulders, and I fall back. A nice, comfortable mattress waits for me, and I bounce a few times before he hovers over me. "No one's ever said that to me before."

I try to wiggle out of his cage, moving up the bed, but he keeps following me. Finally, I stop because I have nowhere to go unless I want to fall off the side. "Probably because they're all scared of you."

His nostrils flare.

I look around. The twisted sheets turn my stomach. "When's the last time you fucked someone in this bed? Are these soiled sheets? Don't ever bring me into a dirty fucking bed," I growl.

He quirks his head, licking his lips. "I don't fuck girls here. You think I bring skanks into this place? This place is for family only."

The way he says family, I know he doesn't just mean him and his dad. He means the gang itself. That's all he has. All he knows.

"I didn't make the bed this morning because I got up early to run with you. Then I watched you train for hours." He presses his body into mine. "Then I get your smart mouth the moment I get alone time with you."

I suck in a breath. Johnny's as hard as a rock. My

workout clothes are skintight, and his joggers leave nothing to the imagination as he presses into me. My body responds to him, licking flames through my core, my muscles tightening. At the same time, my head just doesn't know what to think.

I grip his hips to stop him from pressing into me.

"I want you." His words come out on an exhale.

I take a deep breath, my chest pressing into his. "I can't, Johnny."

He closes his eyes and swallows. "My dad won't find out."

"It's not that," I say. Johnny needs some hard truths. It's better for me if I give them to him because I need to understand who he is. Is he the rough and tough gang guy? Or is he something more? Is there any hope for him at all? "I don't know you," I say, pushing his hips away from me.

His eyes open. His first instinct is to lash out, but I watch as he reins it back in.

I sit up, forcing him to move even further back. "You give out conflicting images of yourself. One minute you say pretty words to me, and the next, you're fucking a dress store worker in a back fitting room. I mean, fuck, Johnny. Does that sound fair to you? I don't know which guy you are."

His response is automatic. "I'm both. I won't make any apologies for who I am."

I slide off the bed, getting to my feet. "I don't want you to."

"But you're still pissed about the girl at the shop?"

"Pissed is an understatement. Ever felt betrayal? White hot rage and embarrassment? That's what it felt like."

"I can't have you yet," Johnny seethes, like it's his reason for everything.

"Then have you ever heard of self-restraint. Fuck, am I allowed to go out and fuck someone?"

"No," Johnny growls. He gets in my face again. "No."

My heart thumps, remembering that perfect moment with Brawler. Here I am being altruistic when I've done the same thing Johnny has. The only difference is, I'm not allowed to get upset if Johnny puts his dick inside someone else. But if I have sex, my partner and I will both end up dead.

I close my eyes. *What am I doing? There's no use trying to make him see reason. This is all he knows.*

Maybe he isn't salvageable. And even if he was, he won't be when he finds out I killed his father.

28

This is my biggest fight yet. Not only does it have the most at stake, but it's my biggest challenge.

I sit next to Johnny in the car on the way to the abandoned mall where the fight is being held. He's holding my hand, but ever since the evening in his apartment, things have been strained between us. Honestly, I don't think he knows what to do with me. Or maybe he's just pissed I turned him down or the fact that Magnum showed up five minutes into the movie we put in and told him he had to come to the meeting after all.

Whatever his reasons for the sour look on his face, I can't worry about it. I need to worry about what's in front of me, and the only thing currently in my way, is taking Evan out. Once I take Evan out, I'm in Big Daddy K's good graces. I'll have the access I need.

Brawler and Oscar are in another car God knows where. Or maybe they're even here already, prepping the space. I attended a meeting yesterday with more members of the Crew than I've seen in one place before. They all looked at me skeptically, but no one outright said anything. Big Daddy K had already made his choice, but he ordered everyone to be on hand during the fight in case they needed anything. In case this went sour. I don't know if he's making contingency plans if I win the fight. Or if I lose.

If I win, maybe I can even save some bloodshed.

The car pulls into the parking lot. It's dark out, so I can't see much through the tinted glass other than a few streetlights in the distance.

"Give us a minute?" Johnny asks Magnum.

Magnum gets out of the car, leaving us alone. Johnny sighs. He turns toward me, so I turn to him, watching him grapple with his emotions.

"I didn't express myself well the other day," he says. "I was angry because you're in this fight at all. That's why I didn't want to talk about it. That's why I didn't want to hear anyone else's opinion on whether you were going to win or not. I don't want you to even be fucking fighting, Kyla. I'm so fucking pissed at my father for getting you in this mess." His hands ball to fists, and he looks straight into my eyes. "I've never expressed that before. Never. My dad makes an order. I follow through. That's how this works. I've never once questioned anything he did, but I did this time. And it's because of you."

My mouth slips open. Right when I decided to harden myself against anything Johnny Rocket had to say or do, he does this. It's not fucking fair, but if anyone knows life isn't fucking fair, it's me.

"Fuck, Kyla," he says, staring at me, his gaze wandering down my clothes. I'm dressed in a tank top and capris, my hair pulled up and out of my face. I wound it into a tight bun, so it couldn't be used against me in the fight. "I only fucked that one girl since I've been with you, and after I did, I didn't feel better. I thought it would, but then I realized who I really wanted was you. So no, it made me feel like shit. Especially when you walked in. Seeing your reaction... I could tell I hurt you."

A knock comes on the car door.

Johnny growls. "Another fucking minute!"

I squeeze his hand. "Thank you for telling me all that."

Johnny's eyes swim with emotion. "Be careful out there tonight. Stick with Magnum after the fight."

I nod, about to turn around to exit the car, but Johnny cups my face. His intense blue eyes soften for a fraction, but then he moves forward, capturing my lips in a kiss. He stokes a fire in my stomach, turning it from nerves to heat. Considering I wasn't able to see Oscar or Brawler this morning like I thought I was, I soak this up like a woman dying of thirst.

Afterward, he pulls away, throws the door open, and then holds his hand out for me. I get out, and as soon as I do, I forget about everything Johnny just said. I peek at my surroundings, taking in every little nuance as I prep for the fight in my head.

There aren't a lot of people here. Mostly members of each gang. There are no crowds hungry for a fight, just those who have a stake in the outcome. Evan is already bouncing on his feet in front of a bunch of strangers I don't recognize except for Roza Fonz. She's sitting in a folding chair, still smoking her cigar, and surrounded by a bunch of men with guns on their hips.

Magnum cocks his head, telling us to go ahead of him. Johnny must sense that I'm in the zone because he doesn't try to talk to me, and he doesn't offer me his arm like he usually does either.

On the opposite side of Roza Fonz's group is ours. I recognize a few from school. Brawler is there, leaning against a folding chair. My heart hiccups when he turns to look at me. He stands up straight, eyeing me as we approach. Oscar is standing in the back, too, talking quietly to someone in the shadows. The only person I don't see here yet is Big Daddy K, but I know he will be. I'm not worried about that at all.

Roza nods at Johnny and me. I nod back at her, then switch my gaze to Evan to watch him as he warms up. He's what I pictured after only seriously seeing him for half a minute. Magnum really was the perfect training partner for this guy. His build is so similar. My confidence ratchets up. I've prepared all I can, now it's just time to lay everything out and see which fighter is best tonight.

Hopefully things will swing my way.

Johnny sits in one of the chairs waiting for him and his father, and I slip into the background with Brawler. His tense jawline tells me everything I need to know. He's worried.

"I got this," I say.

"I know you do," he says, taking the reaction I wish Johnny had the other day and using it to settle my nerves. His gaze says everything else. It apologizes to me for even being in this mess. It tells me he hopes I don't get hurt too badly. It tells me he wishes he was the one going out there instead of me. Instead of saying all that, he asks, "Did you warm up?"

"Yep."

"Do some more," he says. "Big Daddy will be here any moment and then this is on. There won't be any time to talk or discuss."

I start stretching, bouncing on my toes as I go to get the blood flowing. Broken gravel crunches under my feet. I take a moment to check out the area we'll be fighting in. There are a few potholes barely visible in the low light of the old streetlights lighting this area. Dust, rocks, basically shit that might make my shoes slip.

I test the grip of my sneakers, making sure I know how they're going to react in the fight. Not good, but not terrible either. It'll suck if this goes to the ground because all those tiny rocks are going to get imbedded into our skin.

A flash of headlights sweep over us as another car approaches.

I glance away. We already know who it's going to be.

I can hardly even believe I'm here in this moment. I know I have to do it to get in, but who would've thought a daughter of a couple Big Daddy murdered would be fighting *for* him? The irony isn't lost on me even though I should be focusing on nothing but the fight.

I work my shoulders out, rotating one then the other. Brawler's heated gaze settles on me again, but neither one of us is stupid to do or say anything that would put a spotlight on us. Not with members of both the Heights Crew and a rival gang here. Tension is already thick, like a black cloud over us all.

Big Daddy K approaches our side with three guards surrounding him. He sits in the chair, and he and Johnny speak in low whispers to each other before Big Daddy K sits up straight. Johnny turns, giving me a nod. I step forward, but two strong hands on my shoulders stop me for a second. He pulls me back, massaging my shoulders quickly like he's getting me ready for the fight. "Do everything you fucking have to. Do you hear me, Kyla? Everything. Whatever it takes."

I nod, hop up and down a few times, and then make my way out into the center of the area everyone surrounds. Evan moves forward, too. We look each other up and down. I doubt anyone is going to come out and tell us when to fight, so I'm cautious of when he's going to make the first move.

"I have to admit I was shocked when they said I was fighting a girl."

"Yeah?" I ask, grinning. I love being the underdog. I hope he underestimated me. I hope he thought this fight was going to be a walk in the park. "This isn't the first time I've fought an overconfident douche."

Evan's lip curls. "It's sad I have to kick your ass."

I shrug. "What can you do? Life of a fighter."

"You can give in now." His eyes gleam with hope, but I'm not stupid enough to think he wants to stop this fight because he doesn't think he can win. In his head, he'll feel bad if he kicks my ass because I'm a precious girl.

Well, he needs to get the fuck over it.

"Just kick her ass, so we can get on with this, Evan," Roza says from behind him.

That makes me smile even wider.

I know from experience that I have to wait for his move. His reach is far longer than mine, so I have to get through his to the inside. I have to be quick. Strike hard and strike fast before getting out again.

We circle one another, and this time, it's apparent the fight has started. He won't be saying any more remarks to me. He's in his own head, just like I'm in mine.

He's watching every move I make, just like I'm watching his. He has good technique. Unlike Brawler, he's had technical training.

So have I, though.

I fake him into moving forward. I catch a right

hook to the jaw for it, but I also come up on the inside, punching him in the gut and then coming up on the other side of his body, giving him a backfist to the neck. He cranes his neck this way and that, and then we both circle again. Cheers erupt on both sides. Each one calling out words of encouragement for their chosen one.

I fake a punch, wait for his reaction, and then move inside, punching him square in the jaw three times before getting back out again. It's a bare-knuckle fight and my knuckles split for the pleasure of it, but his lip is split too. He reaches up, wiping a smear of blood over his lips and grins.

I know that feeling. You smile, even though it hurts like hell.

Evan rushes, trying to use his strength against me. I know if this goes to the ground, I'm done for. All he has to do is use his weight to hold me down while raining blows down on my head. I sprawl, my forearms cutting into his shoulders, allowing me time to get out of the way. He wasn't ready for the force of my stop, so he puts his hand down to steady himself. I take the opportunity to knee him a few times in the face before getting back out of his reach again.

He bounces around, shaking his head like what I just gave him didn't bother him at all.

"Is it wrong I'm fucking turned on right now?" he asks.

My gaze narrows. Shit like that pisses me off. Don't demean me in a fight between equals, motherfucker.

He comes at me. I block his punches until he kicks me in the gut, and I stagger back. Even with the adrenaline pumping through me, that fucking hurt.

"Come on, Kyla," Johnny says from behind me. His voice is low, growly.

He's rooting for me.

I step forward again, Brawler's words repeating in my head. *Do anything necessary.*

Evan kicks me in the gut again. "How'd that feel?"

"Like you've got a weak kick."

His face tightens. He wipes at his lips, which trickle blood from the center. This time when he comes in, I round house him in the stomach. He groans but catches my foot.

Fuck!

He brings his elbow down into my calf, connecting with a crack. I suck in a breath, wrenching my foot from his hold. As soon as I put my foot down, my leg buckles, a fierce pain emanating from the point his elbow connected with my bone. It's not broken, it just hurts like a bitch.

I flex my toes and absorb the pain as I step back on

it again. I need this foot. It'll hurt way worse after the fight is over when all the energy has died down and I'm not hyped up on the fight itself.

Seeing that I'm injured, Evan goes to kick the same leg, but I block it by bringing my knee up, then faking a kick high to get his guard to rise while I get in another body shot on him.

He starts sucking in air. I wouldn't be surprised if I broke a rib with that one. At the very least, they're bruised, and it's super difficult to breathe with a bruised rib.

"Time to stop playing," Roza says behind Evan.

I hate to say this, but the girl's a dumbass. We're not playing. Unless she really thought he was just going to be able to walk through me, and now she's worried I'm actually still fighting.

We trade blows, each of us getting some solid punches to the face. I have a goose egg on my forehead like the one I got the first day of school.

Aww, Nevaeh. Back when my problems were easy.

I expect Evan to retreat like we've been doing, but he doesn't this time. He stays inside, using me as his personal punching bag. I block and retaliate, waiting for him to make a mistake. He gets overconfident because of the amount of strikes he's been able to get in that he leaves his head unprotected. I elbow him across the nose and blood spurts from it. I get in another blow to his forehead, cracking the skin open before he finally wises up and steps back.

Blood drips down his face and into his eyes. He swipes furiously at it, but I use his lack of vision to my advantage. I step forward, blasting him several times in the nose, and then once to the throat, making him choke.

"Fucking bitch!" he roars as soon as he gets his breath back.

He moves in blindly. His arms moving furiously. I sweep his leg, tripping him, but grab onto his arm, so I can use his leverage to spin me to face him so I can continue to hit him. I drop hammer fists onto his face until he's able to wrangle his arm free and cover up.

Everything goes in underground fighting. And I mean, everything.

When I retreat, I kick his balls, then stomp on his hip.

His hands move to cover his family jewels, and I pounce on him. I use the sharp point of my elbow to do the damage. My focus moves to a pinpoint. I'm on top of him, his arms trapped. As long as I can keep this spot, I'm fine. I don't let up. I don't let him squirm his way out of this. He tries to buck, but I return to what I was doing. Elbow after elbow rains down on him. I split the cut he already had on his forehead wide open. Blood splatters everywhere. I know it's all over me. It's all over his face. It's dripping to the ground.

I go and go and go. I don't let up. I don't stop. I need this. I let my hate for Big Daddy fill me up and fuel my strength. I yell through clenched teeth, like a caged animal, not caring about anyone else but my own safety.

I don't stop for a long time until strong arms grip me. It's then I realize that Evan is limp. As I'm being pulled away, the bloody mess I made comes into focus. Evan isn't dead. He's just knocked out cold. The cut on his head is nasty. His short hair is practically coated in red.

My body starts to shake. I blink, letting my surroundings come into focus little by little.

Roza Fonz's crew looks shocked beyond anything. They're gaping at an unmoving Evan.

"It's okay, it's okay," a voice says next to my ear. It takes me too long to figure out it's Johnny who has me. He brings me back to our side of the circle as Big Daddy K stands, walking toward the center.

Roza looks pissed. She sneers at her guy and throws her cigar to the ground, stomping it out with her feet. When she walks past Evan, she spits on him.

Johnny leans over to say something to me, but I

can't even focus. I can't believe she disrespected her own fighter like that.

She turns an angry glare to Big Daddy K. "What are you playing at, old man? Who is that girl?"

"We had a deal," he says. But he doesn't give her a chance to respond.

Everything melts into slow motion. His hand moves first. It sneaks to his hip, and then he holds his hand out. His body blocks my view, but I don't have to see the gun to know it's there. The gunshot that sounds shortly after tells me everything I need to know. As does Roza falling to the ground, a bullet hole between her eyes.

I exhale, and all hell breaks loose as a trail of blood leaks from the single bullet wound in Roza's head, running through the parts in her braids like water trickling through a stream.

29

Gunshots ring out. I'm shoved to the ground from behind. The gravel eats at my palms, digging in deep. Unlike before, time doesn't slow like when the first shot rang out. It speeds up, like I'm looking at everything through fast forward. Guards rush to Roza while firing randomly in the air. Grunts of pain fill the all but deserted parking lot, but then dissipate.

"Come on," a voice says in my ear while I'm getting tugged away.

I turn to find Magnum pulling me back. The small stones are embedding into the skin of my stomach as I'm being dragged, my tank top inching upward, leaving my skin exposed. I look past him, searching the area for Brawler and Oscar, who I knew were just here seconds before the fight started, but I don't see them anymore. Bodies lie on the ground, and I cry out, hoping it's not them.

He drags me right into a hedge that lines the parking lot and then pulls me upright. "We've got to get out of here."

He shakes me, and all I can see is the chaos of the shootout still in full swing. My heart gets stuck in my throat. Brawler's brother and sister died in a shootout. He must be so scared. I shrug Magnum off and start for the parking lot again, but he grabs me from behind and lifts.

"Let me fucking go! Magnum!"

He runs, holding me in his arms. The branches of the wild bushes scrape at my body. The sounds of cars starting and peeling out of the parking area reverberate through me. I'm running through the images in my head, wondering if I can remember seeing Oscar or Brawler. Hell, even Johnny. He was right there. Right fucking there.

Now, where are they?

Magnum pulls me out onto a side street, and we crouch next to a dilapidated garage. I push him. "You knew that was going to happen. What the fuck?"

He staggers back but catches himself. Ignoring me, he looks around the side of the building.

"What's going on?" I hush out. "Shouldn't you be helping Johnny? What about Big Daddy K?"

Why I'm asking that, I don't know. I don't give a flying fuck if that fucker got hit. He just shot someone in cold blood. Oh my God. My stomach revolts, and this time, I really do wretch. It's been building and building ever since I first saw him in real life, in his skin. He shot Roza without a care in the world. Talking one second. Dead the next. Her eyes so wide as she went down. Surprise captured in a moment in time while she fell backward, dead before she even hit the ground.

"We need to get out of here," Magnum says. "Johnny told me you were the number one priority."

"Where is Johnny?" I ask, looking behind me.

Magnum shakes his head. My stomach plummets. I don't know if he's shaking his head because Johnny didn't make it or if he's shaking his head because he doesn't know.

"Here. This car."

Magnum jumps into the middle of the road, holding his hands out. He pulls the gun from his holster and points it in the windshield. "Get out of the car," he orders.

The woman inside shrieks.

"Get the fuck out!" Magnum yells.

The woman scrambles out of the car, tears already running down her face. "Don't shoot. Don't shoot. I have kids. Please."

Magnum waves the gun, telling her to get to the side of the road. With it still pointed toward her, he comes back over to me, yanking me up by the shoulder and shoving me into the front seat.

The woman falls to the ground, sobbing, shaking. I'm numb to her pain. I should be having a reaction to this, but I can't think about anything other than what I'm leaving behind in the parking lot.

"Fuck!" Magnum yells. He jumps into the car and pins my head down. A moment later, the windshield in front of us explodes in fireworks of glass. Magnum presses on the gas, peeling out. "Keep your head down," he grinds out, wrestling with the steering wheel.

We're already at the end of the block when he finally reaches out and pulls his door closed before he takes a sharp right. I slide in the seat, tucking my head between my knees. I only know what's happening by the way my body moves over the front seat. More shots ring out, but they must miss us because I don't hear the explosion of them hitting their target.

The woman's car is meticulously clean except for a receipt on the floor. It's from McDonald's. The print says "Happy Meal" in all uppercase letters. I close my eyes.

None of this makes any sense. I won the fight. Why would he kill her? What the fuck?

Within a few minutes, Magnum slows the car. He places his gun on the seat. "They're gone but stay down just in case."

"Where are they?" I ask, panic rising inside.

"I don't know where anyone is," Magnum says. I glance up. His eyes are sharp, calculating. His copper stubble disheveled. Before long, he pulls the car to the side of the road. No one glances our way, like people driving around with a smashed windshield is a regular occurrence. "Get out," he says.

I slide out of the car, my knees wobbling. I try to stand, but my leg is still injured from Evan's well-placed elbow. I hiss in a breath.

"Can you walk?"

"I can limp," I tell him.

He slides the gun into the waistband of his pants. I lean on him as we walk to the Heights Crew building where Johnny and Big Daddy K live. When I glance up at it, he says, "We'll be safe here. If Roza's group reforms, they'll come for us. This is the safest place."

"Don't they know where this is? We should go to my apartment."

"You think they don't know where you live?" he asks. "They've known about you since Big Daddy K threw you to the wolves. This place is engineered with so much security it's basically impossible to penetrate. It would take a bomb to get to us and none of Roza's guys are as smart as Rocket."

My heart skids to a halt inside my chest. "You shouldn't have left them."

Inside, my heart splinters. Where's Brawler? Where's Oscar? Brawler wouldn't know to come here. He'd head home if he's alive at all. He was only there for me.

Wait. Did Oscar fucking know about this?

We make our way onto the elevator. When the doors open on the Penthouse floor, Magnum calls out before we step over the threshold. "It's Magnum."

Eerie silence meets us.

"Where are they?" I breathe out again.

Magnum runs a hand through his copper hair. He takes me into Big Daddy K's suite and sits me on the couch while he checks the rooms like I've seen people do on cop shows. When he returns, he says, "No one's here."

"No fucking shit. I—" I stop mid-rant. Blood drips from Magnum's arm, sliding off his fingertips in rivulets. "You're shot."

"I know." He grimaces when he turns his arm to look at the wound. "Dick got me when we were getting in the car." He pulls his shirt over his head and wraps it around the entry point. "I think he just grazed me."

I watch him patch himself up, and my mind goes blank. It looks like he's done this far too many times. This whole way of life is fucked up. "Why did he do that?" My voice signifying the barest grip I have on sanity right now. "I won the fight. I fucking won. No one had to die."

"You'll have to ask K."

"If he's even fucking alive."

The barest of happy thoughts flits through my brain. If he's dead, I can leave. I can put all this shit behind me. It would be a perfect ending to this mess. I can take Brawler and Oscar. We could get the hell out of the Heights. I have money saved up, and I'm sure my aunt and uncle would help us. They just love doing charity work. I'm their greatest charity of all. What are two more guys with horrific childhoods?

"Did you see what happened to any of the others?"

Magnum's lips purse. He sits on the coffee table, his fingers still wrapped around his gun like a lifeline. "I watched you the whole time. You were my assignment."

"So, they knew this was going to happen? They knew things were going to end up like this anyway."

Magnum's quiet. His gaze keeps tracking to the door. It's like I'm not even here until he turns hazel green eyes on me. "You should leave," he says. "I'll tell them you got shot. They'll never know. If you leave now, disappear, you can actually have a life, Kyla."

Why does everyone want to save me? "I can't leave."

"Because of Johnny?" he asks, disappointment, confusion, and outright shock coloring his features. When I don't say anything right away, he says, "Fuck that. Leave. I'll wipe the footage of us coming in. I'll tell them you got hit in the car in case that gets out, and then I'll tell them I had to ditch the car, so it won't come back on us. You can get the fuck out of here and have a new life."

"I have a life," I tell him. I have a whole other life no one even knows about, but I don't want that fucking life. I never did. I wanted the one God sent me to Earth with. The one where I had parents.

Now, though, I know in my heart I have people here who will help me make a life. I can't leave.

My heart rips down the center. Being here changed me. Even now, if I close my eyes, I can feel the memory of Brawler's arms around me. I'm not going to just up and leave him. He's had enough of that in life.

And Oscar? He needs someone here who believes in him. Who tells him that he can play football if he wants. He's not stuck. And hell, maybe one day, they both need someone to help them escape this shit.

In the back of my mind, my head keeps repeating a terrible thought. A single word my life has been filled with. A word I hate to even think might have happened to Brawler, Oscar, or even Johnny. None of them deserve this life, they're just caught up in the tangles, like a spiderweb. Eventually, the spider's going to get us. We just don't know when.

My leg jumps up and down, and I look Magnum square in the eye. "I'm not going."

Magnum reaches out, his fingertips trailing over my cheek. He frowns, then his lips pull down when his gaze tracks lower. "You're bleeding."

I stare down, noticing blood has seeped through my shirt. I lean back and lift it. There's a nasty scrape on my stomach. Dirt and pebbles stick to my skin. "You dragged me through the parking lot."

He swallows, his tender touch hovering over my skin before he gets to his feet, leaves the room, and then returns with a First Aid kit. He kneels between my knees and opens the kit on the couch next to me. He pulls out an antiseptic pad and rips the pouch open. "This will sting."

His touch is soft, reassuring. It's like I'm seeing a whole different side to the aloof, mysterious guard who's always around. "You're worried about my wounds? You're the one who was shot."

"You're more important than I am."

"No one's more important than anyone else."

His gaze moves up to meet mine. "Not true," he says. I see the truth in his eyes. I am wrong. Because if I had the chance to pick and choose who dies in that shootout, I wouldn't have picked Brawler or Oscar or even Johnny. I would've chosen Big Daddy K. I would've thrown others into the bullet's paths, people I don't even know, but the sacrifice would be worth it. Because then, I would know the people I care about most would be walking through that door.

It's not up to me to play God, but I would. I would if it meant keeping the ones I care about alive.

Tears prick my eyes. Magnum reaches up, flicking the first away, but then they come so freely there's no way he can keep up. "I'm sure they're alive," he says.

They? My stomach twists. He can see right through me, can't he?

"Kyla, I—" He pauses and swallows, like what he's about to say is some monumental declaration.

My heart skips. His words hang in the air between us. I want to take the end of the rope and keep pulling until I free every single one of the words he wants to say from his mouth.

But I never get the chance.

The suite door swings open.

In one swift movement, Magnum gets to his feet, gun raised.

I turn, lowering myself into the leather, but peeking around the couch to see who walks in.

My stomach sinks as in walks the reason for me even being here. He was so close to the foray that I imagined he would die, but he's not dead at all. In fact, he's in better shape than us. He's not nursing a gun wound or bleeding from his stomach. He certainly wasn't knocked around in a fight and then dragged through a parking lot to avoid being shot at.

"Magnum."

Bodies usher in behind him. I get to my feet, my heart hammering in my ears and at the pulse in my wrists. I blink several times, trying to take in the faces as they come in. Some are wounded. Some are being carried by others, but my eyes refuse to focus.

Where are they? Where are they? They have to be here.

Flashes of the gun fight flick through my head. For the first time, I allow myself to think that people don't just survive shit like this. There are probably more dead than alive. It wasn't a game to any of them out there. They were shooting to kill. They didn't care who.

Their family had been wronged, and they were out for blood.

"Kyla?"

The world stops. I search for the owner of the voice in a sea of distraught faces until I find him.

Him.

And then I fall to my knees, watching the open door for others, but no one comes.

About the Author

E. M. Moore is a USA Today Bestselling author of Contemporary and Paranormal Romance. She's drawn to write within the teen and college-aged years where her characters get knocked on their asses, torn inside out, and put back together again by their first loves. Whether it's in a fantastical setting where human guards protect the creatures of the night or a realistic high school backdrop where social cliques rule the halls, the emotions are the same. Dark. Twisty. Angsty. Raw.

When Erin's not writing, you can find her dreaming up vacations for her family, watching murder mystery shows, or dancing in her kitchen while she pretends to cook.

Printed in Great Britain
by Amazon